Copyright

The right of Peter Jay Black as
been asserted in accordance with the ct
1988.

All rights reserved. No part of this book may be reproduced, stored in or transmitted into any retrieval system, in any form on, or by any means (electronic, mechanical, photocopying, recording or otherwise) without permission in writing from the publisher, except by a reviewer who may quote brief passages in a review. Any person who does any unauthorised act in relation to this publication may be liable to criminal prosecution and civil claims for damages.

This is a work of fiction. Names, characters, businesses, brands, titles, places, events, locales, and incidents are either the products of the author's imagination or used in a fictitious manner. Any resemblance to actual persons, living or dead, or actual events is purely coincidental.

1 2 3 4 5 6 7 8 9 10

OAKBRIDGE
K280525
ISBN 9781068482618 (paperback)

A CIP catalogue record for this book is available from the British Library

Black, Peter Jay
Murder at the Osborne Outlet / Peter Jay Black

London

Note to the reader
This work is a mid-Atlantic edit.
A considered style choice of both British and American spelling, grammar, and terms usage.

Ruth Morgan Investigates...

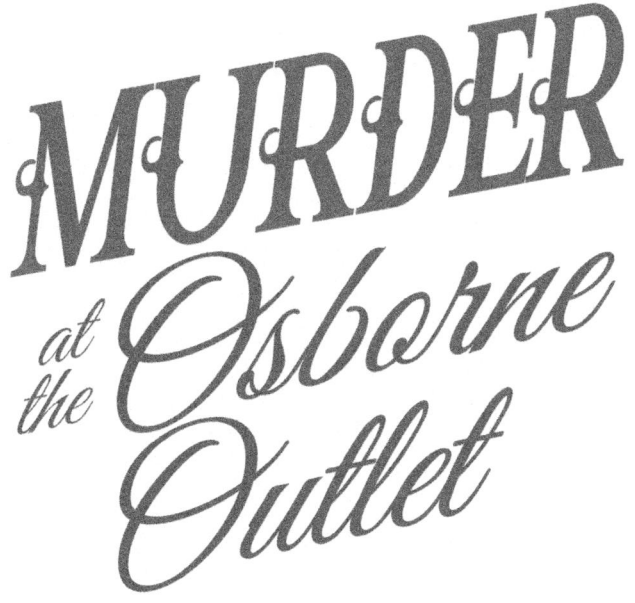

MURDER at the Osborne Outlet

PETER JAY BLACK

1

Greg glared at Merlin, Ruth Morgan's cat, who returned the favour by shooting daggers at him from the confines of his bubble-domed pet carrier. "Grandma?" Greg called, not taking his eyes off the midnight-furred feline. "Can I go in front and steer for a bit, please?"

Ruth glanced at him in the tandem bicycle's side mirror. "Not long now." She gripped the handlebars. "Keep pedalling. You're doing splendidly." Ruth adjusted a shoulder strap on the carrier. For some strange reason the cat felt a lot heavier on her back than in his usual box. "How's Merlin?"

"Plotting my demise."

"Great," Ruth said. "Normal, then." Ignoring the chorus of impatient horns and the stream of slow-moving traffic behind them, she expertly navigated the tandem around a pothole.

Greg snarled. "Could you stop doing that?"

"What? Steering?"

"Swerving." He'd lost their game of rock, paper, scissors, which meant Greg got the rear seat.

Ruth checked the bike's other side mirror, ensuring the trailer remained firmly attached. It did. Their suitcases, and Merlin's custom-built mahogany travel box, towered precariously. It had taken some creative bungee cord work, but they held fast.

For now.

However, a knot of anxiety tightened in Ruth's stomach. A niggling doubt about those bungee cords plagued her ever since the overly enthusiastic garage mechanic—a man with biceps bigger than Greg's head—had assured Ruth they were 'As strong as a ferry chain, love.'

What if the trailer detaches? Ruth mused. *Everything could end up sprawled across the road, luggage scattered, Greg moaning and groaning, Merlin making a dash for freedom...*

The image of a traumatised cat fleeing into the countryside, never to be seen again, filled Ruth with dread.

"Do I have to wear this one?" Greg pointed to his fetching crash helmet.

"Of course. Safety first." Ruth wore a matching helmet. "The man at the garage only had these. You do know plenty of boys wear pink, right?"

"Sure," Greg said. "But mine has all these cartoon stickers, and that lady we passed just now literally pointed and laughed."

"Don't be ridiculous," Ruth said. "You're imagining it."

Although, now he mentioned it, she had heard something as they'd zoomed past.

Behind them, a brave white van pulled out to overtake them.

Ruth redoubled her grip on the handlebars, bracing for the inevitable wind buffeting.

Instead of passing, however, the van drew alongside, matching their speed—all of about ten miles an hour.

The passenger, a bald man sporting more ink than a comic book, rolled down his window and leaned out. He grinned at Greg. "Whatcha doin', mate?"

"What does it look like?" Greg pedalled harder.

"That's a nice ride." The man nodded at Ruth. "This your girlfriend?" He took a picture with his phone.

The driver let out a hearty chortle, and they sped off.

Greg gnashed his teeth and muttered a string of expletives no grandmother should ever have to hear from a sweet, cherished grandchild, even if he was, *technically*, an adult.

"The motorhome breaking down wasn't my fault," Ruth said in a defensive tone. "Anyway, we're almost there." She frowned at a passing road sign. "Although, I don't recognise any of the place names."

"I thought you said you've been here before."

"That's right. I have." Ruth then murmured, "Forty-four years ago."

The roads looked very different now—less countryside, more concrete.

The motorhome had, fortunately, chosen to conk out less than a mile from a repair garage. Unfortunately, their courtesy car was unavailable, leaving them with a tandem bicycle and its ever-so-handy trailer. *The cherry on top of this disastrous cake?* The garage was still ten miles from their ultimate destination.

Greg had suggested a taxi, but their remote location would've meant a lengthy wait. Ruth, determined not to miss her appointment with Reverend Michael, especially with a storm brewing, had dismissed the idea.

One of the things Ruth prided herself on, especially when travelling up and down the United Kingdom for her job, was being on time to all her food consultancy appointments, no matter what.

Besides, she'd thought it would be a grand adventure. As Ruth had convinced Greg before they'd set out: 'A once-in-a-lifetime opportunity to ride a tandem bicycle with my adorable grandson, enjoying the fresh country air and the magnificent scenery.'

In all her sixty-five years, and Greg's nineteen, neither had ridden a tandem before. Now, legs burning and threatening to detach at the hips, Ruth vowed this would be the last time.

"Do you even know where we're going?" Greg asked, his tone edging toward *decidedly grumpy*.

"Of course," Ruth lied. "East."

"The sun's behind us. We're going north."

"Precisely. That's what I meant. Northeast. *Ish*."

In fact, their destination was in the northeast of England, a few miles outside Whitehaven. *If I can find a landmark, a familiar road, anything* . . . Despite herself, Ruth's internal unease began to rise. She couldn't afford to get lost, especially not with the ominous storm clouds gathering.

"We should pull over," Greg said.

"Why?"

"So I can check the map on my phone . . . and throw up a little bit."

Ruth sighed, and was about to agree, when a sign swung into view:

OSBORNE OUTLET VILLAGE

"Here we go," she called over her shoulder, a tad relieved. "Lean."

"Which way?"

"This way. *Now*."

They swung a hard left into a narrow road, barely

avoided an oncoming bus, and almost flipped onto their side as the trailer popped onto one wheel.

Ruth and Greg both yelped and leaned the other way. As the trailer slammed back down on two wheels again, it sent a jolt up their spines.

"Ouch." Greg's voice hit a new octave.

By some miracle, the tandem-riding daredevils avoided catastrophe, dived into a car park, and finally slid to a halt alongside a bicycle shed.

"Never again." Greg clambered off, snarling, "Not in a million years."

Ruth winced as she extricated herself from the death trap. "It certainly is a unique mode of transport." She sighed as her grandson backed away, shaking his head. "I hate to break it to you, but we must ride it back to the garage in a couple of days."

Greg pulled off his helmet. "Not doing it. No way. Find someone else."

Ruth chose not to press the matter. Besides, they had no choice—they needed to return the tandem to the owner. Then hand over an exorbitant amount of money in exchange for a repaired motorhome.

In theory.

Ruth's brow furrowed. The garage owner, a greasy-haired man with shifty eyes and a penchant for muttering rude words under his breath, had given her a bad feeling.

What if he overcharges us? For that matter, what if he never intends to fix the motorhome at all?

Since their recent outing at Hadfield Hall, Ruth found herself more distrusting of strangers than usual.

While Greg wrestled with the trailer and bungee cords, Ruth took off her helmet and looked about. Ten-foot-high faux stone walls topped with battlements surrounded the outlet village, leaving only the tops of slate roofs visible, along with a glorious tower in the distance.

Greg set Merlin's custom box at Ruth's feet, and then, with a series of exaggerated grunts and expelled air, tugged the suitcases free of the trailer.

"Well done." Ruth picked up Merlin's box and strode toward the entrance. "This way."

"Where are we going exactly?" Greg huffed and puffed as he waddled along, a bulging suitcase in each hand.

Ruth glanced up at a security camera. "The Silver Thimble Café."

Greg's pace increased as they crossed a drawbridge and through an archway with a portcullis. *Rather dramatic for a discount shopping centre,* Ruth thought, amused nonetheless.

Indeed, the Osborne Outlet Village's narrow lanes, Tudor-style buildings, gingerbread house, and a charming thatched cottage filled with magical-looking trinkets, plus a babbling brook, created a fairy-tale aesthetic. As if that wasn't impressive enough, what was clearly Rapunzel's tower—with a long rope of braided hair cascading from a window—stretched high above, dominating the scene.

After several market stalls selling fruit and veg, chocolate, fudge, temporary tattoos, and mugs with '*I heart the Osborne Outlet,*' Ruth and Greg strode past Cinderella's Slipper Emporium.

It was a shimmering shop appearing to be held aloft by nothing but glitter, with a giant glass slipper in the window, and overflowing with discounted designer shoes.

Bargain hunters, laden with shopping bags, rushed from one boutique to another as though on a time limit. Ruth squinted up at the overcast sky, which grew darker by the minute, and thought they had a good point.

Next up was The Emperor's New Threads: A menswear

shop with everything from suits to T-shirts. The Poison Apple was a sleek, modern juice bar with a wicked twist, selling detox blends with names like '*Evil Queen Cleanse*' and '*Sleeping Beauty Slumber Smoothie.*'

Then there was the Three Little Pigs BBQ: a rustic smokehouse built of faux straw, wood, and brick, offering platters of ribs, pulled pork, and other cardiac-arrest-inducing delights.

Ruth pointed to a bakery shaped like a giant loaf of bread. "See, Greg? Not only discount clothes. Plenty to eat." She held up a hand before he dropped the suitcases and asked for an advance on his inheritance. "We need to meet my client first. We're very nearly late." Ruth stopped at a village map near a wishing well: a beautifully crafted structure with glowing runes. "Here we go." She traced a route on the map with her finger, then looked up to match landmarks. "Ah. This way."

As they headed along another brick-paved street, a woman adorned by a flowing green and purple dress, matching scarves, sandals, hair so tall and messy it looked like the aftermath of a tornado, and enough jewellery to sink a ship, stepped into their path.

The woman waved incense sticks about, as if the smoke would scare away bad mojo. "There's an impending storm coming," she said in a mystical voice. "Blue skies, happy faces. Blue skies, happy faces. Chase away the clouds."

Greg glanced up at the sky, and then frowned at her.

The woman locked eyes with Ruth. "I sense you're a bargain hunter, looking for a new pair of sensible walking shoes."

Ruth cleared her throat. "No, I—"

"Wait, wait." The woman flapped her arms about, and her eyes rolled into the back of her head. "It's coming through. I feel it in your aura." She gasped and looked back at Ruth, her eyes wide and unblinking. "You're hunting for a set of candles. A gift for a loved one. Very reasonable price. Lovely scents. Seven-day money-back guarantee."

"I'm here for—"

"No, no, there's more." She squeezed her eyes shut, took several deep sniffs of the air, swayed from side to side, and then her eyes suddenly snapped open again. "You want to help someone. I can see. Yes. Help someone in need. It's coming through now." The woman spread her arms wide. "You're here for the Silver Thimble Café."

Ruth gaped at her. "That's right." Perhaps the woman was a real, bona fide mystic. "I'm a food consultant."

The woman nodded. "As I suspected all along." Her expression hardened. "What about those candles? Very reasonable prices. Limited-time deal: two for three."

Greg blinked. "Don't you mean three for two?"

"Sorry. No candles today," Ruth said. "Maybe later."

The woman deflated, stepped aside, and muttered, "The Silver Thimble is that way." She thrust a thumb over her shoulder.

Ruth smiled as she strode past with Greg in tow.

"You'll be back," the woman said, her voice regaining its earlier mystical tone. "I predict your return. Yes, you will come back very, *very* soon."

"Not likely," Greg muttered.

At the end of the lane stood a rickety facade of brown bricks and leaded windows. It wasn't the bricks themselves that gave the Silver Thimble its charm, but rather the way they leaned this way and that, as though perpetually midjig.

Ivy, threaded with white blossoms, clambered over the walls, softening the edges of a crooked chimney that puffed out plumes of lavender-tinged smoke.

Windows, each wonkier than the last, served as the café's beckoning eyes—a mismatched collection of stained glass panes in hues of emerald, ruby, and sapphire.

Above the door hung a crooked sign that read:

THE SILVER THIMBLE

Ruth pushed open the door and stepped into a whirlwind of warmth and an intoxicating aroma of cinnamon, vanilla, and freshly brewed coffee.

The café's interior was a delightful jumble—a shrine to comfortable chaos. Sunlight, fragmented by the stained glass windows, painted a rainbow on the worn wooden floor in a mosaic of jewel tones. Wooden beams hung low, with mismatched tables and chairs beneath, each bearing a heavy patina.

A magnificent stone fireplace crackled at the far end of the room, flanked by bookshelves overflowing with well-loved novels, and plush velvet armchairs with faded floral prints.

Walls of exposed brick held all manner of objects, from patterned plates, copper pots, and oversized wooden spoons, to porcelain signs, vintage car number plates, and even a CCTV camera in the corner.

The air hummed with the quiet murmur of conversation, punctuated by the clinking of cutlery against china, and the occasional burst of laughter.

Behind a counter crafted from reclaimed wood, a man with silver hair, a kind face, and a flour-dusted apron arranged pastries within a glass display.

He smiled at Ruth's approach. "You must be Mrs Morgan."

She returned the gesture. "How did you know?"

The café owner circled the counter. "A lucky guess." He extended a hand. "Reverend Michael O'Connell. Although, I'm retired." He motioned around the café—"As you can see"—and chuckled. "I'm pleased to meet you in person."

"Likewise." Ruth shook his hand. "And this is my grandson, Greg. He's on a gap year, travelling the country with his dear grandmother before he starts university later in the year." As they shook hands too, Ruth glanced about again. "A fine establishment."

"Isn't it? Took it over a couple of years ago." Reverend Michael eyed the suitcases. "Had some trouble?"

"We broke down," Ruth said. "Greg and I ventured the rest of the way on a bike."

"Bike? Really?" Reverend Michael rubbed his chin. "Motor?"

"Pedal," Greg muttered. "Lots and lots of pedalling."

"Oh dear." Reverend Michael looked sympathetic. "Then you'll be wanting a place to rest."

"Is the bed and breakfast still nearby?" Ruth asked, hopeful. "My husband and I stayed in it many years ago."

"It is," Reverend Michael said. "But you're more than welcome to stay here. In fact, due to the inclement weather, I'd already planned on it." He took the empty mahogany box from Ruth. "Wasn't sure you'd want to stay in your motorhome with a storm rolling in. I have a spare flat above the café that's not in use."

"I have a cat." Ruth turned so he could see Merlin in the pet carrier.

"That's no problem," Reverend Michael said. "As long as you keep him away from the kitchen."

Raised voices drew their attention to the corner of the room where a man and woman sat, both red-faced.

The man appeared to be in his fifties, slender, wearing a

tailored suit with a vibrant purple Hermès silk pocket square, a matching neck scarf, and Italian leather loafers.

The woman sat ramrod straight, the crisp lines of her white blouse accentuating a tasteful silver and turquoise necklace, above tailored black trousers and low-heeled, but undoubtedly designer, pumps.

Their sharp city clothes jarred against the café's worn wood. They leaned forward, faces flushed, fists clenched, about ready to punch one another.

"What's going on there?" Ruth whispered.

"Believe it or not, a peace summit." Reverend Michael nodded to the man. "Julian J Jasper. According to Hattie, it was his idea to meet. Wanted to clear the air once and for all." A crease furrowed Reverend Michael's brow. "Doesn't seem to be working. Julian runs the Enchanted Loom, whereas Kathy Fellows"—he indicated the woman—"owns Kathy's Klassics." He sighed and shook his head. "They've been at each other's throats since Julian's shop burned down and he moved opposite."

"Fire?" Suspicion flickered through Ruth's mind, but she suppressed it. "What are they arguing about?"

"I'm not entirely sure," Reverend Michael said. "He's a fallen fashion star relegated to running a discount shop. Julian has not been happy recently. Was quite a big deal back in the day."

Ruth could believe that because Julian's face was etched with bitterness and longing. She sensed a deeper conflict brewing beneath the surface.

Julian erupted from his chair. "I don't have to listen to any more of this nonsense." His words were clipped, vowels rounded, overlaid with an Irish lilt. "When you want to put an end to all the bickering and talk sensibly, you know where I am." And then he stormed from the café.

Kathy stared at the wall, grinding her teeth.

"Never a dull moment." Reverend Michael motioned for Ruth and Greg to follow.

They circled the counter and stepped into a spacious and light kitchen with more exposed wooden beams, walls painted a soft, creamy yellow, and cabinets crafted from knotty oak.

Open shelving displayed a collection of mismatched pottery and vintage enamelware, above a butcher's block. A butler sink sat under a window that overlooked a compact herb garden, while a vintage cooker, its porcelain speckled with age, stood against the opposite wall.

Finally, a kitchen table sat on the flagstone floor, its worn pine surface complementing the natural materials throughout the space. Cakes, sandwiches, pork pies, Cornish pasties, and all manner of savoury and sweet snacks filled every inch of the table, arranged with obvious care, each perfectly aligned under plastic wrappings.

"A party tonight," Reverend Michael said, clearly noticing Greg's slack jaw. "The whole village are turning out. Brought forward from Sunday, due to the weather. You're both invited." He passed through a door and headed up a flight of narrow stairs.

At the top was a hallway lined with watercolour landscapes.

Reverend Michael gestured to the left-hand door. "My rooms." He nodded to a door at the far end. "Bathroom." Then he opened a door on the right. "Guests' accommodation."

They stepped into a spacious sitting room with soft furnishings, a TV, a coffee table, and windows overlooking the back of the café and the remaining village.

Reverend Michael placed Merlin's box on a table and

then opened doors on the other side of the room. "A bedroom each. They're rather on the small side, I'm afraid." He indicated the single beds.

"Absolutely perfect," Ruth said. "Thank you." She peered out the window at the brewing storm clouds, while Greg set the suitcases in the rooms.

"Would you care for some tea before we start?" Reverend Michael asked.

"Yes, please," Ruth said, never one to turn down a brew.

"Are you hungry? It's about lunchtime. You must be famished after all that pedalling." When Reverend Michael received an eager nod from Greg, he added, "I'm sure I can rustle something up." He addressed Ruth. "As for the purpose of your visit, I've taken the liberty of making an extra batch of cakes and pies for you to sample. Come down when you're ready." He bowed and left the room.

Ruth slipped the kitty carrier off her back, unzipped it, and lifted out a disgruntled Merlin, who leapt from her arms onto the sofa. "I'm sorry," she said. "Won't happen again." Ruth then muttered, "Apart from the return journey." She filled Merlin's water and food bowls to His Lordship's satisfaction, then unpacked her suitcase.

In the corner of her bedroom sat a wardrobe, which Ruth loaded with three pairs of trousers, black; three blouses, black; three pairs of socks, bright pink; undergarments and nightwear; boots and walking shoes, along with a waterproof coat, also black; and a matching knitted hat and scarf in pink.

She studied her assembled attire and muttered, "I'm sensing a theme, Morgan." Ruth then extracted her copy of *Mrs Beeton's Book of Household Management* and set it on a bedside table. "I'll see you later, Isabella."

Raised voices drew Ruth to the window. In the street

below, clearly not finished with their argument, Julian Jasper and Kathy Fellows squared up to one another, their faces contorted. Kathy held a box of colourful bunting, while Julian grasped several bunches of flowers.

Ruth opened her window a crack.

"I know you did it, Ju-li-an." Kathy said his name in a sarcastic staccato, each syllable dripping with venom.

His face reddened, a mottled patchwork of indignation. "What did I do now?"

"Scratched my freshly painted shop door." Kathy's voice was sharp, accusatory.

"Your evidence?"

Kathy thrust a finger at a nearby security camera. "Don't make me ask Alex. You know I'm right."

Julian shifted the flowers to one arm and adjusted the silk scarf at his neck, a gesture that seemed both defensive and an attempt to maintain his composure. "You're being absurd. As always."

"Am I?" Kathy set the box at her feet and folded her arms.

"Why would I scratch your door?" Julian motioned to passing shoppers. "Could've been anyone. An accident, I'm sure. Tip of an umbrella, perhaps."

"No accident." Her eyes narrowed. "I know you did it. Same with knocking my bins over."

"Wind," Julian said.

Kathy's eyebrows shot up. "Excuse me?"

Julian sighed. "The wind tipped over your bins, Kathy. You're seeing conspiracies where there are none. Perhaps you've been talking to Leana and Hattie too much."

"What about the dead mouse on my car?"

"For goodness' sake." Julian rolled his eyes. "That was a stray cat's doing."

Kathy waggled a finger in his face, her crimson nails flashing. "Funny how all this started as soon as you moved opposite. I know it was you. All of it. Told Mrs Vanderlin. She'll keep an eye on you, Julian. One more step out of place and you're gone."

He shook his head. "You'll push too far one day."

Kathy took a step toward him, eyes blazing. "What will you do?"

Julian hesitated, opened his mouth to say something, then spun on his heel and marched away.

"Just as spineless as ever," Kathy called after him. She snatched up the box and trotted after him. "Come back here. We're not finished."

"Wow. No love lost there." Ruth closed the window and vowed not to cross paths with either of them.

2

Greg sat on the edge of his bed, thumbs a blur across his smartphone screen.

Ruth leaned against the open doorframe, with Julian and Kathy's argument still ringing in her ears. "Mia?"

"Yep," Greg mumbled, eyes glued to the display.

"How is she?"

"Fine."

"Did you invite her to the family wedding next week?"

"Yes."

Ruth tilted her head, suppressing a sigh. "So? Is she coming?"

"Yep."

"Riveting conversation, Gregory. Thanks." A breath escaped Ruth's lips, a mixture of amusement and exasperation at her teenage companion. "Lunch?"

He bolted upright, shoving the phone into his pocket.

Ruth smirked. "If you had to choose between Mia or burgers, which would it be?"

Greg's brow furrowed. "Cheeseburgers or plain?"

"Cheese."

"Double stacked with gherkins and burger sauce?"
"Sure. Why not? Throw some French fries in too."
Greg squeezed past her. "Do you have to ask?"
Ruth padded after him. "Can't wait to tell Mia."
"Don't you dare."

Downstairs in the Silver Thimble's kitchen, Reverend Michael had transformed the space. Gone was the party food, replaced by plates loaded with sample-sized cakes, buns, and sandwiches—a miniature feast laid out for Ruth's inspection.

Greg gaped at it all, wide-eyed.

"How many girlfriends is this worth?" Ruth murmured out of the corner of her mouth.

"I wasn't sure what you wanted to look over," Reverend Michael said to her. "So, I made a fair representation of what's on those." He indicated copies of the café's menus, along with a notebook and a pen. "All ready for you, Mrs Morgan." He smiled at Greg, his eyes crinkling. "I made enough for you too. Hope that's okay?"

"You don't need to ask him twice," Ruth said. "My grandson is like a stray dog—instantly friends with anyone offering food." She settled at the kitchen table, her gaze sweeping over the delicacies.

Greg sat down too, practically drooling.

Ruth jotted notes on their presentation first. Even in this simple buffet, Reverend Michael's attention to detail showed with the presentation of his comfort food, and part of her consultancy covered appearance. "Julian and Kathy were at it again outside."

Reverend Michael clucked his tongue as he set more plates. "Those two are relentless. I've tried talking to them, but it's to no avail. Shame, really. They're both lovely people. Julian especially."

Lovely? Ruth thought, recalling Kathy's sharp tongue and aggressive stance. "What's their story? Before working at the village? You mentioned Julian being a fallen fashion star?" Ruth picked up a cheese and pickle sandwich and examined it before taking a bite and savouring the ingredients.

"Let me see." Reverend Michael set down a jug of ice water and glasses, his movements practised and precise. "Julian worked for a world-renowned fashion house, known for their high-end, meticulously crafted suits. He headed a new line, endorsed by a major film celebrity." Reverend Michael glanced into the café, where a few customers lingered over coffee and cake, and then he sat at the kitchen table with Ruth and Greg as they tucked in. "Julian worked day and night, ensuring the celebrity received a special suit in time for a big red-carpet event."

"Amazing," Ruth said. "I'd love to meet a celebrity."

"What are you on about?" Greg mumbled through a mouthful of bacon sandwich. "You and Grandad met loads."

"A film star, I mean." Ruth motioned for Reverend Michael to continue as she sampled the food and made notes.

He leaned back, his expression thoughtful. "It all went south when the celebrity had a major wardrobe malfunction in front of the gathered crowds and cameras."

"What happened?" Ruth cut open a sausage roll and prodded the contents with the knife.

"The suit ripped in an embarrassing place. Millions saw it. He became an instant laughingstock in the tabloids."

"Wait." Greg's eyebrows lifted, a flicker of recognition in his eyes. "I think I know who you're talking about. It was all over the internet too. Became a meme, not because of the ripped suit, but the way he reacted."

Reverend Michael nodded solemnly. "He was fuming.

Deleted all his glowing posts about the fashion house and issued a scathing statement, vowing never to work with them, and especially Julian, ever again."

"How was an accident Julian's fault?" Ruth asked.

"Investigations revealed he'd used cheaper, less durable fabrics to meet an unrealistic deadline. He rushed." Reverend Michael watched Ruth make more notes. "Tarnished Julian's reputation. No other fashion house would touch him after that fiasco." He then paused, his gaze distant. "Julian's a good guy, though. Didn't deserve what happened to him."

"And Kathy?" Ruth asked.

"Kathy is a shrewd businesswoman." Reverend Michael leaned forward, and his voice dropped to a conspiratorial whisper. "She knows retail inside and out, can spot a deal a mile away, and isn't afraid to negotiate ruthlessly." He sat back. "Years of running another successful outlet store gave her a network of connections."

Ruth's curiosity flared. "She had a shop before moving here?"

"Weymouth. When she discovered the Osborne Outlet was expanding, Kathy met with the owner, Celia Vanderlin, and apparently wouldn't take no for an answer. Walked away with a ten-year lease for about half what everyone else pays." He shook his head, his expression of admiration mixed with disbelief. "Kathy is a tough negotiator. I admire her tenacity." Reverend Michael then nodded to the pies Ruth sampled. "How are they?"

"Overall, very good." She picked up a steak slice, her expression thoughtful. "This one could use a tad more seasoning, perhaps a hint of smoked paprika. I've made a note."

"I think it's all great," Greg declared, having demolished

the sandwiches and pies and now working through pastries and cakes. "Gets my seal of approval."

Reverend Michael smiled. "Glad to hear it." He hesitated, a flicker of uncertainty in his eyes. "I bought this place from a lovely couple. I've stuck to their old recipes. It's long due for an overhaul, which is why I wanted you here, Ruth." He sighed. "My only fear is alienating my loyal customers by making drastic changes."

"You don't have anything to worry about," Ruth said. "I can tell you right now there are no drastic changes needed. I like the traditional theme. It works well. Perfect for this setting." She glanced at the notes so far. "We can revamp it here and there without losing any of its current simplicity and charm." Ruth paused, an idea forming. "Where do you source your ingredients?"

"Axminster Wholesale."

"How about sourcing more locally?" Ruth noted the reliance on prepackaged offerings—a culinary misdemeanour in her eyes. "We could use seasonal produce, create a menu that reflects the region's character. Keeps things interesting. Offers fresh choices."

"I love that." Reverend Michael's face lit up.

"I noticed a fruit and vegetable stall on our way in, and a bakery."

He nodded. "Know both owners. I'll talk to them."

Ruth made more notes. "Once I'm done here, may I have some time to mull it over? I like to cogitate before making final suggestions. Then, tonight and tomorrow, I'll work on some tweaked recipes and ideas." She glanced around the compact kitchen, assessing the layout and equipment. "After that, we'll talk through the Health and Safety."

"Sounds perfect. I look forward to it." Reverend Michael stood. "How about you spend the afternoon perusing the village?" His eyes darted to the café. "Excuse me." He walked through the door, and his brow smoothed, a warm smile replacing his thoughtful frown as he served a customer.

Greg nodded to the remaining food near Ruth. "Done?"

She slid the plates toward him. "Be my guest."

An hour later, Ruth and Greg explored the maze of narrow brick-paved lanes and charming storefronts. The air buzzed with excited chatter, and gentle melodies drifted from speakers disguised as flowerpots overflowing with red, white, and blue petunias.

They passed the bigger shops: *Sleeping Beauty's Mattress Market*, its entrance a giant four-poster bed, complete with a snoring Teddy bear; the *Beanstalk Garden Centre*, a sprawling greenhouse with the aforementioned beanstalk stretching skyward; and *Rapunzel's Hair Emporium*, a salon and wig shop housed at the base of a crooked stone tower. Its windows displayed discounted hair extensions, braiding services, and a bewildering selection of hair care products with scientific names Ruth couldn't pronounce, let alone understand.

She opted for a narrower cobbled lane that curved out of sight between a fish and chip shop called *Gape Cod* with American-themed décor, despite the distinctly British culinary offerings; and an old-fashioned sweet shop, its windows filled with brightly coloured jars.

A sign swung into view, painted in flowing script:

Mystical Flames
Discount Candles & Homemade Soap

Its chipped and faded paint lent an air of whimsical deterioration. Another sign in the window advertised aromatherapy candles guaranteed to make you feel a decade younger.

Intrigued, Ruth stopped. "I need a wedding present for Bernard and Betty's daughter."

Greg raised an eyebrow. "A candle?"

Ruth peered through the window at the eclectic array of goods. "Not only candles in there, but soap too."

"Wow. Soap." Greg rolled his eyes. "Exciting."

Ignoring his overt negativity, Ruth opened the door and stepped inside. A bell tinkled softly to announce their arrival.

The air hung thick with incense and essential oils in the shop's narrow, long, and dimly lit interior. Candles of every shape and size lined the shelves on the left, some lit, their flames casting flickering shadows.

On the right, arranged on rustic wooden shelves, glass jars crammed with fragrant herbs and dried flowers jostled for space alongside incense sticks—their exotic aromas mingling.

In the middle of the shop, crystals filled a display case, their facets catching the light and throwing rainbows across the floor.

Ruth peered at a green gemstone carved into a dragon, mounted on a silver chain. "Do you think they would like this?"

Greg pursed his lips, his expression dubious. "Are you calling the bride a dragon?"

"Good point." Ruth straightened. "My sister never forgave me for buying her that stuffed bat." She smirked.

"Perhaps a beeswax candle." Greg nodded to a nearby shelf.

Ruth wasn't sure if he was being sarcastic.

As she moved deeper into the shop, she eyed two old security cameras in the corners. Behind a wooden counter cluttered with receipts and price tags, a young woman with long dark hair straightened a display of handmade soaps.

She wore baggy black clothes, and a silver ankh necklace rested on a T-shirt depicting Edgar Allan Poe. The young woman looked up as Ruth approached, pausing a true crime podcast on her phone, her finger hovering over the screen. Her name badge, shaped like a pentagram, read, 'Leana.'

"Good afternoon." Ruth picked up a bar of lavender and chamomile-scented soap. "Did you make these?" The soaps were lumpy, uneven—clearly handmade.

"Aunty Hattie did." Leana tucked a strand of hair behind her ear as she noticed Greg. "I just work here."

Ruth nodded at Leana's phone. "You like true crime?" She glanced toward the door as a tall, elegant woman with silver hair and a stern expression swept past the shop. The woman wore a tailored suit and a string of pearls. Her every movement radiated authority—she walked with a straight back, chin raised, acknowledging no one.

"That's Mrs Vanderlin," Leana whispered. "The owner of the village. I call her the Black Widow."

Ruth's eyebrows lifted. "Why on earth would you call her that?"

"I think she poisoned her husband." She leaned closer, her voice barely audible above the tinkling of wind chimes hanging outside the door. "And I bet she burned down Julian's shop last year. He had to move because of it. Was really upset."

Ruth put down the knobbly soap and tried to sound

casual, even though her pulse quickened. "A fire? Why would she do that, if she owns the place?"

Greg rolled his eyes, and muttered, "Here we go."

"I don't know why," Leana said. "Insurance, maybe?" She shrugged. "She's really suspicious, if you ask me. Mrs Vanderlin had an argument with Kathy only yesterday. I heard it all. Mrs Vanderlin was—"

A sharp voice, laced with disapproval, cut through their conversation. "Leana." A woman emerged from a back room, the same mystical lady in the flowing scarves they'd met earlier. She balanced a stack of peach soap bars in her arms.

"Sorry, Aunty Hattie." Leana took the bars.

Hattie eyed Ruth with curiosity. "We have a new batch of aura-cleansing candles for only ten pounds each." She smiled and indicated a nearby display.

Ruth forced a smile in return. "I'm afraid my aura is beyond redemption."

Greg coughed. "Truth."

"I do love a good soap bar, though," Ruth added, choosing to ignore him. "Especially lavender." She poked a finger at the misshapen bars.

Hattie opened her mouth to respond, but her eyes darted to the street as a shaven-headed security guard, in his fifties, with a lean physique and an air of quiet authority—his posture upright, his gaze straight ahead—marched past.

Alex, perhaps? Ruth wondered. *Kathy Fellows' security camera contact?*

"Excuse me." Hattie hurried from the shop and went after him, her flowing scarves trailing behind her like colourful streamers.

Ruth picked up two bars of warped soap and placed them on the counter. "You were saying? Julian's shop fire?"

"He was forced to move opposite Kathy." Leana scanned and bagged the items. "I think Mrs Vanderlin might have done it on purpose," she said as Ruth handed over the money. "Knew they hate each other. Mrs Vanderlin is trying to force Kathy out."

"Why would she do that?" Ruth asked.

"I don't know," Leana admitted. "But isn't it bizarre?" She handed Ruth her change. "It's like musical shops around here."

Ruth glanced about at all the lit candles. "And yet, this one seems most primed to burn down."

Leana nodded. "Exactly. Aunty Hattie's always leaving them. I keep telling her to be careful, but she never listens."

Ruth thanked the young woman and stepped back outside with Greg, the fresh air a welcome relief from the heady scents of the shop.

They rounded the corner to *Kathy's Klassics*, a woman's fashion outlet store. Ruth looked to the shop opposite: *The Enchanted Loom*, where a mechanical loom in the window worked back and forth. "This must be Julian's, and that one is—"

"Kathy's?" Greg said with a deadpan expression. "You're not thinking about sticking your beak in other people's business, are you?" He gave her a stern look.

"How dare you." Ruth sniffed. But as they continued along the narrow lane, she thought there was a lot more to the Osborne Outlet than met the eye, and she definitely itched to stick her beak in places it didn't belong.

Greg scowled at her. "Don't even think about it."

~

That evening, after spending a couple of hours going through Reverend Michael's menus, suggesting tweaks to existing recipes, and adding new ones, Ruth and Greg helped him carry food for the party, their arms laden with platters of savoury snacks and sweet treats.

They followed the narrow lanes to a giant lake, its surface shimmering in the fading light. Shops lined one side, the glow of their windows sparkling off the water, creating a magical, ethereal atmosphere, while a dense forest loomed on the other, its shadows deepening as dusk settled.

In the middle of the lake sat an island with a willow tree weeping over the water's edge and a gazebo perched on a small rise, its white paint gleaming in the twilight, above a row of thatched cottages.

Back on this side of the lake, a grassed area, shaded by a gnarled apple tree, had trestle tables set up, along with colourful bunting and fairy lights.

"What are we celebrating?" Ruth asked Reverend Michael as they set the plates down and uncovered them.

"Twenty years since the Osborne Outlet's founding." He nodded to a passing man with red hair. "Evening." And then said, "We brought it forward from Sunday due to the inclement weather rolling in."

Ruth glanced up at the darkening sky.

People began to arrive, their laughter and chatter filling the air. The party appeared to be a mix of shop owners and their invited friends and family.

"Ruth, let me introduce May Thomas." Reverend Michael gestured to a woman with purple hair styled in a gravity-defying beehive and a flamboyant dress that shimmered and changed colour with every movement. "She owns the Storybook, an excellent bookshop."

Ruth extended a hand. "Pleased to meet you."

May beamed. "Likewise." She had a high-pitched, musical voice.

"This is my grandson, Gregory."

"Greg." He shook May's hand too. "It's a pleasure to meet you."

May's eyes twinkled. "The pleasure's all mine, young man." Her attention returned to Ruth. "I hear you're the culinary wizard who'll sprinkle some magic on Michael's café."

"I'll do my best." Ruth glanced at Julian as he strode through the guests, giving Kathy a wide berth and pretending not to notice her as he adjusted a red and white rose pinned to his lapel.

May spotted him too, grabbed his arm, and pulled him over to them. "Ruth and Greg, this is Julian."

A flicker of recognition crossed his features. He cleared his throat and muttered, "Nice to meet you."

Ruth smiled. "That's a lovely rose."

"My family ancestry has ties to the Tudors."

"The union of the House of Lancaster and the House of York," Greg said.

Julian's bored expression vanished. He turned to Greg, giving the young man his full attention.

"Greg is all about history." Ruth beamed. "He's off to study it, along with archaeology, later in the year."

Julian's eyebrows lifted, his expression filled with curiosity.

Greg nodded to the flower. "White represents the House of York, and a red rose signified allegiance to the House of Lancaster."

Julian smiled. "The War of the Roses."

"King Henry VII created the Tudor Rose as a joining of the two," Greg said. "It was one of the first ever hybrids."

And then they were off: chatting about the history of the monarchy and various related topics that went way over Ruth's head. Julian's eyes now sparkled as he talked about the influence history had on his craft and fashion creations.

Ruth left them to it, and as the evening progressed, she met a variety of colourful characters, including Alex, the stoic security guard—expressionless face, brief nods—who seemed to observe everything with a watchful eye, and only muttered the odd word to her.

However, Ruth found herself drawn to Celia Vanderlin most of all, the outlet's matriarch, the one whose aura of power and mystery was both intriguing and unsettling. Ruth studied Celia as she moved through the crowd, her every word and gesture commanding attention, and couldn't shake the feeling there was more to this woman than met the eye.

Would she really have arranged for one of her own shops to be burned down?

Ruth fought the urge to ask her directly; however, Celia swept past without a glance. Following in her shadow was a tall, imposing man in his forties, with dark hair slicked back from his forehead, accentuating sharp, angular features.

"Oliver Vanderlin." Reverend Michael handed Ruth a Champagne flute. "Celia's son."

Ruth caught Oliver's eye and smiled, but he quickly looked away, and continued to follow his mother through the party guests.

∽

Later that night, after a long soak in the bath, Ruth sat on the sofa with Merlin curled up beside her, his soft purring a comfort.

On her lap lay *Mrs Beeton's Book of Household Management*. However, a light outside the window caught Ruth's eye.

Beyond several rooftops, Julian worked late above his shop. Illuminated by the glow of a work lamp, he removed a shimmering purple gown from a dummy and placed it carefully in a wicker basket, along with several silk scarves. He then left, turning out the light.

A soft knock came at Ruth's door.

"Come in."

Reverend Michael appeared with two mugs of steaming hot chocolate. "Am I disturbing you?"

"Not at all."

He set the tray down. "Settled okay?"

"Perfect. Thank you." Ruth gestured to the window. "Quite a view."

"It has its charms."

"I saw Julian just now, working late," Ruth said. "He seems very passionate and dedicated."

Reverend Michael's gaze drifted to the window. "It's his Friday ritual. Everyone expects it." He refocussed on Ruth and clearly noticed her inquisitive expression. "A local tradition, I suppose. Julian, perhaps a little desperate to reclaim his former glory, spends his nights crafting haute couture masterpieces. Every Friday, he displays his work on the village square's famous mannequin." A crease furrowed Reverend Michael's brow as he stared, unseeing, out the window. "He can be a bit obsessive. Pours his heart and soul into those creations."

Ruth chuckled. "I know the feeling."

Reverend Michael blinked, his gaze refocussing on Ruth. "Have you always been a food consultant?"

"Believe it or not, I was once a police officer. Many moons ago."

His eyebrows shot up. "Really? How fascinating."

"It had its moments."

"Perhaps you could share some stories tomorrow." Reverend Michael bowed his head. "I'll see you in the morning." He left, his footsteps fading down the hallway.

Ruth returned to Mrs Beeton and her bohemian ideas, her mind buzzing with extra culinary possibilities for the café, while the question burned in her mind: *Did Celia Vanderlin really start that fire?*

3

Dawn crept over the Osborne Outlet, and Ruth woke to the insistent meow of Merlin, his internal clock synced to early breakfast time down to the nanosecond. Her thoughts, however, came up with more ideas for Reverend Michael's café.

A tweaked menu could really draw in more punters, she thought, envisioning bustling tables and the chatter of happy diners.

After tending to Merlin and her own morning ablutions, Ruth spent a focussed twenty minutes jotting down suggestions.

Still keeping the core of the menu intact, as promised, she added some simple extras: *Avocado toast? Sure. A few vegan options? Great. A signature cake? Absolutely.*

Perhaps a decadent chocolate fudge, or a light-as-air Victoria sponge . . . The possibilities were exciting, but Ruth, ever pragmatic, curated a list of the most cost-effective and appealing options.

She then meticulously detailed easy recipes to follow,

adding tips for presentation—a sprig of parsley, a delicate dusting of icing sugar.

Then, remembering a more unusual recipe from the night before, she grabbed her copy of *Mrs Beeton's Book of Household Management*. In it was 'Spaghetti Pudding,' which involved breaking pasta into short lengths, dropping them into boiling milk, and simmering. Then the recipe called for adding sugar, butter, egg yolks, and lemon rind. Lastly, one introduced the egg whites and baked the concoction in a buttered pie dish for thirty minutes. *Easy*.

Ruth added the recipe to her suggestions for the café, half smirking to herself.

Downstairs, the aroma of coffee and sizzling bacon hung in the air. Reverend Michael, looking remarkably fresh in a crisp white shirt and a rather fetching brown leather apron, greeted her with a warm smile.

"Morning," he said, his voice bright. "Breakfast?"

"Didn't expect anyone up yet." Ruth pointed to the kettle. "May I?"

"Of course. Mugs are in the cupboard above."

She dropped her notebook onto the table and flicked on the kettle. "Would you like one?" Ruth extracted the largest, builder's-sized mug she could find and located the tea and sugar barrels.

"I've had two coffees already," Reverend Michael said with a sheepish expression, working with quiet efficiency. "Any more and I'll be bouncing off the walls."

Must be used to early mornings, Ruth mused.

He gestured to a stack of bread. "Toast and marmalade? Or would you prefer cereal? Full English?"

"Toast and marmalade will be fine, thanks." Ruth leaned against the worktop and peered into the café. Even at this early hour, several bleary-eyed figures were already seated, sipping coffee. Shop owners, she guessed, by their easy familiarity with one another. "What time do you open?"

"Five, usually." Reverend Michael shrugged. "I don't sleep much."

Ruth tried to imagine rousing Greg at such an ungodly hour. *A crowbar and heavy machinery might do the trick.* However, he had the sleep habits of a hibernating bear, surfacing only when the promise of food or WiFi was strong enough to rouse him.

"How about you?" Reverend Michael buttered the toast and spread liberal amounts of marmalade. Clearly a man who believed in generous portions. "Sleep well?"

"Like a log." Ruth made her tea, adding a scandalous amount of sugar, and sat at the table.

Reverend Michael set the plate in front of her and looked as though he was about to ask another question when a knock sounded at the back door. He opened it to a young postwoman clutching a parcel.

"Sorry to disturb." She glanced over her shoulder. "Have you seen Mr Jasper this morning?"

"Julian?" Reverend Michael frowned, a flicker of concern crossing his features. "Now that you mention it, no." He rubbed the back of his neck. "Odd. Julian's usually the first in for his java."

"Mr Jasper's not at his shop either," she said. "I started there, knowing he's usually open by now. Didn't mention he'd be away, did he?" She held up the parcel.

"Not that I know of," Reverend Michael said. "Would you like me to sign for that? I can take it over later."

"Thank you." She set it on the table as he signed her electronic device. "See you Monday." She touched the brim of her cap and left, unease lingering in her wake.

Reverend Michael stared at the parcel. "It's unlike Julian

not to be here." He sighed and motioned to a laptop. "I was working on getting the first things we've discussed underway." He looked genuinely apologetic, as though he'd somehow failed Julian by not noticing his absence sooner.

Ruth nodded to her notepad. "More ideas here, if you're up for it." She sipped her tea, savouring the sugary goodness, before moving on to her toast and marmalade. She perked up. The marmalade was homemade, with a delightful tang of Seville oranges.

Reverend Michael stared into the café.

"I can take the parcel over to Julian's shop, if you like?" Ruth offered, intrigued by the missing shopkeeper. "The Enchanted Loom, right?"

"That's the one." He turned back. "I don't want to put you out."

"It's no problem. I'll pop over there as soon as we've gone through the notes and I've finished my tea." *And maybe I can find out what that argument with Kathy was about.*

After checking the café again, Reverend Michael spent the next ten minutes with Ruth, going through more suggestions. He seemed very receptive to her ideas—apart from the spaghetti pudding, which he spotted as a joke immediately—nodding enthusiastically, clearly eager to make the café even more of a success.

"And we'll talk about the health and safety regulations once you're ready," Ruth said.

Reverend Michael stood. "I can get through this in the prelunch lull. How does three o'clock sound?"

"Perfect."

The main door opened, and Alex, the security guard, stepped in, yawning. "Morning, Reverend," he said as he approached the counter. He wore a dark blue uniform, and his gaze swept the café with a quiet intensity.

He'd been a mostly silent presence at the party, watching everything but saying little.

"Good morning, Alex." Reverend Michael gestured. "Alex, you've met Ruth Morgan? She's helping me spruce up the menu."

Alex nodded, his eyes lingering on her. "Last night."

Reverend Michael's expression turned serious again, and he said in a hushed voice, "Have you seen Julian? He appears to be missing."

Alex's eyebrows rose a fraction. "Missing?"

"Didn't come in for his usual." Reverend Michael pointed to the parcel on the kitchen table next to Ruth. "Nor does he seem to be at his shop." He poured a black coffee, his hand steady despite his obvious worry.

Alex took a sip, his eyes fixed on the parcel. "Did Julian mention any plans? An extra-long weekend? Anything out of the ordinary?"

Reverend Michael shook his head. "Not that I'm aware of. Not to me, at least. Seemed his usual self last night. A little preoccupied, maybe, but nothing unusual. Ruth saw him working late, as he always does on Fridays."

Ruth finished her tea and recalled seeing him through the window the previous evening, the single lamp casting long shadows as Julian carefully packed away his latest creation. He'd seemed lost in his work. "Could he have slipped and hurt himself on his way to dress the mannequin?" she asked, hoping that wasn't the case. The image of Julian lying injured, alone in his shop, sent a shiver down her spine.

"Only one way to find out." Alex downed his coffee.

Ruth stood. "I was about to take this over for him." She motioned to the parcel. "Care to escort me? I could do with some fresh air."

Alex hesitated, then, after a glance at Reverend Michael, shrugged. "Sure. Why not? You'll need a coat." He handed over a card, which the reverend swiped. Not a credit card, but an Osborne Outlet Village loyalty card.

Reverend Michael caught her eye. "Village employees get their drinks and food paid for. Courtesy of Mrs Vanderlin."

"Nice perk." Ruth chuckled. "Wouldn't let my grandson have one. You'd be bankrupt by the end of the day. Back in a minute." She rushed upstairs. Greg's bedroom door was still closed, and loud snores emanated from the other side. *Best not to disturb him.* Ruth grabbed her coat, scarf, and hat.

After checking on Merlin, who barely acknowledged her, Ruth headed back downstairs, eager to unravel the mystery of the missing shopkeeper.

She picked up the parcel and circled the counter. "Ready." Ruth headed to the door with Alex, a strange anticipation tightening her chest.

Reverend Michael called after Ruth, "When he comes down, I'll tell your grandson where you've gone."

"Not to worry. Greg won't be up for at least another three hours." She stepped outside with Alex, and they strode around the building, heading into the main part of the village, the crisp morning air invigorating her.

"We'll check Julian's shop first," Alex said, his voice clipped and professional. "His last known location. Then we'll retrace his steps to the village square."

"How long have you worked here?" Ruth asked as they walked.

"Two years."

"Seen some changes, I imagine?"

His lips twitched in what might be a wry smile. "Changes are inevitable."

"Didn't Julian move because of a fire?"

"He did." Alex glanced at her, a hint of suspicion in his eyes. He opened his mouth to say something, but quickly closed it again and looked away.

He's holding something back, Ruth realised. *He knows more than he's letting on.* "You suspect foul play?"

Alex let out a breath as they turned a corner. "Not my place to speculate. The police found no evidence of arson. Julian swore he'd not left a wet towel anywhere near the electric heater, and that the appliance should've been unplugged. Knew how dangerous they can be."

"If it was deliberate, any suspects?" Ruth pressed, her sleuthing instincts kicking in.

Alex shook his head, but Ruth had a good idea of one potential suspect—Julian's nemesis, Kathy Fellows. Ruth had seen the animosity between them at the party too, the barely concealed disdain in Kathy's eyes. *Could she have set fire to Julian's shop? But why? After all, it resulted in him having to move close to her.*

As they continued on, Ruth glanced around at all the buildings. "You know, I was here many years ago, and I'm sure it was all fields back then."

"It was," Alex said. "I've lived here all my life." Again, he looked as though he was about to say something else, but stopped himself as they reached Julian's shop. The loom in the window chugged away, weaving back and forth.

Behind it, bolts of fabric were stacked to one side, along with spools of thread and boxes overflowing with buttons and beads. However, the interior of the shop stood in darkness, no welcoming lights to beckon customers inside.

Alex tried the handle. "Locked." He peered up at the windows above, which were also dark.

Ruth cupped her hands to the glass, making out

mannequins, their plastic limbs frozen in various poses. A chill ran down her spine. The stillness unsettled her. "He's not here," she confirmed. "Any other way in?"

Alex produced a ring of keys. "I have access to all the shops." He unlocked the door with a small numbered brass key.

The scent of sandalwood and cotton wafted out.

"Julian?" Alex shone his torch inside. He stepped over the threshold, his movements cautious. "Julian, are you here?"

Ruth followed him in, the floorboards creaking beneath their feet, the sound amplified in the otherwise silent shop.

Alex flipped on a bank of light switches.

The shop was surprisingly spacious, with a high ceiling and exposed brick walls. Displays of scarves, dresses, and blouses filled the area, each item carefully folded and arranged.

Ruth ran a hand over the length of an emerald green silk scarf draped around a mannequin's neck. "Such beautiful material."

"He makes those." Alex shone his torch into a back room, his beam illuminating shelves with boxes.

Ruth eyed a vase filled with white lilies. "A shame he didn't maintain his previous success, but he seems to be flourishing here."

"Ambition can be a double-edged sword," Alex muttered.

"You can say that again." Ruth recalled her years on the force; the drive for justice often came at a personal cost. She'd seen firsthand how ambition could twist and corrupt, leaving a trail of broken lives in its wake. She shook herself back to the present.

As with the other shops in the Osborne Outlet village, this one too had a CCTV camera.

Alex's gaze swept the interior again, taking in every detail. "Nothing looks out of place."

"Julian works above, right?" Ruth peered at a slender staircase.

"Actually, he has a small apartment up there," Alex said. "A lot of the shop owners live in the village." His eyes narrowed. "You may be the last one to have seen him."

"Perhaps he's still asleep or unwell." Ruth tried to sound optimistic, though a knot of unease tightened in her stomach. "Do you have his phone number?"

"Never needed it." Alex led the way upstairs.

Ruth followed close behind, still clutching the parcel.

A door at the top stood ajar, casting a sliver of light into the otherwise darkened stairwell. Alex pushed it open and turned on the lights, revealing a workshop with a workbench overflowing with sketches and fabric samples, and more shelves stacked with bolts of silk and linen in every imaginable colour. A sewing machine sat next to the window, along with a work basket crammed full of yet more rolls of fabric.

The air hung heavy with Julian's absence.

Alex turned on the spot. "Not here either."

Ruth's gaze darted around the room, taking in the personal touches: a framed photograph of a younger Julian stood on a catwalk, surrounded by beautiful models. *A stark reminder of his past successes,* she thought with a pang of sympathy for the man.

A table overflowed with stacks of well-thumbed fashion magazines, and a collection of vintage sewing machines was displayed on a long sideboard. *A man who clearly loves his craft.* Ruth admired his dedication.

A cutting table sat in the middle of the room, with fabric scissors, embedded brass rulers, and tailor's chalk lined up along one edge.

There was a poignant sadness to it all, a sense of a life lived with passion, now hanging by a thread.

Alex crossed to a kitchen area and placed his hand on the kettle. He shook his head. "Cold. He's been gone a while."

"Maybe." Ruth set the parcel on a sideboard, next to an arrangement of flowers, with growing dread. "But he usually grabs his first coffee from the Silver Thimble." She brushed the petals. "Fresh. No more than a day old."

Alex went to the bedroom door, which stood open, revealing a neatly made bed and a wardrobe with its doors slightly ajar.

Ruth joined him, her pulse quickening. The bed was made, the covers taut. *Did Julian rise early and tidy up, or has he not slept in it at all?*

"His phone and wallet are here." Ruth pointed to a bowl by the door.

"Car keys are missing, though." Alex opened a window and peered down. "Car's missing from the staff car park." He let out a breath, and his shoulders relaxed. "Must've gone on an errand."

"Without his phone and wallet?" That didn't make much sense. Ruth peered closer at his phone. "No missed calls or messages."

They stood in silence for a moment, each lost in their own thoughts. The only sound was the distant hum of traffic from the motorway beyond the village.

A piercing scream outside shattered the stillness.

Alex ran to the front window and threw it open.

Heart in her mouth, Ruth joined him.

"Something's going on in the village square." Alex pointed to a spot between the buildings where an agitated group gathered. "Wait here." He raced to the door.

"Not likely." Ruth hurried after him, down the stairs, and across the shop.

They burst outside.

"This way." Alex jogged down the street, with Ruth hot on his heels.

The two of them reached the village square—a picturesque space surrounded by quaint shops with flower-filled baskets hanging from lampposts and the wishing well Ruth had spotted the day before. It was a scene of tranquillity, shattered by the knot of people gathered, their faces twisted with horror.

To one side of the wishing well sat a stone pedestal with a mannequin displaying Julian's latest creation: a flowing gown and a wide-brimmed hat. The one he'd been working on late the night before.

The group of people clustered in front of it, their faces pale with shock, their voices a jumble of panicked whispers.

"What happened?" Alex pushed through the crowd.

"It's— She's—" A woman dissolved into sobs.

Alex exchanged a grim look with Ruth, then followed their horrified gazes.

Ruth's stomach lurched.

The mannequin, draped in Julian's gown, was no mannequin at all, but the lifeless body of Kathy Fellows, propped up and tied to a pole around the waist and chest. Her face was contorted in a mask of terror, her eyes wide and staring blankly at the sky. A single red and white rose, identical to the one Julian had worn at the party, lay at her feet.

4

The vibrant purple gown, which Julian had meticulously crafted the previous night, now clung to Kathy's lifeless form. The luxurious fabric, meant to shimmer in a shop window or on a runway, accentuated the stillness of her body with a chilling finality.

Kathy's head lolled at an unnatural angle, her usually vibrant face now ashen, her lips tinged an unsettling shade of blue. A silk scarf, the exact emerald green of the one Ruth had admired moments earlier in Julian's shop, was cinched tightly around her neck. The sight sent a shiver down her spine.

Collective gasps and murmurs rippled through the growing crowd as more people arrived, the reality of the scene sinking in. Faces, previously alight with the cheerful bustle of the Osborne Outlet, were now contorted with shock and horror, mirroring the darkening sky.

Alex pushed through the onlookers. "Touch nothing." His gaze swept over the stunned faces, and landed on a man in a long coat—a newcomer to Ruth. "Call the police."

The man fumbled for his phone, his hand trembling as

he pressed it to his ear, and he muttered something about a tragedy.

Ruth stepped in front of Kathy's body, her eyes taking in the scene with a practised intensity. Years on the force had instilled in her a meticulous attention to detail, a habit she couldn't shake, even after all this time.

A wave of suspicion, cold and sharp, cut through the initial shock. Julian was gone. Kathy was dead. And the scarf, his creation, was now an apparent murder weapon.

The details formed a picture too clear to ignore, yet something felt off. *Too staged,* Ruth mused, her mind already racing through possibilities.

Is this a crime of passion, or something far deeper?

"Dear me." Reverend Michael's voice, tight with shock, pierced the whispers of the crowd. He stood behind Ruth, one hand clutching at his chest. "That's... that's Kathy."

Ruth backed away from the body, her gaze darting to the surrounding buildings, searching for any CCTV cameras. A flicker of hope ignited within her when she spotted one perched high on the wall down a street opposite.

"Police are on their way," the man in the long coat called out, his voice steadier now.

Sure enough, a few minutes later, the distant wail of sirens cut through the air, growing closer, more insistent, as the quiet morning shattered under the weight of a murder.

The idyllic peace of the outlet village, the charm that had drawn Ruth in, was now tainted with grim reality. She studied each and every face, looking for any hint as to who could've carried out such a heinous act.

Alex motioned to the crowd. "Everyone back, please." He waved Ruth and Reverend Michael over. "Hold the fort for a moment. I need to unlock the main gate for the emergency vehicles." He then jogged down the nearest street.

Ruth and Reverend Michael faced the onlookers, their arms outstretched. But no one dared to draw closer. Instead, the crowd continued to buzz with a mixture of shock and morbid fascination.

"Murder," someone breathed, the word hanging heavy in the air.

"Julian," another said, his voice laced with venom. "He hated her. Everyone knows that."

"I knew it would come to this," a short elderly lady wearing a bright yellow raincoat declared, her tone self-satisfied, her eyes narrowed, as if privy to some dark secret. "Didn't I warn you all? Didn't I say this would happen?"

"What did you warn them?" Ruth stepped forward. "Do you know something about this? About Julian and Kathy?"

The woman, startled by the direct questioning, shrank back, shaking her head, her bravado evaporating. "No, no, nothing. Only— Only talk, that's all. It's silly, really."

"What talk?" Ruth pressed, but the woman continued to shrink away, now staring at the ground.

After what seemed an eternity, the crowd parted as a police car—its blue, white, and yellow livery a jarring contrast to the quaint charm of the village—pulled into the square. Several officers climbed out.

Alex, having returned from unlocking the gate, jogged over to meet them.

The lead officer—judging by his bearing, a detective inspector. He acknowledged Alex with a curt nod. "Kensington. What do we have here?" He surveyed the scene before his gaze landed on Kathy's posed body and bound body.

"No one's touched anything," Alex said, his voice tight. He turned to the crowd. "Who was the first to find her?"

The lady in the yellow raincoat raised a trembling hand,

her eyes gleaming with a strange mixture of fear and self-importance.

The inspector motioned to his colleague, a younger officer who pulled a notepad from his pocket. "Take her statement. Get all the details." He nodded to his other officers. "Everyone moves back, and cordon off the scene."

"Yes, sir."

"Anyone unaccounted for?" the inspector asked Alex.

"Julian J Jasper. He runs the Enchanted Loom. Didn't show up this morning, which is highly unusual. He's always here, without fail."

The inspector nodded to his younger colleague. "Give Sergeant Nielsen Mr Jasper's details. I want him found. Now."

As Alex walked over to Sergeant Nielsen, Ruth approached the inspector, her hand outstretched. "Ruth Morgan."

"Detective Inspector Barnes." They shook hands, his grip firm, his eyes assessing. "You knew the deceased?"

"No. I only arrived yesterday," Ruth said. "I'm a food consultant. Hired to assist the Silver Thimble."

His brow furrowed. "What can I do for you, Ms Morgan?"

"I have an observation, if I may." Ruth pointed to Kathy's body. "The scarf around her neck, although one of Julian's, appears to have been tied with a single knot. However, from what I've seen in his shop, Julian uses a double loop. All the scarves are tied the same way. I noticed them earlier."

Inspector Barnes stared at her, his expression hardening. "Ms Morgan, I hardly think a killer, in the heat of the moment, will be meticulously tying a scarf a certain way."

"I beg to differ," Ruth countered, keeping her tone firm but not combative. "It would be second nature to Julian. A craftsman like him, meticulous in his work, wouldn't deviate from his established practise, even under duress. It's a matter of habit, of muscle memory."

Inspector Barnes glared at her, his patience clearly wearing thin. "Thank you for your input, but I suggest you leave the crime scene. You're wasting valuable police time. We'll handle this investigation." He ushered her back.

Ruth hesitated, her instincts screaming that something was amiss. *He's too quick to dismiss it.* Frustration rose within her. *Already made up his mind about Julian's guilt.* But arguing would do no good at this stage, so she backed away, and stepped outside the cordon.

More police cars and an ambulance arrived, their flashing lights adding to the chaos of the scene. Officers began to shoo the onlookers farther from the square. A doctor headed over to Kathy's body, accompanied by Detective Inspector Barnes.

With nothing more to contribute at the scene, Ruth, along with Reverend Michael and Alex, returned to the Silver Thimble Café.

The air inside hung heavy with the weight of the morning's events, the usual comforting scent of coffee and freshly baked goods unable to dispel the lingering unease.

They sat at the kitchen table in a daze, hands wrapped around mugs of coffee and tea, the silence punctuated by the occasional sip or sigh.

"I know this is asking a lot," Reverend Michael said to Ruth, his normally cheerful face downcast. "But considering your background, your experience as a former police officer, would you consider looking into Kathy's death too? For Julian's sake?"

"Hold on a minute," Alex interjected. "You were a police officer?"

Ruth nodded. "A long time ago."

Alex's voice was now laced with caution. "We're talking about a murder investigation. It's not our place to get involved. We need to let the *current* police do their job."

"I disagree," Reverend Michael countered. "It's everyone's place. Especially when an innocent man will be wrongly accused. We can't just stand by and watch that happen."

Alex frowned. "You think Julian is innocent?"

"Of course I do." Reverend Michael inclined his head, his gaze unwavering. "Have you ever known Julian to be anything but kind and gentle? He wouldn't hurt a fly." Without waiting for an answer, he refocussed on Ruth. "What do you think?"

"I don't have an opinion either way," she said, choosing her words carefully. "And I think Alex is right—I shouldn't get involved. I'm sure the police will conduct a thorough investigation. They have the resources, and the expertise."

Even so, her doubts grew with every passing moment. Something still felt off. *Why would Julian stage Kathy's body like that? Why so obvious?*

The door to the café opened, and Inspector Barnes strode in, his face set with determination. He beckoned to Alex. "Kensington, a word, please."

As Alex rose from the kitchen table, he leaned in to Reverend Michael, his voice low and urgent. "Look, I understand your concern for Julian, but we need to trust the process. Let the police do their job. We can't afford to interfere." He then crossed the café and followed Inspector Barnes outside, leaving palpable tension in his wake.

Reverend Michael stared after him, his jaw clenched. "I still think someone else should—"

The door to the stairs creaked open, and Greg padded

into the kitchen, yawning and running a hand through his tousled hair. "Morning," he mumbled, dropping into a chair at the table. He blinked, his bleary eyes taking in their sombre faces. "What's wrong? Something happened?"

Greg's face paled as Ruth and Reverend Michael recounted the events of the morning, the discovery of Kathy's body, the arrival of the police, and Julian's implied involvement.

"But Julian seems like a really nice guy," Greg said, echoing Reverend Michael's earlier sentiment.

"Exactly." Reverend Michael began to prepare him a breakfast of eggs, bacon, sausages, and beans, his movements almost mechanical, as if trying to find solace in the familiar routine. "I've always considered Julian a kindred spirit, someone who doesn't quite fit in, who marches to the beat of his own drum. Yet, he possesses a unique talent, a quiet strength. There's more to this than meets the eye, I'm sure of it." He fixed his gaze on Ruth. "I've known Julian for years, and I can vouch for his character. He's a kind, gentle soul, incapable of violence."

Ruth opened her mouth to answer, but Reverend Michael continued in a rush, "Why, just last month, when a pipe burst in Mrs Henderson's shop, causing a section of her ceiling to collapse, Julian was the first one there, offering her shelter in his apartment, helping her salvage what they could from the water damage." He paused, his voice thick with emotion. "The thought of Julian being accused of such a brutal act is simply incomprehensible."

"I think I now agree." Alex strode back into the kitchen. He lowered himself into a chair with a heavy sigh. "They've arrested Julian, even though he says he's innocent."

Ruth, who had been staring at the table, trying to remember everything she'd overheard Julian saying at the party and his general placid demeanour, looked up sharply. "They've already arrested him? On what grounds?"

"He was apprehended while trying to reach his sister, who lives out of town. They found Kathy's handbag in his possession."

Ruth cringed. "That's damning evidence. Circumstantial, but damning." She avoided eye contact with Reverend Michael.

"Julian claims Kathy left it in his shop after an argument yesterday," Alex continued. "He says he panicked when he discovered her body this morning, fearing he would be implicated, that no one would believe him."

Reverend Michael set a plate piled high with breakfast goodies in front of Greg.

"Thanks." Greg tucked in with his usual gusto.

Alex reached for his coffee, but Reverend Michael stopped him, his eyes filled with a steely determination that surprised Ruth. "In that case, Julian thinks someone has framed him?" he asked, tipping away Alex's stale coffee and pouring him a fresh mug. "Does he have any idea who might want to do such a thing?"

"Officers will interview him soon." Alex sipped the coffee, his brow furrowed in thought. "They'll have the square cleared in the next hour, and we can open the village as normal."

"They're done with the crime scene so soon?" Ruth asked, her eyebrows raised in surprise. "That seems awfully rushed, especially for a murder investigation. Surely, they need more time to process the scene properly."

"They think they have their guy." Alex shrugged. "But I'm sure they've collected the necessary forensic evidence. They wouldn't be so careless."

Ruth nodded slowly, but a knot of unease continued to

tighten in her stomach. This was all moving too fast. And despite her initial reluctance, she found herself drawn into the unfolding drama.

The inconsistencies she'd observed at the crime scene, the seemingly rushed conclusion of the police, and the genuine distress of Reverend Michael all pointed to a deeper mystery, one she felt increasingly compelled to unravel.

Greg glanced at her. "So, will you investigate?" he asked, his voice laced with a mixture of apprehension and anticipation.

She closed her eyes as an unwelcome memory rose to the surface. An interrogation room, the harsh glare of the overhead light, the young man, barely more than a boy, his face pale with fear as he insisted on his innocence.

The boy, Danny, had been accused of robbing a local shop, a crime he vehemently denied. Ruth had believed him, had fought for Danny tooth and nail, but the evidence, or rather, the interpretation of the evidence, had ultimately condemned him.

It had taken years, and a chance encounter with a colleague who had mentioned a prison confession never followed up on, to finally uncover the truth, to expose the real perpetrator and clear Danny's name.

The guilt of failing Danny, of not seeing through the deception sooner, had haunted Ruth ever since.

She opened her eyes, the memory fading but the sting remaining. Ruth had vowed never to let that happen again, to listen to friends and family who knew the accused best, and to fight for those who couldn't fight for themselves.

I can't stand by and watch another potentially innocent person be punished. Her resolve hardened. But Ruth needed to tread carefully.

"We must help him," Reverend Michael insisted. "We can't let Julian go to prison for something he didn't do."

"I understand your concern," Alex said before Ruth could answer. "But as I've already said, we must not interfere with a police investigation."

"What if they're wrong?" Greg muttered, surprising Ruth. He usually hated getting involved in anything remotely mysterious.

Ruth's eyes unfocused as the image of Kathy's lifeless body, draped in Julian's creation, flashed in her mind's eye again. And that emerald scarf. "If we do get involved, we must be careful."

Greg snorted.

Ruth cleared her throat. "No silly mistakes."

Her grandson raised an eyebrow, his scepticism evident. "But you're still planning on jumping in, feet first, risking everyone's lives in the process, though, right?"

"Of course." Ruth smiled. "This will be fun," she added to inject a note of levity into the tense atmosphere.

Reverend Michael's shoulders relaxed, and his face brightened. "Thank you, Ruth. You won't regret this. I know you can help us find the truth."

"Don't thank me yet," Ruth cautioned. "This won't be easy."

"Detective Inspector Barnes seems convinced of Julian's guilt," Alex said. "He won't appreciate any interference."

"Then we'll have to be discreet."

Alex shook his head, his disapproval evident. "I can't allow—"

"May I remind you of the unfortunate shoplifting incident?" Reverend Michael interjected, his voice low, his gaze fixed on Alex. "When you accidentally let the shoplifter go? We all rallied around you then, did we not?

Everyone stood up for you against Mrs Vanderlin. Julian included."

Alex stared back at him, his expression unreadable.

"We can be discreet," Ruth said. "We'll ask a few questions, see if anything comes up. That's all. We will report any findings to the police. No interference, I promise." She shot Greg a sidelong glance, a silent warning not to contradict her.

Alex took another gulp of his coffee, his internal conflict evident in the deep worry lines on his face. "Earlier, you asked if I suspected foul play in Julian's shop fire." His gaze darted toward the café to ensure they were alone. "I told you the police didn't find any evidence of arson. That was true." He paused, his eyes now drifting to the nearest window, as if searching for something beyond the glass. "But I did find something that bothered me at the time. I handed it over to them, of course, but... they didn't take it seriously enough."

"What kind of evidence?" Ruth asked.

"Nothing concrete," Alex said. "Just inconsistencies. Things that didn't add up. The way the fire seemed to start in the middle of the workroom, surrounded by flammable materials."

"Julian is meticulous about safety," Reverend Michael said. "Always has been. We all knew it was suspicious."

Alex nodded. "He swore he kept the electric heater against the wall, near the window, well away from any fabrics."

"He would never have placed it in the middle of the room like that," Reverend Michael agreed. "And the back door was found unlocked. Again, something Julian would never have done. He's always so careful about security."

Alex looked at Ruth. "I told the inspector it didn't make sense. Someone else must have done it. Of course, Mrs

Vanderlin also refused to hear of it. Said it was an accident, that Julian was careless."

Reverend Michael rolled his eyes. "His workshop was overflowing with expensive fabrics and equipment. Someone clearly wanted him to suffer."

"Kathy?" Greg asked.

A logical question, Ruth thought.

Alex shrugged. "I can't see Kathy doing something like that. She's outspoken at times, a bit brash, but not an arsonist. She wouldn't stoop that low."

"We all know she wasn't exactly Julian's biggest fan," Reverend Michael said. "They argued constantly, especially after he was forced to relocate his shop opposite hers. That made things ten times worse."

Ruth had witnessed that tension the previous day, along with the barely concealed disdain in Kathy's eyes.

But could that animosity between them have escalated to murder?

"If she was responsible for the fire," Ruth said, thinking aloud, "did Kathy know beforehand that Julian would have to move to the shop opposite? If so, that wouldn't make any sense. Why burn down his shop only for him to end up right across the street, where she'd have to see him every day?"

"Maybe she wanted to make Julian's life a misery," Greg suggested. "Kathy might have planned it that way, have Julian close by so she could keep an eye on him, wind him up to the point of wanting to leave the village entirely."

A slow, calculated campaign of harassment, Ruth thought. *Plausible. But why?*

"Does Julian have any other enemies?" she asked, trying to encompass all possibilities.

"None," Reverend Michael said with complete conviction. "Everyone loves Julian. He's a pillar of the community."

A memory from the previous day struck Ruth, a conversation that now seemed imbued with a new significance. "Leana. The girl in the candle shop. She mentioned something about Celia Vanderlin. Said she was trying to force Kathy out of her shop. Is that true?"

Alex's brow furrowed. "That's the first I've heard of it. Why would Mrs Vanderlin want Kathy out? Kathy's shop is one of the most successful in the village. She's been here for years."

"Leana didn't know the reason," Ruth said, "but she mentioned something about 'musical shops,' as if there was some sort of rotation going on behind the scenes, with owners being shuffled around at Celia's whim."

Alex shook his head. "Other than Julian's relocation after the fire, no one has moved in the last six months. And Kathy's shop has been in the same spot."

Reverend Michael sat down and leaned back in his chair, a thoughtful expression on his face. "I'm afraid Leana is prone to a conspiracy theory or two. She's a sweet girl, but her imagination sometimes runs away with her."

"She called Celia Vanderlin 'The Black Widow,'" Greg said, his voice tinged with a hint of amusement.

Reverend Michael sighed. "Yes, well, we've all heard Leana's crazy rumours about Celia's husband's untimely demise. But none of it is true. He died of a heart attack, not poison."

"Celia is formidable," Alex said. "She runs a tight ship, and she doesn't suffer fools gladly. But she's not a murderer. That's ridiculous."

"Indeed. Utter nonsense," Reverend Michael echoed, although his tone lacked conviction.

"I still think it wouldn't hurt to ask a few discreet questions," Ruth said, returning to her earlier point. "With your help, Alex, we can do it quickly, and efficiently. We'll be gathering information, seeing if anything comes to light. As I said, we won't interfere with the official investigation."

Reverend Michael poured Alex another coffee, a conciliatory gesture.

Alex stared down at his mug, his expression conflicted. He took a deep breath and sighed. "Fine. We'll ask around, see what we can find out. But I'm serious"—his expression hardened—"if it gets too risky, if I say stop, we stop. No arguments."

"You have my solemn promise," Ruth said, crossing her fingers under the table.

Greg noticed the gesture and shook his head in obvious exasperation.

5

Ruth finished her tea, her mind already racing with various avenues of investigation they could hope to explore. The outlet village, with its multitude of shops and tenants, suddenly felt like a wealth of secrets.

"First thing's first." She pushed her chair back with a decisive scrape across the tiled floor. "We need to retrace Julian's steps from last night. Someone must have seen him after he left his shop to go to the party, and vice versa." Her gaze sharpened as it landed on Alex. "What about the security cameras?"

"I gave Sergeant Davies access. He shouldn't be too long. He's only taking copies. Said he'll review the recordings back at the station. I'm to keep the originals. Give him an hour, and then we can take a look."

Ruth pointed up at the camera mounted in the corner of the café's main room. "What about internal CCTV? I noticed them in all the shops."

Alex shook his head. "No go. Old system. Deactivated. Only the newer cameras in the public areas work."

A sigh escaped Ruth's lips. *Of course. It wouldn't be that easy.* She swivelled to face Greg, who was currently engrossed in the glowing rectangle of his phone, no doubt relaying the morning's grim events to his girlfriend, Mia. "Greg, are you coming with us?"

He glanced up, a flicker of resignation in his eyes. "Sure." He knew it was a rhetorical question.

Greg might grumble, but beneath the teenage apathy, he possessed a sharp mind and a surprising willingness to get involved, if nothing more than to try and prevent Ruth from doing something foolish. *An asset during times like these.*

Besides, with a potential killer on the loose, Ruth wanted her grandson close.

As Greg unfolded himself from the chair with a series of dramatic groans, Ruth turned to Reverend Michael. The colour had yet to return to his cheeks, betraying the lingering shock of the morning's discovery.

"Thank you for breakfast." Ruth offered him a reassuring smile. "We'll let you know what we find. And I'll be sure to finish up with the consultancy later today."

Reverend Michael managed a weak smile in return, his earlier anxiety replaced by a look of fragile hope. "Please, be careful."

"Not likely," Greg mumbled, pocketing his phone. "Grandma loves danger."

Ruth shot him a warning glance. "That's not even remotely true, Gregory," she said, hoping to intercept Alex's stern glare before it could fully materialise. "I am the definition of safety." A blatant lie, of course, but necessary.

Ruth and Greg donned their coats and followed Alex out of the warmth of the café into a dark and overcast world that mirrored the sombre mood. Ruth pulled her collar in tight against the biting wind that whipped between the buildings and along the narrow streets.

The sky threatened a downpour at any moment.

"Only going to get worse," Alex said.

"Then we need to be quick," Ruth replied, eager to get investigating. "Do you have a list of the shop tenants?"

"In my office. We can look at it when we review the CCTV footage."

Ruth's intuition buzzed. "In the meantime, let's go back to the square. I need to examine the scene again. Maybe I missed something." She couldn't definitively say Julian was innocent, not with the current evidence, or lack thereof, but something wasn't right.

The outlet village square, once a vibrant hub of activity, was now eerily quiet, the cheerful chatter of shoppers replaced by an unsettling hush.

The police had removed the cordon, but the ghost of the tragedy lingered, a palpable weight that settled over the quaint cobbled streets.

The initial shock seemed to have subsided, replaced by subdued, almost hesitant activity as a few brave shopkeepers opened their doors and prepared for the day ahead, their movements cautious, dreamlike.

Ruth approached the wishing well, the focal point of the square, and then turned to the stone pedestal where Kathy's body had been tied up and displayed on the pole. As she circled it, a speck of red glitter caught Ruth's eye, clinging to the edge, shimmering in the weak light of a nearby streetlamp that remained on beneath the grim sky.

She pointed it out to Alex. "Did the crime scene officers miss that?"

Alex's brow furrowed with concern. "They shouldn't have."

Greg offered a possible explanation. "Might have blown in since. There's a breeze, after all."

Ruth knelt and leaned in close. Despite the strengthening wind, the glitter remained stubbornly adhered to the rough stone, held fast by a tiny drop of what looked like dried oil or wax. She took several pictures with her phone, careful not to disturb the potential evidence. "We should tell the police." She straightened up. "It might be important."

"I'll call them." Alex pressed his phone to his ear and strode away.

Ruth scanned the nearby buildings: a quaint pottery shop with lace-curtained windows; a brightly coloured sweet shop, its doors flanked by candy canes; and down the alleyway between them, a CCTV camera, discreetly positioned.

Greg followed her gaze. "If they've caught Julian on that, it's an open-and-shut case, right?"

Ruth pursed her lips, sifting through the possibilities. "Look at the way it's angled." She motioned to the stone pedestal. "Kathy was facing away from it, and the camera's view is obscured by the wishing well. It's possible someone could have placed Kathy there unseen, especially from the lane opposite."

Alex returned. "I passed on your finding to Sergeant Davies. He says he's almost done copying the CCTV recordings and will come here next to collect the evidence."

Ruth scanned the square again, but nothing else seemed out of place. "Who was closest to Kathy? Who knew her best?"

"That'll be May, at the Storybook Store." Alex gestured down a nearby alleyway.

The three of them strode along the narrow alley, the wind whistling through the gaps between the buildings. They reached May's shop, a welcome splash of colour against the greyness of the day.

The Storybook Store lived up to its name: a storefront painted in cheerful shades of blue and green, adorned with illustrations of children's book characters: a grinning Cheshire cat perched precariously on a stack of oversized books, a sleepy-eyed owl wearing spectacles, and a mischievous-looking pixie peering from behind a toadstool.

Ruth peered up at the rooftops, getting her bearings. "This street runs parallel to Julian and Kathy's shops?"

"Right," Alex confirmed. "Julian's is over there."

Ruth took a deep breath, steeling herself, and opened the door, and a tinkling bell announced their arrival.

The interior was a book-lover's paradise, with shelves stretching two floors high, filled with thousands of novels, everything from classic literature and contemporary fiction to biographies and cookbooks.

The air hung thick with the scent of old paper and leather, a comforting aroma that momentarily transported Ruth to her time spent with her late husband, poring over ancient manuscripts.

Greg settled into a comfortable armchair by the window, surrounded by stacks of books. He picked up a hardback on ancient Egypt, his fingers tracing the embossed cover.

May Thomas, a woman in her fifties with a warm smile and kind face, greeted them from behind the counter. Her hair was still styled in the impressive beehive of the night before, but now, instead of a designer dress, she wore a beige cardigan and black trousers. Her eyes, though tinged with sadness, held a spark of resilience.

"You left the party early last night," Alex said as they approached the counter.

May sighed. "Sorry. Cleaner alerted me to a minor flood in the back room. Needed my attention."

Alex's face fell. "Everything okay? Want me to take a look?"

"It's all taken care of." May managed a weak smile. "Thank you." The smile then vanished. "It's the least of my worries today."

"Good morning," Ruth said. "We're so sorry about Kathy." She gestured to Alex. "We were hoping to ask you a few questions, if you don't mind?"

May looked off into the distance, her expression sorrowful. "I've already spoken to the police." Her gaze flickered back to Alex. "But of course. Anything I can do to help." She hugged herself, wrapping her cardigan tightly around her body as if to ward off a chill. "It's horrible, what happened. I can't believe she's gone." May's voice trembled. "Sh-She was such an effervescent presence. We'll all miss her terribly."

"You knew her well?" Ruth asked, keeping her tone soft.

Tears welled in May's eyes. "We were close friends since childhood. Even when she lived in Weymouth, we stayed in touch." She plucked a handkerchief from her pocket and dabbed her eyes. "When Kathy said she wanted to move back to Osborne, I negotiated her shop lease."

"With Mrs Vanderlin?" Ruth asked, confusion furrowing her brow. "Reverend Michael seemed to be under the impression that was all Kathy's doing. That she was a shrewd businesswoman."

Despite the circumstances, a ghost of a smile touched May's lips. "She was terrible. Barely kept afloat. I had to help her a lot. She was nothing but tenacious, though."

"So, you spoke to her often?" Ruth asked.

"Kathy and I had lunch together every day." May blew her nose. "It's a small place, you know. Plenty of gossip to share over coffee."

"Did you notice anything unusual about Kathy's behaviour recently?" Ruth pressed.

Alex added, "Anything that might have indicated she was in trouble?"

Ruth was caught off guard by his question.

Does he know more than he's letting on?

May's eyes widened in surprise. "Trouble? Oh, goodness, no. Kathy was always so positive. Full of life. Boundless energy." She sniffed. "I'll miss her terribly."

Ruth glanced at Alex, a fleeting expression of doubt on his face. She refocussed on May. "Nothing bothered her at all? Especially recently?"

May shook her head vehemently. "Kathy seemed her usual self. Always busy, of course. Always on the go. She wanted to succeed so badly." She paused, a thoughtful frown creasing her brow. "Now that you mention it, though, she did seem a bit preoccupied lately. Distracted. Kathy mentioned having some disagreements with Julian, but didn't go into detail."

"You don't know what their arguments were about?" Ruth asked.

May shook her head again, her beehive swaying.

Ruth wasn't convinced Kathy's best friend wouldn't be privy to Kathy's arguments with Julian, especially when they shared more general village gossip so freely. Her lack of knowledge regarding Julian seemed unlikely.

Ruth changed tack; a different approach would yield better results. "Did Kathy mention anyone else she might have had a disagreement with?"

May's gaze drifted to a set of shelves lined with colourful children's books, her eyes unfocussed. "Not that I can recall. Like I said, Kathy was a very private person, despite her outgoing nature. She didn't often share her personal problems." She looked back at Ruth and Alex, a hint of defensiveness in her tone. "I helped when I could."

This was proving more difficult than Ruth had anticipated. "Is there anything at all you can tell us? No matter how insignificant it might seem."

When May merely shrugged, apparently unable or unwilling to offer any further information, Alex stepped in, his voice taking on a sharper edge. "What about Oliver Vanderlin? Celia's son. I'm sure you two had a lot to discuss about him."

May recoiled a step, and stared at Alex, her eyes widening with a mixture of surprise and apprehension, before she finally let out a small shaky breath. "I have nothing to say about that man." Her shoulders then slumped as if the weight of the village's problems had suddenly landed on her. "I don't know why this happened to Kathy. It's awful." She gripped the edge of the counter. "Kathy and Celia had a few heated exchanges about something. Nothing physical, mind you. Just words."

But words can lead to more, Ruth thought. *Could this be the motive? A dispute turned deadly?*

"Beyond that, I can't think of anything else. Everyone loves Kathy." May's voice cracked again, her grief palpable. "*Loved* her. I cannot believe I'll never see her again." She wiped away tears with her handkerchief. "Do you think Celia has something to do with Kathy's murder?"

"Thank you for your time." Ruth gave her a sympathetic smile. "We appreciate your help. If you think of anything else, please let us know."

As they left the shop, the tinkling bell announcing their departure, Ruth felt a pang of disappointment. May had been their first real lead, and she had yielded little in the way of concrete information, only hearsay. Ruth, however, refused to be discouraged. "We learned that Kathy and Julian's disagreements weren't the only petty squabbles going on."

"The issues with Celia Vanderlin?" Greg asked.

Ruth pulled her coat collar tighter against the wind. "There's something deeper there, something we may need to uncover. Speaking of which . . ." She turned to Alex, her eyes narrowed with suspicion. "What was with that comment about Kathy being in trouble? Do you know something you'd like to share?"

"No," he said, a little too quickly, and averted his gaze.

Ruth didn't believe him, but she wouldn't press the matter right away. She'd bide her time.

They continued their walk, the wind picking up, whipping their hair and coats around them like unruly banners. The sky had darkened considerably, and the first fat raindrops began to fall, splattering against the cobblestones.

"Sergeant Davies should be finished with the CCTV." Alex motioned down another alleyway. "Let's go to my office and review the footage there."

Ruth and Greg followed him along a winding alleyway, past overflowing bins and the backs of shops, their footsteps echoing in the confined space.

"I told you individual shops used to have their own interior CCTV cameras, but they were deactivated when someone complained about privacy," Alex said as they passed a delivery van parked haphazardly across the alley, its side door hanging open, revealing a jumble of boxes. "But there are several newer cameras covering the communal areas. That's what we'll look at now."

"And don't forget the list of tenants," Ruth reminded him.

Alex led them around the back of the garden centre, past

a display of wilting plants and chipped gnomes, to the base of the giant beanstalk. He opened a discreetly hidden door. "Follow me."

Ruth and Greg exchanged bemused expressions.

"If I get murdered to death in here," Greg murmured, "Mum will kill you."

Ruth stared back at him, unblinking. "You have my word, Gregory, the moment Alex pulls out a gun or a knife, I'll leap in front of him, so you have time to run away."

"What about a rope?" Greg asked.

"That too."

"Wrench?"

Ruth nodded.

"A lead pipe taped to a candlestick?"

"Sure. Why not?"

Greg furrowed his brow. "Okay, what if he throws a hand grenade at me?"

"Don't push your luck." Ruth took a deep breath and stepped through the door, hoping Alex didn't have a secret stash of hand grenades, otherwise they were *both* done for.

6

Ruth and Greg followed Alex down a flight of stairs and along a dimly lit corridor with a strong odour of damp—a stark contrast to the charming storybook atmosphere of the village above.

At the end of the concrete hallway, Alex stopped before a nondescript metal door and, with a pointed look at Ruth and Greg, pushed it open. He stepped aside, gesturing for them to enter.

Ruth motioned to her grandson. "After you."

Greg mumbled something unintelligible, casting a wary glance at Alex before stepping through.

The room beyond stood twenty feet square, with a small window propped open to allow ventilation, and a large cluttered desk piled high with paperwork, technical manuals, and several half-empty coffee cups.

Next to the desk sat a rack filled with rolled-up blueprints, and a table beneath with a couple laid flat, showing plans of the village.

A worn faux leather swivel chair sat facing monitors,

each displaying images from security cameras throughout the Osborne Outlet Village.

Alex scooped up a ring of keys—the ones Sergeant Davies had evidently left behind—and gestured to one screen in particular that showed a wide-angle view of the village square.

Ruth peered at the image, her eyes adjusting to the dim light. Sure enough, Sergeant Davies, partly obscured by the wishing well, bent over, no doubt collecting the glitter evidence.

"This is the only camera covering the village square?" Ruth asked.

Alex nodded in confirmation and pointed to the screen. "And as you can see, the wishing well obscures where Kathy was found."

"Why so few cameras?" Greg asked. "Isn't shoplifting a thing here?"

"Mrs Vanderlin doesn't see the need for an extensive camera system," Alex replied, his own frustration evident in the tightness of his voice. "When the old system went down, she only approved these ones overlooking the communal areas. Declined my request to add more. Said it would ruin the village's atmosphere. Someone is due to remove the old cameras next week." He navigated through files. "These recordings are from last night."

The largest screen shifted, dividing into nine smaller squares, each displaying footage from different areas of the village.

The recordings showed a steady stream of shoppers milling about during the day, their faces blurred and indistinct.

Greg frowned. "These are new cameras?"

Alex sighed. "Mrs Vanderlin bought them cheap, but they're still better quality than the old ones."

As evening approached, the crowds thinned, and the streets grew quieter. Darkness fell, the shops closed one by one, their windows going dark, until the village was empty.

The recording continued, the timestamp in the corner of the screen ticking away the minutes and hours.

"There." Greg pointed at a view aiming toward the Enchanted Loom. "That's Julian."

Ruth leaned closer. The figure, tall and slender, was unmistakable. He walked with a purposeful stride, his head held high, and carried a wicker basket, its contents obscured by a dark cloth.

"Where's he going?" Greg scanned the other images.

Alex pointed to a display in the middle row, far right. It showed Julian striding past more darkened shops, disappearing down a narrow lane between Gape Cod, the garish fish and chip shop, and the gingerbread-house sweet shop. "No cameras down there."

"That's the lane that leads to Mystical Flames," Ruth said, recalling their visit to the candle shop the previous day.

"Why would he go there?" Greg asked, his brow furrowed. "You think that's where he picked up the glitter?"

The minutes ticked by on the screen, five, ten, fifteen... and finally, Julian reappeared at the edge of the village square. Without hesitation, he made his way across the cobblestones, passing behind the wishing well, and stopped in front of where Kathy's body had been found.

A cold dread washed over Ruth. "As I feared. We can't see what he's doing. The angle of this camera is completely useless."

The three of them watched in silence as Julian carefully removed a dress from the wicker basket and fitted it to what could have been either a mannequin or Kathy's lifeless corpse.

There was no way to tell.

After finishing by tying a scarf around what could only be the figure's neck, he stepped back, appraising his work with a critical eye.

Alex rewound the footage again and again, while Ruth scrutinised every detail, every movement. There was nothing in Julian's demeanour to suggest he had just committed a murder. He seemed calm, almost serene, as if he was merely performing his usual weekly task.

Perhaps he really is innocent.

Ruth's gaze darted over all the other images, but the rest of the village was quiet, with no signs of another person. The lanes and alleyways appeared deserted, the shops dark and lifeless.

"There's no one else around," she said, unable to keep disappointment from her voice.

"Not necessarily," Alex countered, resuming normal playback. "Like I said, the cameras we have don't cover every inch of the village. There are blind spots. Lots of them. Someone could have slipped in and out unnoticed."

"And even if Julian met someone first," Greg added, his voice thoughtful, "it doesn't mean they had anything to do with Kathy's murder. Maybe he was meeting a friend, or a supplier."

Ruth nodded, acknowledging the possibility. "We can't jump to conclusions."

Julian, his task completed, walked away from the wishing well and headed down another alleyway that snaked its way through the back of the village.

"What's down there?" Ruth asked.

"Staff car park," Alex said.

"I don't understand," Greg said. "Julian lives above his shop."

Alex shrugged. "He often stays with his sister over the weekend."

Ruth cocked an eyebrow, her suspicion growing. "Let me guess—no cameras in the staff car park?"

Alex sighed. "No cameras."

Blind spots everywhere. Ruth gnashed her teeth. This was proving more challenging than she'd anticipated. But she wasn't one to give up easily. "Bodies don't just appear out of thin air," she muttered, more to herself than anyone else. Ruth took a deep, steadying breath. "Let's continue with these recordings."

Alex sped the footage forward. The monochrome night bled into a grey dawn, with no other movement in the village until shopkeepers unfurled their awnings and switched on lights.

A familiar figure appeared: Julian, striding purposefully across the cobbles, heading toward the wishing well. He stopped abruptly, his body going rigid. Even in the grainy footage, his shock was palpable. He stared up at the stone pedestal, his face a mask of horror, then stumbled backward, almost tripping over his own feet.

"He sees Kathy," Greg breathed, his eyes glued to the screen. "So her body did just appear, then?"

"Impossible," Ruth said, more confused than ever.

Julian stood there for a moment, frozen in place, before turning and running back the way he had come, disappearing down the alleyway toward the staff car park.

"Lines up with what he told Inspector Barnes," Alex said. "Panicked when he saw her and ran off."

Ruth glanced at the timestamp: 08:15. It coincided almost exactly with the moment Alex had shown up at the

Silver Thimble to start his shift. A tiny seed of suspicion took root in her mind, but she pushed it down, for the time being.

Sure enough, a few minutes later, Ruth and Alex appeared on screen, walking toward Julian's shop, Ruth clutching the parcel. Alex unlocked the door, and they entered.

The minutes ticked by.

"Look." Greg pointed to the image of the village square.

The woman in the yellow raincoat threw her hands up and stumbled backward, almost tripping over her own feet. Other people came running, their faces a blur of confusion and alarm.

Moments later, Ruth and Alex appeared in the square, their body language quickly turning from initial confusion to horror as they realised the true nature of the scene before them.

"No one swapped out the mannequin for Kathy's body," Alex said, his brow furrowed. "Julian must have done it."

"But when?" Ruth asked, her voice rising in frustration. "And how? There's no one else on these recordings. No sign of anyone near the square after Julian left Friday night." She motioned to the controls. "Rewind to the moment he returned to the square and continue back from there. We'll look for any other movement, shadows, anything at all. We must have missed something."

Alex did as she suggested, and the three of them leaned in, their eyes glued to the screen as the scene played out in reverse, from before Julian returned that morning the shop keepers walking backward, their movements unnatural.

"Someone would've noticed a body earlier, though, right?" Greg asked. "Before Julian? And then that lady in the rain mac afterward?"

Ruth's gaze remained fixed on the screen. The recordings continued to rewind, back through the Saturday morning, and the previous Friday night. "Stop. Play it forward. Normal speed."

Alex complied, and a young couple, their faces blurred by the low resolution, stumbled into the square, clutching each other and laughing.

"We saw them at the party," Greg said.

"Josh and Connie," Alex said. "Connie is Dave Jones' daughter. He runs the bakery."

Ruth nodded to the timestamp: 23:23. "After the party, and long after Julian had left for the night."

The couple looked up at a spot where the mannequin must have been, laughed and pointed, then staggered off, disappearing down one of the alleyways.

"Not fans of Julian's creation, it would seem," Ruth murmured, folding her arms.

"Right, but I think we can safely say that means there was no body there at that time either," Alex said.

Ruth pursed her lips. "How did the murderer do it, then? It's not magic. Must have been from the lane that's obscured by the wishing well. It's the only way to reach the pedestal unseen."

"Someone hoisted Kathy up there between 11:23 last night and when Julian showed up this morning?" Greg asked. "They must be strong, right? To lift a body up onto the platform?"

Alex sped the recording forward again, but slower this time, and all three of them huddled around the monitor, their eyes scanning the screen for any sign of movement.

Ruth kept her attention fixed on the buildings and cobblestones around the wishing well.

Nothing.

No shadows, no sign of anyone approaching the square.

They watched in silence, all the way back to morning again, and Julian's shock discovery.

"This is ridiculous." Ruth huffed and stepped back from the monitor. "Return to the previous night, when Julian dressed the mannequin."

Alex did as she asked, rewinding the footage all the way back to when Julian entered the square with the wicker basket, and he hit play.

Julian worked, lifting out the dress and placing it on what they could only assume was the mannequin obscured by the wishing well. Once done, he pulled out the scarf and reached up, then finally stepped back to admire his handiwork.

"Hold on," Ruth said in realisation. "Where's the other one?"

Greg frowned at her. "Other what?"

"When Julian dressed the mannequin with his new creation, he didn't remove the old one. Why? Where is it? Was the mannequin naked?"

Alex rubbed his chin. "I don't know. And Kathy's body was found with the dress pulled over her normal clothes."

"So, what does it mean?" Greg asked. "Julian did kill her?"

Ruth studied the image of the village square as the recordings continued backward through the previous day, her mind grappling with the implications of their discovery.

Could Julian really have somehow managed to swap the mannequin for Kathy's body without being seen? Or did someone else do it? What happened to the old dress? Did Julian not bother removing it from the mannequin, only pulled the new one over the top, as with Kathy's body?

The camera angle didn't cover the lane on the other side

of the square, so it was impossible to know what had really happened. *Could someone have used that as an access point to frame Julian?* Right now, it seemed the only plausible conclusion.

Ruth straightened up, her resolve hardening. The lack of adequate security cameras was infuriating. "Wait." As Alex hit a button to resume normal playback speed, she pointed to the alleyway behind the Silver Thimble, where Julian and Kathy stood, arguing. The memory of that heated exchange was still fresh in her mind. "I saw that happen."

Kathy pointed up at the security camera, her face contorted in anger.

"What is she saying?" Alex asked.

"Threatening to fetch you," Ruth said. "Kathy was accusing Julian of something."

"Maybe she thought there was evidence on these recordings that could incriminate him," Greg said in a hopeful tone.

Alex shrugged. "We can keep going back through them. See if we can find anything."

Ruth held up a hand.

In the recording, Julian turned his back on Kathy and marched away. She shouted after him—Ruth recalled her calling Julian spineless—and Kathy marched after him as he headed into his shop.

Kathy went in too, slamming the door behind her.

Ruth, Alex, and Greg watched the screen intently, the silence broken only by the hum of the computer.

A few minutes later, Kathy stormed out, her face flushed, across the road, and entered her own shop.

"Handbag." Ruth waved a finger at the screen. "Kathy had it going in, but not when she came out."

Alex rewound the recording a few minutes, scanning the

footage. Sure enough, Ruth was right. Kathy had entered Julian's shop with her handbag and box of decorations but emerged only with the box.

He let the recording continue backward, watching them argue and head from the Silver Thimble earlier. "Let's see what else there is."

"So Julian was telling the truth?" Greg asked Ruth. "Kathy did leave her handbag there earlier."

But what if that isn't the whole story? Ruth thought. *What if Kathy returned for her handbag later, and that's when the killer, perhaps Julian, struck?*

"There's nothing here to prove someone else was involved," Alex said, his voice tinged with disappointment.

"But there's also nothing to show how Julian got Kathy's body to the square without anyone seeing either," Ruth countered, taking a picture of the CCTV image of the square with her phone. She needed to study this later, see if there were any clues she'd missed.

"Hold on. What's this?" Alex stopped the recording on the previous morning.

In one of the side streets, Kathy and Celia Vanderlin squared up to one another. Despite the poor image quality, their body language left no doubt as to their hostility. Celia's face was a mask of fury, while Kathy seemed to be holding her own, her chin held high.

"Kathy sure liked to argue," Greg said.

Ruth pointed to the doorway of the candle shop. "Leana heard them. Just as she said." She stepped back from the monitors. "I think it's time we spoke to Celia Vanderlin." Ruth was about to leave when a thought struck her, and she faced Alex again. "Could this footage have been tampered with?"

He frowned, obviously considering the question. "I

suppose it's possible, but the timestamps all match up. There are no jumps or glitches in the recording."

"Someone with enough technical know-how could do it," Greg said, his brow furrowed. "After all, this equipment is pretty old." He nodded to a bulky computer case with a tangle of wires connected to it.

Ruth thought it through. If there was missing footage, that would explain how someone had managed to swap the mannequin for a body undetected. And this immediately raised more suspicions about Alex.

He had permanent access to the security system, and likely the knowledge to manipulate the recordings. *What about a motive?*

Ruth took a breath, forcing herself to think rationally. Although she couldn't rule him out, Ruth struggled to believe that if Alex was involved, he'd happily show them the security footage. Not unless he was supremely confident in his ability to cover his tracks.

Despite her misgivings about his guilt, Ruth sensed Alex was still hiding something, and she chose not to reveal her suspicions yet. She needed more evidence before she could confront him.

Ruth looked about the room, searching for anything out of the ordinary. "Who else has access to this place?"

"No one," Alex said. "Well, I think Mrs Vanderlin has a spare set of keys in her office, but she wouldn't hand them over to anyone else without telling me first."

Ruth's gaze fell on a small air duct near the floor, a sudden intuition hitting her. "How could someone sneak in without you knowing?" She pointed at the vent. "Where does this lead?"

"There's a storeroom on the other side," Alex said.

"Who has access to that storeroom?"

Alex hesitated for a moment. "Everyone."

Ruth pulled on a pair of gloves, her intuition kicking into high gear. She knelt in front of the vent and ran her fingers around the outside of the metal grate, feeling for any irregularities. "The screws are in place," she said, noting the small silver heads securing the vent cover. "But they don't look properly seated, as if they've been messed with." She gripped the edges of the cover. "So I shouldn't be able to..." She gave the metalwork a firm tug, and the vent came away with ease, the screws remaining in place, held loosely in their holes. "Well, well, what do you know?"

7

Still knelt on the floor of the security room, Ruth turned the vent cover around and motioned Greg over.

He joined her and traced his fingers along the inside of the frame. "The screws have been cut out, and then the heads glued back in to make it look like they're still intact." He glanced up at Ruth, a flicker of understanding in his eyes. "Someone went to a lot of trouble to make this look undisturbed."

"What?" Alex exclaimed, his voice filled with genuine surprise, or perhaps it was a convincing act. He hurried over and knelt beside them, his eyes fixed on the vent. "But why? What's the point?"

"Look at these too." Greg indicated two small metal handles that had been stuck to the top and bottom of the grate on the inside. They were crudely fashioned but effective. "That's so someone can pull it closed from the other side."

The precision of the modifications suggested someone with a plan, someone who knew what they were doing. More than just a spur-of-the-moment idea.

Ruth set the air vent cover to one side, leaning it against the wall, and then motioned to Alex's torch. "May I borrow that, please?"

He handed it to her, and Ruth flicked it on, the sudden beam of light cutting through the dimness of the room. She shone it into the air vent, illuminating the interior of the duct, revealing the smooth texture of the metal and the accumulation of dust.

Ruth could make out another grille further down. "That's the storeroom on the other side?"

"It must be," Alex said, his voice tight with a hint of unease. "But I don't understand. Why go to all this trouble to break in here?"

"What is that?" Greg pointed to a spot halfway down the duct.

Ruth leaned in, her eyes narrowing as she focussed on something caught on a protruding rivet between the two air vents. It was a snag of shimmering gold fabric.

"Is that from one of Julian's pieces?" Greg asked.

"Maybe," Ruth said. Although, Julian seemed to favour bold, vibrant colours in his designs, jewel tones and rich hues that demanded attention. She pictured the bolts of fabric in his workshop, neatly arranged and categorised, but couldn't recall seeing anything gold, at least not prominently displayed. "Might have to take another look at Julian's place. See if we can find a match, something that fits."

"We can't," Alex said. "The police have sealed it off, pending examination. We must not go in there without their permission. It's linked to a crime scene."

Ruth sighed, frustrated by the limitations placed upon them. She took a picture, then set the vent back over the air duct, the metallic clang echoing in the small room.

"Don't you want to grab the fabric?" Greg asked.

Ruth stood and brushed the dust from her knees. "We must leave it for the police." She knew, all too well, that tampering with evidence, even with the best intentions, could jeopardise the entire investigation.

"I should tell them about this," Alex said. "I'll call them again." He reached for his phone.

"Not yet." Ruth stopped him. "Let's see what other evidence we can gather first. We need as much as we can before handing over our findings." She removed her gloves. "One thing's for sure. Someone must have done this days in advance." She motioned to the air vent.

"If not weeks," Greg said to Alex. "They must have sneaked in here, cut those screws, and glued them back, all without you knowing. Do you ever leave this room unlocked?"

"I have done before, when on my rounds," Alex said. "Not every time. But no one would come down here."

"Clearly, they have . . ." Ruth thought of the cut screws, the added handles, the meticulous thought that had gone into creating the secret access point where they could tamper with the CCTV recordings at their own leisure. "This was not a crime of spontaneous passion, or an argument gone too far. And that leads me to believe there's far more going on beneath the surface than we initially thought."

Alex looked at his watch, his expression troubled. "Speaking of which, I need to do my morning rounds. Check on the shops, make sure everything is secure." He paused, his gaze shifting between Ruth and Greg. "Shall we meet in the square in fifteen minutes, and then visit with Mrs Vanderlin? I'll tell her to expect us."

Ruth nodded, her mind already racing ahead to their

next encounter, and the questions she wanted to ask. As she followed her grandson out of the security room, a surge of determination balled her fists. She would get to the bottom of this mystery, no matter what it took.

Now she believed Julian was innocent.

Back at the village square, Ruth circled the wishing well and the pedestal, scanning the surrounding area, trying to visualise the events of the previous night, to see through the eyes of the killer.

She glanced over at the only security camera a few times, noting its limited field of view, the way it failed to capture the crucial spot where they'd found Kathy's body. It was a glaring oversight, a blind spot the killer had known about and exploited.

She pictured a shadowy figure sliding out of the air vent and sitting at Alex's desk, studying the CCTV images night after night, planning...

Upon reaching the far side of the wishing well for the fourth time, and clearly masked by the structure's pitched roof, Ruth peered up at the spot where Kathy's body had once rested, the image of her lifeless form still vivid in her mind.

Then Ruth faced the opposite direction, her gaze drawn to the alley and a green door set into the side of a building, half-hidden in the shadows. It was an unobtrusive entrance, easily overlooked, but it offered a potential route, a way to approach unseen.

Greg joined her, his eyes narrowing. "Someone could have easily come from there, swapped the mannequin for Kathy's body, all out of view of the camera."

Ruth had taken a step toward the green door when someone called her name, the sound cutting through the quiet morning air.

"Mrs Morgan?" May, the bookshop owner, hurried over, her face pale and drawn. She clutched a book to her chest, her knuckles white against the worn leather cover. "Sorry to bother you, but you said to let you know if anything else sprang to mind, no matter how insignificant it might seem."

"You have some information?" Ruth asked.

"It might be nothing." May's eyes darted around as if she was making sure no one overheard. Her gaze landed on the green door for a second, before looking away. "I couldn't say anything earlier because *he* was there," she added in a whisper.

Ruth glanced at Greg, who shrugged, and back to May. "You mean Alex?"

May leaned in, her voice dropping further, her words laced with a mixture of fear and suspicion. "I've caught him sneaking about the village, at night, when he thought everyone had gone home."

Ruth's mind reeled, her suspicions about Alex, which she had tried to dismiss, resurfacing with renewed force. "He's a security guard," she pointed out, stating the obvious.

"Yes, of course," May continued. "Alex checks doors and gates are locked, makes sure the cameras are in good working order, supposedly, but why would he keep going into shops' storerooms without permission? Through the back doors and into them. It's not part of his job, is it? To snoop around where he doesn't belong?"

"I don't know." Ruth stared at her. "Have you asked him about it?"

"Once." May grimaced. "He got very angry and denied it, said I was imagining things." She took a deep breath, as if steeling herself. "I'm sorry, but I don't trust Alex. I think he's up to something. Has been ever since he joined as the new security guard a couple of years back. He's always been . . . off, somehow."

"Did you ever see him take stock from the storerooms?" Ruth asked. "Anything that might suggest he was stealing, that he was using his position for personal gain?"

May shook her head.

"So, as far as you know, Alex has never stolen anything?" Ruth pressed, wanting to be absolutely sure.

May shook her head again, more firmly this time. "If he had, I would've told Mrs Vanderlin immediately. She wouldn't tolerate that sort of behaviour."

"Have you thought about changing the lock on your shop's storeroom?" Greg asked. "Just to be on the safe side."

May frowned, clearly considering the suggestion, her fingers tracing the worn edges of the book she held. "I don't have anything to hide in there, really. Just old books and stock, nothing of value. If he wants to sneak in, read a few, then so be it." She looked about, her gaze sweeping across the square. "I—I just thought, given what happened this morning, you should know. I'll never get over what happened to poor Kathy. It's just awful."

"I promise to do everything I can to get to the bottom of what happened," Ruth said. "You have my word. Thank you for bringing your suspicions to my attention."

May's shoulders relaxed. "Can I tell you a secret?" After an encouraging nod from Ruth, she glanced about and said, "I hope Julian is guilty."

Ruth blinked, taken aback by the unexpected sentiment, and a little confused. "Why would you say that?"

May's voice trembled. "B-Because the thought of a k-killer still being on the loose in the village is t-terrifying."

She swallowed. "It's bad enough knowing Kathy's gone, but to think that whoever did it might still be out there, walking among us . . ." May shuddered. "It's too much to bear." She offered a tremulous smile, and hurried away, her retreating figure disappearing into the maze of shops.

Ruth watched her go, pondering May's words.

At that moment, Alex strode across the square, his face grim, his usual stoic demeanour replaced with an air of urgency. "I'm finished with my rounds." He motioned to a nearby street, his gaze fixed on some distant point. "Mrs Vanderlin has agreed to meet with us. She's waiting in her office."

"Find anything out of the ordinary?" Ruth asked as the three of them headed past a shop called the Lavender Room, its windows filled with an array of dried flowers and handmade soaps that would rival Hattie's creations.

Alex shook his head. "No, nothing unusual. A lot of frightened and bewildered people. Everyone's talking about what happened, of course. It's the only thing on anyone's mind, trying to make sense of it all."

Ruth sighed, her heart heavy with the knowledge that this tragedy would cast a dark shadow over the peaceful outlet village for years to come.

They rounded a corner, heading up a shallow incline of cobblestones flanked by rows of colourful flower boxes and charming half-timbered faux-fronted cottages on one side, a view across the lake on the other. The water rippled under the overcast sky, reflecting the dark clouds.

"Where is Celia Vanderlin's office?"

Alex pointed straight ahead. "Right there."

Ruth smiled. "Of course it is."

Rapunzel's tower, a cylindrical structure of rough stone blocks, rose majestically from the heart of the outlet village.

Its design and grandeur fit perfectly with the fairy-tale-themed architecture surrounding it, a testament to Celia Vanderlin's vision and ambition.

Greg let out a low whistle.

"It certainly is something," Ruth said.

Alex opened a heavy oak door in the base of the tower.

The three of them stepped into the tower's core—a circular space, twenty feet across, stretching high above and ending in a wooden floor some fifty feet overhead.

A compact elevator stood nestled against the wall, its intricate ironwork casting imposing shadows in the dim light.

The scent of cold stone hung thick in the air, and Ruth pictured her husband, John, climbing a castle's spiral staircase, some forty years prior, his fingertips tracing the damp stonework, his footsteps echoing.

Ruth eyed the elevator and and a familiar tightness constricted her chest. The thought of being enclosed in that metal cage, hurtling upward, sent a wave of panic washing through her.

She gestured to a metal ladder opposite, one fixed to the wall, leading all the way to the top of the tower. "I'll take this."

Alex's brow furrowed. "That's for emergencies only."

Ruth nodded. The walls seemed to close in.

"Grandma has cleithrophobia," Greg said. "Hates lifts."

Alex's frown deepened. "Claustrophobia?"

"No, it's different." Greg shot Ruth a supportive glance. "She has a fear of being trapped."

"It's not so much the size of the space that bothers me," Ruth said, forcing herself to breathe deeply, to calm the rising panic. "It's more about getting stuck somewhere with no escape. The feeling of being confined, with no way out, that's what triggers it."

Greg smiled at Alex's puzzled expression, a hint of amusement in his eyes. He knew Ruth's fear was not easily understood by those who had never experienced it.

She studied the metal rungs of the ladder: each had a knurled surface, giving extra grip, a small comfort. A ladder Ruth could control, a way up and a way down, accessible at all times. "I'll be fine. You go on ahead. Besides"—she cleared her throat—"a little exercise never hurt anyone." Although Ruth's knees already ached at the prospect of the climb, and her heart pounded in her chest, but anything was better than the infernal lift.

Alex, clearly realising arguing with her would do no good, merely shrugged. "Suit yourself." He opened the elevator door and stepped inside. The metal grating clanged shut behind him, his face betraying a flicker of concern as he glanced back at Ruth.

"Please be careful, Grandma." Greg peered up the ladder. "That's a long way to fall."

"I'll be fine," Ruth said, her voice stronger than she felt. *Famous last words.* Her head was already swimming at the thought of the dizzying heights.

"We could ask Mrs Vanderlin to come down," Greg suggested.

Ruth shook her head, her resolve hardening. She wanted to get a good look at Celia's office, to absorb the atmosphere, to see her in her natural environment, to look for any subtle clues that might shed light on any village drama and on Kathy's murder. It was a chance she couldn't pass up, a risk she was willing to take. "I'll be fine," Ruth repeated, more to herself.

She took a deep breath and placed her foot on the first rung of the ladder, then the other, and began her ascent.

The cold, solid metal beneath her hands provided a welcome sense of stability, along with the rhythmic clang of her shoes on the rungs.

The elevator rattled past, with Greg and a bemused Alex staring back at her.

A prickle of unease ran through Ruth.

Am I being paranoid, or is there something truly unsettling about Alex? The thought lingered.

Determination coursed through her, each step bringing Ruth closer to Celia Vanderlin and, hopefully, closer to the truth behind Kathy Fellows' murder.

She pressed on, doing her absolute best to ignore the burning in her legs, the growing ache in her muscles, and failing miserably.

Ruth paused halfway up, catching her breath as a wave of dizziness gripped her. The height suddenly seemed much more significant, the ground far below a dizzying abyss.

She closed her eyes, took a deep pull of air, and focussed on the task at hand, repeating the mantra in her mind like a prayer; *Celia Vanderlin. Answers. Justice for Kathy. Free Julian.*

"Get moving, Morgan." Ruth forced herself up the ladder, pushing past the fear, refusing to look down, and as she finally reached the top, a trapdoor above her head swung open.

Strong hands reached down, gripped her arms and pulled her onto the floor above.

A wave of relief washed over Ruth, and she panted, "Thanks," as Greg and Alex assisted her to her feet, the solid floor a welcome change from the narrow rungs.

They now stood in a circular space with large windows that offered a breathtaking 360-degree view of the entire outlet village stretched out below; a miniature world of cobbled streets and whimsical buildings, with the odd figure of an employee scurrying from door to door.

The storm clouds cast a dramatic shadow over the scene, turning the bright colours of the village into muted hues.

The office itself was furnished with a minimalist elegance that spoke of wealth and taste. A plush white rug partially covered a polished wooden floor, and two sleek modern chairs, upholstered in a grey fabric.

A collection of abstract paintings adorned the walls, their bold colours and intricate patterns providing a striking contrast to the otherwise neutral palette of the room.

Finally, Ruth's gaze settled on the large mahogany desk that sat in the middle of the room, its polished surface gleaming beneath the glow of recessed lighting.

Behind it, in a high-backed leather chair, almost throne-like in its grandeur, sat Celia Vanderlin. Her silver hair was swept back into an elegant chignon, accentuating her sharp, aristocratic features. She wore a tailored black suit that accentuated her slender frame. A single strand of pearls shimmered against her pale neck.

Her expression was cool and composed as she studied her guests, her posture radiating an aura of power and control. Celia Vanderlin looked every inch the queen of her miniature kingdom.

Ruth nodded to the desk, catching her breath, her legs still trembling from the climb. "How— How on earth did you get *that* up here?"

"Crane." Celia's dark eyes assessed Ruth with a mixture of curiosity and suspicion.

"This is Mrs Morgan," Alex said. "And her grandson, Greg."

"Call me Ruth." She approached the desk, hand outstretched.

Celia didn't take it. "What can I do for you?" Her eyes, sharp and intelligent, held a glint of challenge.

Ruth retracted her hand and lowered herself into one of the comfortable-looking chairs opposite Celia, while Greg and Alex remained standing, both keeping a wary distance.

Probably a wise move.

8

After taking a few deep breaths and composing her thoughts, Ruth began to explain the reason for their visit with Mrs Vanderlin. She detailed their concerns about the police investigation, and their growing suspicion that Julian might be innocent. Ruth described the inconsistencies they had found so far: the strange placement of Kathy's body, the scarf around her neck, the speck of glitter, and the lack of concrete evidence tying Julian to the crime.

As Ruth spoke, she watched Celia intently, searching for any flicker of reaction, any telltale sign that might betray her true feelings. ". . . and that's when we found someone had modified the air vent in the security room. So they could come and go as they please, tamper with the CCTV recordings."

Celia's expression remained unchanged. She sat perfectly still the whole time, like one of Julian's mannequins, her gaze unwavering, her face a mask of composure. Then, her eyes finally shifted to Alex. "When I agreed to you being here, you assured me there would be no trouble." Her voice was soft, almost a whisper, but the underlying threat was unmistakable.

Alex stared back at her, his jaw tight. "A murder isn't my fault." A bead of sweat trickled down his temple.

Celia's cold gaze moved back to Ruth. "Why are you really here? Ah, yes, the food consultant, working with Reverend Michael, correct?"

Ruth refused to be baited by the woman's condescending tone. "I used to be a police officer." And then she instantly regretted saying it.

Celia leaned forward, her lips curving into a thin, humourless smile. "You're of the opinion that modern policing is inferior to that of your day?" She inclined her head. "You have far superior investigative skills to DI Barnes? You'll have this all wrapped up before afternoon tea, no doubt."

"Officers are still investigating," Alex interjected. "But we thought you could shed light on Kathy's relationships within the village. Any arguments, any disagreements, any reason someone may want to harm her."

Celia shot him a withering glance. "I'm sure Mrs Morgan is more than capable of answering for herself."

Alex took a step back, his face flushed.

Celia returned her attention to Ruth. "You believe Julian has been wrongly accused, and the killer is still at large."

Ruth nodded and fought to keep her annoyance out of her tone. "Like I say, we've found several inconsistencies that suggest he may not be responsible for Kathy's death. They're worth pursuing."

Celia leaned back in her chair, elbows on the armrests, her fingers steepled beneath her chin. "Tell me, Mrs Morgan, what is your interest in all this? Why inject yourself into an active murder investigation? Other than your *past* as a police officer, of course."

Ruth met Celia's gaze, her own expression resolute. "If there's even the slightest chance Julian is innocent, then I must look into it. Kathy deserves justice, and I won't stand by and watch an innocent man be punished."

Celia's eyebrows arched. "The police have their suspect, and they seem quite convinced of his guilt."

"But what if they're wrong?" Greg said.

Celia shrugged a single elegant shoulder. "Then I suppose Mr Jasper will have to prove his innocence, will he not? In a court of law. As everyone else must do." She paused, her eyes flicking toward the window, where rain lashed against the glass, blurring the world outside into a hazy grey watercolour. "I find it difficult to believe that a man who held such animosity toward Kathy would be incapable of such an act."

Ruth furrowed her brow. "Arguments happen all the time. That doesn't make someone a murderer." She leaned forward, her voice dropping to a low, confidential tone, trying to appeal to Celia's better nature. If she had one. "Mrs Vanderlin, did you see or hear anything unusual last night? Or in the days leading up to Kathy's death? Anything at all that might help us understand what happened."

Celia's lips tightened into a thin line. "Everyone within the village loved Kathy. I can see no reason why someone would commit such a heinous act, other than Julian J Jasper."

Despite her words, Ruth sensed a lack of genuine emotion in Celia's voice. Her eyes still held a coldness.

She's withholding information, Ruth thought, her suspicion growing with each passing moment. *But why? Is she protecting someone, or is it the village's reputation she's so concerned about?*

Ruth pressed on. "You had an argument with Kathy the day before her murder. Can I ask what it was about?"

Celia waved the question away with a dismissive flick of her wrist. "A minor disagreement. Nothing of consequence." Her eyes narrowed, a glimmer of something—perhaps calculation, perhaps a warning—flickering within their depths. "I have already explained everything to DI Barnes. He knows the details." She straightened a folder on her desk, her movements precise and controlled. "Business is business, Mrs Morgan. I'm not running a charity here. Kathy had financial issues, which in turn led to her missing several rent payments."

Even though Reverend Michael painted Kathy as a successful businesswoman, her best friend, May, had said quite the contrary, which tallied with what Mrs Vanderlin said now.

"And you gave her an ultimatum?" Ruth guessed.

Celia's voice hardened. "I told her, in no uncertain terms, that if she missed another payment, she'd be out. Evicted." She stared at Ruth, her jaw set, a clear indication their conversation was over. "Now, if you'll excuse me, I have a great deal of work to do."

Ruth got to her feet, and muttered, "Thank you for your time." She turned to leave, frustrated and feeling the weight of Celia's gaze on her back.

"Mrs Morgan?"

Here we go.

Tensed, Ruth turned around.

"I will offer you one piece of advice." Celia's face darkened further. "I strongly suggest you stick to your pies and cakes. Stay out of police business, out of this village's business, or I'll be forced to have you removed. By force, if necessary." She eyed Alex with undisguised disdain. "I have no patience for those who stick their noses where they don't belong."

As Ruth, aided by Greg and Alex, carefully started her descent down the ladder, her legs still shaky from the climb, a surge of anger coursed through her. Celia's words echoed in her mind—flippant, dismissive, and filled with barely concealed hostility.

Is it simply a case of a businesswoman protecting her interests, or is there something more sinister at play?

Ruth continued down the ladder, the metal rungs cold and unforgiving beneath her hands. The elevator rattled past, carrying Alex and Greg to the ground floor. Her mind churned over the conversation with Celia. She hadn't said much, but the revelation that the argument with Kathy was over rent payments was significant.

Could it be more than a landlord-tenant dispute?

One thing was for sure, Ruth's commitment to uncovering the truth had only solidified. Despite the gathering storm clouds, both literally and metaphorically, her resolve remained unshaken.

The lack of concrete evidence against Julian fuelled her desire to expose the real killer. She owed it to Kathy, to the village, to find the truth. Even if it meant facing the wrath of Celia Vanderlin.

Back at the Silver Thimble, the wind howled outside, rattling the panes, and whistling through the cracks in doorframes.

The café was now eerily deserted.

After checking in on Merlin and giving him his lunch, Ruth sat at the kitchen table with Greg, while Reverend Michael busied himself making cups of tea, coffee, hot chocolate, and sandwiches.

Alex left to check around the village, to make sure everything was secure and escort any remaining shoppers safely out. His departure had been abrupt, almost hurried, which only served to deepen Ruth's suspicions of him too.

She couldn't shake the feeling there was something going on with Alex, something he was deliberately hiding. She decided to pick her time carefully to confront him.

And as for Celia Vanderlin—her icy demeanour and thinly veiled threats had done little to quell Ruth's misgivings. In fact, they'd only intensified them.

"She's hiding something," Ruth murmured, more to herself than to Greg or Reverend Michael. "I'm certain of it."

Greg, perched on a stool by the counter, idly flipping through the internet on his phone, looked up. "Definitely gives the impression she has a few skeletons in her closet."

Reverend Michael, his face etched with worry, placed a steaming mug of hot chocolate beside Greg and a cup of tea in front of Ruth. "It didn't go well with Mrs Vanderlin?"

Ruth sipped her tea, the sugary warmth a welcome comfort. "I fear I've done more harm than good. Her influence clearly extends far beyond the walls of that tower. She'll be watching us closely now." Ruth sighed, the exhaustion of the traumatic morning weighing heavily on her. "Celia told us Kathy was in financial trouble."

Reverend Michael sat opposite her, his expression thoughtful. "I'm not sure I can believe that." As Greg joined them at the table, Reverend Michael slid a plate piled high with sandwiches toward him.

"May also said she wasn't the successful businesswoman Kathy made herself out to be," Ruth added.

"I find that quite surprising." Reverend Michael rubbed his chin. "Kathy always seemed so confident . . ." He trailed off, shaking his head, his eyes filled with a mixture of confusion and concern.

"Not according to Mrs Vanderlin." Greg tucked into a chicken sandwich with his usual unbridled gusto.

Reverend Michael's gaze drifted toward the rain-streaked window. "Although Kathy never mentioned any specific figures, I know she often gave money to a local cat shelter, and the church restoration fund." His eyes became distant. "I wonder if anyone else in the village knew about these financial woes." He refocussed on Ruth. "It's a small community. Word travels fast. If Kathy was struggling, someone else, other than Celia and May, would have known."

"Julian?" Ruth asked, thinking aloud.

Reverend Michael pursed his lips. "Well, given the circumstances, and their . . . strained relationship, I would imagine he'd be the last person she'd confide in."

Greg swallowed the last mouthful of chicken sandwich and moved on to a cheese and ham one. "Someone else could've let slip. Maybe Julian does know. May could've told him."

Reverend Michael leaned back in his chair, lifted a fruitcake from the kitchen counter, and held it up for Greg to see.

Greg smiled and nodded.

Thoughtful silence settled over them as they ate, the only sound the rhythmic drumming of the rain against the windows, the mournful howl of the wind as it whipped through the narrow streets outside, and the occasional rumble of thunder in the distance.

Ruth's mind wandered, drifting back to her own experiences running a family business. She thought about the enterprise she'd inherited after her husband's death, the one her daughter, Sara, now ran with such competence and dedication.

What had started out as a small well-respected cat breeding enterprise had expanded, under Sara's guidance, into a mini empire supplying not only pedigree felines but also food, accessories, and offering boarding and grooming facilities.

It had been a part of Ruth's life at Morgan Manor for decades, a source of pride and satisfaction for both John and then Sara.

But it had also been demanding, requiring long hours, unwavering dedication, and the occasional cash injection during leaner times.

Ruth knew firsthand how quickly financial stability could crumble, how easily a thriving business could fall into difficulty, be brought to its knees by unexpected expenses or a sudden downturn in trade.

Perhaps Kathy's situation wasn't as improbable as it first seemed. Maybe the pressure of running a business, coupled with personal issues or unforeseen circumstances, had taken its toll.

Could Kathy's combative nature have led her to make some bad decisions, choices that had ultimately cost her life?

"Okay," Ruth said, bringing her attention back to the task at hand. "What about the rumour Celia poisoned her husband? Do you think there's any truth to it?"

"That's all in Leana's head." By the look on his face, Reverend Michael understood exactly where Ruth was going with her questioning. He was about to say something further, but the back door banged open, sending a gust of wind and rain swirling into the kitchen.

"Sorry." Alex, now wearing a heavy, rain-soaked mac, stepped into the room. "Front way's locked." He closed the door behind him with a decisive click, water dripping from his coat onto the tiled floor.

Reverend Michael's brow furrowed. "I forgot to unlock before lunch. What with everything that's going on, it completely slipped my mind." He started to stand, but Alex waved him back down.

"Don't worry about it. There's no one out there. Streets are deserted. Everyone's battened down the hatches." He shrugged out of his wet coat and hung it on a hook by the door.

Reverend Michael poured him a cup of steaming coffee.

"Thanks." Alex sat at the table with a heavy sigh. "Weather's getting worse by the minute. Some roads are already flooded. No one's getting in or out for a while."

Reverend Michael slid another slice of cake toward Greg, a faint smile touching his lips. "I guess you're all stuck here, then."

"Fine by me." Greg tucked in.

"It's very gracious of you to let us stay, but you might live to regret it," Ruth said to Reverend Michael. "If you keep giving Greg free food, you'll be out of business in a week. And if you bill me, I'll be bankrupt." She turned her attention to Alex. "Would you be willing to go to Kathy's shop and look at her accounts with me? Maybe there's a clue as to why she was in financial difficulty. Something that might point to another suspect."

Alex shifted uncomfortably in his seat and glanced at Reverend Michael. "I'm sorry, but that's taking things too far.

Mrs Vanderlin is right—it's police business, not ours." He stood abruptly, his chair scraping against the floor. "Now, if you'll excuse me." Alex slipped his wet coat back on and headed out into the storm, leaving a trail of puddles in his wake.

Ruth stared after him. His reaction was . . . *unexpected*.

An hour after Alex had left the Silver Thimble, and showed no signs of returning, Ruth insisted on washing up while Reverend Michael took a break. Once finished, she slipped on her coat, her determination hardening. "I'll see if Alex is all right," she said, trying to keep her voice light.

She and Greg couldn't continue to investigate alone. They needed Alex's knowledge of the village, its people, its layout, and, most important of all, his access to Kathy's shop.

"You're going out in this weather?" Reverend Michael asked with obvious incredulity. "Are you sure that's wise?"

He was right, of course. The wind whipped the rain against the window with renewed ferocity, and the sky had darkened further by the minute, but Ruth's gut told her to go after Alex.

Greg wiped his hands on a tea towel. "I'll come with you, Grandma."

She shook her head. "Stay here. I won't be long."

Greg's eyes narrowed. "You can't just go—"

Ruth held up a hand. "Alex is more likely to confide in me if I'm alone. Besides, you have that silly family app thing."

Reverend Michael looked puzzled. "Family app?"

Ruth rolled her eyes. "My daughter, Sara, forced me to download it last week." She pulled her phone from her pocket. "Tracks my every move. Any family member can see where I am at any given moment. Big Brother is watching my every move."

"It's for your own safety," Greg said, and then muttered, "Mine too."

Ruth tutted and put away her phone. "People seem to think I make a habit of running off and getting into trouble."

Greg stared at her. "You do. Remember the Finsbury Flyer? Would've been a lot easier to find you with the app installed."

Ruth grumbled under her breath, and before Greg could argue some more, she opened the back door.

Howling wind knocked her back a step, startling Ruth with its ferocity. It took a moment to catch her breath as the rain stung her face, plastering Ruth's hair to her forehead.

"Are you okay?" Reverend Michael called.

"I'm fine." Ruth stepped outside and closed the door. She lifted her collar and pulled her woolly hat down low over her ears. "Here goes nothing."

The outlet village streets, once bustling with activity, were now deserted. Some shop fronts stood dark and lifeless; others were shuttered, their brightly painted facades now hidden behind a veil of rain.

The few remaining lit shops revealed glimpses of people inside, peering out at the madwoman as she passed by, their faces a mixture of curiosity, pity, and astonishment.

The rain, now a relentless downpour, hammered against the quaint, fairy-tale-esque buildings, sending rivers cascading down the slick cobblestones. Ruth concentrated on remaining upright, her shoes slipping on the wet surface.

Keeping as close as she could to the storefronts, she shivered, and pulled her coat tighter around her body, already regretting her impulsive decision to venture out.

She navigated the narrow lanes and alleyways, her footsteps—each splash in a puddle—swallowed by the howling wind. Gusts rattled shop signs.

After all this, what if Alex isn't in his security office? What if he's wandered off somewhere else?

One problem at a time, Morgan.

Ruth then took a wrong turn, realised her mistake, and doubled back, only to find another unfamiliar street. "This place is like a maze." The rain really wasn't helping with her navigation. She was about to admit defeat and call Greg, or press the emergency button on the family tracking app, when she spotted Rapunzel's tower in the distance.

Ruth hurried toward it, and after another couple of turns, passed the darkened windows of Julian's shop. The mechanical loom, usually a hypnotic dance of threads, stood frozen, its intricate movements stilled. The vibrant fabrics within, normally so eye-catching, looked dull and lifeless.

Ruth pictured Julian's gentle smile, his passion for his craft, and the way his eyes had lit up when he spoke about his creations and his shared interests with Greg. The thought of him being wrongly accused, trapped in a police cell while the real killer roamed free, spurred her on.

Finally, and with no small measure of relief, Ruth reached the entrance to the security office, tucked within the imposing bulk of the beanstalk. The rain hammered against the giant leaves, cascading around her in waterfalls.

Ruth pushed open the heavy door and hurried down the steps, the dimly lit corridor offering a welcome respite from the storm's fury. She opened the door at the end, and a wave of warm air washed over her.

Alex sat hunched over his desk, headphones on, his

back to Ruth. He stared intently at one of the monitors, his shoulders tense.

"Alex?"

He didn't answer, seemingly lost in whatever he was doing, oblivious to her presence.

Ruth peered over his shoulder to see what he was up to.

The main screen showed a recording of the previous day —Julian dressing the supposed mannequin in the village square. The image sped forward, then back, forward and back, then jumped to an hour prior, repeating the same jerky motion with each click of the mouse.

What's he looking for? Ruth wondered.

"Alex?" She rested a hand on his shoulder.

He jolted upright and spun in his chair, fists raised, eyes wild.

9

Inside the security room, Ruth recoiled from Alex, her heart hammering against her ribs. A disconcerting flash of something—guilt, perhaps—flickered across Alex's face before he regained his composure, lowering his raised fist.

He yanked off his headphones, strains of heavy metal thumping from the tiny speakers. "You frightened the life out of me."

"Ditto." Ruth panted. "Thought you were about to hit me." Her gaze shifted to the monitors, her curiosity now tinged with a healthy dose of suspicion.

"What are you doing here?" Alex asked in a tight voice. The screens cast an eerie glow on his face, accentuating the deep lines around his eyes and the rigid set of his jaw. He looked utterly exhausted, as if he bore the weight of the world on his shoulders.

"I wanted to make sure you were all right," Ruth said, bringing the temperature back down. "You left so abruptly."

Alex hesitated. His gaze darted toward the door and then to Ruth again. "I—" He swallowed. "I needed to check something." He gestured vaguely to the CCTV images, a faint blush creeping up his neck.

Ruth edged closer, scanning the screens. "What?"

Alex turned to face them again. "I've been meticulously examining this morning's recordings. If someone went to all the bother of creating a way in here, they must have a reason. I've been searching for any signs of tampering, painstakingly comparing recordings to previous days. Maybe they copied and spliced them together." He clicked the mouse, toggling between the different feeds.

Ruth leaned in to scrutinise the displays. She focussed on the individual shops, searching for any subtle hints of unusual movement, any flicker or glitch that might betray a digital manipulation.

So far, nothing stood out.

At least not to her untrained eye.

Alex rubbed the back of his neck, his frustration evident. "If someone has used previous recordings to overwrite parts of the current footage, they've done an immaculate job." He pinched his chin, brow furrowed. "They'd also have to painstakingly modify the time and date stamps. I'm starting with the recordings themselves, looking for any inconsistencies and working from there."

"It would be a clever idea, if that's what they've done, but a complex undertaking," Ruth conceded. "Even accomplishing that, they would need to be incredibly precise with their editing." Her gaze flickered to the air vent. "Who here would have the expertise to tamper with the security system in such an intricate manner?"

"Well, it is definitely far more involved than simply deleting footage," Alex said. "We'd notice the abrupt jump. To seamlessly splice recordings from previous days, they'd require considerable technical skill. I can only surmise they must have used an editing program to accomplish it, along with modifying the time and date. No easy task."

"Do you have such a program?" Ruth asked.

Alex shook his head. "I don't need that kind of thing for my job. CCTV files are sacrosanct; they shouldn't be tampered with. They record directly to the hard drive, untouched."

"A program capable of seamlessly cutting recordings and altering the time and date..." Ruth exhaled a puff of air, her breath misting in the coolness of the security office. "I didn't know such a thing existed. Perhaps Greg could conduct an internet search. He might be able to tell us what software is capable of such a feat."

Alex shook his head again. "I strongly suspect it has to be a bespoke piece of software, meticulously designed specifically for this task, not something you could acquire off the shelf."

Ruth's eyebrows shot up, and she couldn't help a wry smirk. "That implies some seriously shady underworld connections, doesn't it?" When Alex didn't return her smile, she straightened her face again.

Could someone in this otherwise tranquil, sleepy outlet village possess that level of technical sophistication? It seemed far-fetched.

However, Alex appeared to think so, his gaze fixed on the screens as he continued to work with grim determination.

Ruth studied him, her intuition screaming that he was still concealing something. "What do you know?"

"Hmm?" He didn't look up, his attention riveted to the monitors.

"Alex," Ruth pressed, her voice unwavering. "What aren't you telling me?"

"I don't know what you mean." Alex leaned closer to the main screen, his body tense.

Ruth changed her approach, for the time being. "Since you now concur that something more sinister is going on here, how about we take a closer look at Kathy's shop?" She braced herself for his answer, fully expecting him to try and dissuade her once again, but this time, Ruth was prepared to plead her case.

"I'm not sure that's—"

"It is not a crime scene, Alex. We are perfectly within our rights to conduct a thorough examination of the premises, as long as we don't disturb any potential evidence we might uncover."

Besides, even if that isn't entirely true, a little bit of harmless snooping never hurt anyone.

Alex sighed. "You don't give up easily, do you?" The tension in his shoulders eased, his troubled expression replaced by one of newfound purpose, however grudging. "Fine. Let's go to Kathy's shop and examine those ledgers." He stood. "It's not as if Mrs Vanderlin is likely to catch us in this atrocious weather."

Ruth, relieved that he had finally acquiesced, couldn't help but wonder if Celia, from her lofty vantage point in the tower, could still observe their movements.

It was a disquieting thought.

Alex and Ruth stepped outside, plunging back into the tempestuous storm. It raged on unabated as they made their way to Kathy's shop, their heads bowed against the driving rain. The wind howled around them, making it nearly impossible for Ruth to hear anything other than her own musings.

They dashed from one meagre source of shelter to the

next, the village streets having transformed into a treacherous obstacle course.

At long last, they reached Kathy's Klassics, its once vibrant and inviting window display now obscured by a curtain of rain and the encroaching darkness.

Alex unlocked the door, and they slipped inside, profoundly grateful for the temporary respite from the elements.

The shop's interior sat quiet and still, a stark contrast to the chaos outside. The air hung thick with the lingering, cloying aroma of potpourri—a clashing blend of dried lavender, rose petals, and cinnamon sticks.

"People really love their strong scents around here." Ruth glanced about, taking in the racks of clothes, each meticulously organised by colour and style. Mannequins, frozen in various unnatural poses, stood sentinel throughout the shop, their vacant eyes seeming to follow Ruth's every move.

Alex flicked on a bank of light switches, but the harsh, fluorescent glare did little to dispel the gloom or bring life into the space. "This way," he said, his voice subdued.

Ruth followed him to the rear of the shop, her eyes diligently scanning for anything out of place, any subtle clue; a misplaced item, a stray button, anything that might offer a shred of insight into Kathy's attacker.

But everything seemed as it should be. Nothing appeared disturbed, no glaring signs of a struggle, no overt clues to suggest why Kathy had been so brutally targeted.

Alex stopped at a nondescript door tucked away in the back corner, almost hidden from view. He produced a ring of keys from his pocket, selected one, and unlocked the door.

After a glance at Ruth, he pushed it open, revealing a small, cramped office, cluttered with a chaotic jumble of paperwork and dog-eared fashion magazines.

A single desk, piled high with files and folders, dominated the room. A small window overlooked the back alley, offering a bleak view of the storm raging outside.

Ruth scanned the room, taking in every minute detail. "Let's locate her financial records," she said, her voice brisk and businesslike, determined to push aside the unsettling feeling steadily growing within her. Going through a deceased person's files never got any easier, but needs must.

She pulled up a chair and gestured to a stack of imposing ledgers on the desk. "We first need to ascertain if there's any truth to Celia's claims about Kathy's financial difficulties."

Alex fetched another chair from the corner and joined her. He grabbed a ledger, and his finger traced columns of numbers. "This will take a considerable amount of time," he said, his voice laced with frustration. "There's so much to go through."

Ruth picked up a ledger with the current year prominently displayed on the spine. "I'll work backward from today. Her supposed difficulties were recent." She flipped through the pages until she reached the very end, and then searched for any discrepancies, any anomalies that might shed some much-needed light on the perplexing mystery.

She scanned the columns of figures, her brow furrowed in concentration.

The next hour crawled by at an excruciatingly slow pace. The only sounds were the rhythmic rustling of papers, the insistent click of Kathy's calculator as they checked and rechecked the figures, and the relentless drumming of the rain outside.

The oppressive darkness within the office seemed to deepen with each passing minute.

To Ruth, the walls themselves were closing in, suffocating her. She kept glancing at the door, her unease growing with each tick of the clock, and she reminded herself she could leave whenever she liked.

"Wait a minute." Alex tapped the page. "What's this?" He indicated a deposit from several months prior, his finger underlining a specific figure.

Ruth leaned in, her heart quickening with anticipation. "What have you discovered?"

"A substantial deposit paid in by an unknown contributor."

"Twenty thousand?" Ruth widened her eyes in astonishment. "That's an extraordinary amount of cash for such a small business." She scanned the rest of the page. "All the other deposits are relatively minute amounts, nothing exceeding a few hundred, undoubtedly payments for items purchased in the shop." She tapped the ledger with her forefinger. "All except for this glaring anomaly." She squinted. "It's written in blue ink. All the others are black."

"Her last three payments to Mrs Vanderlin are blue too," Alex said. "Anyway, maybe it was a personal loan. A member of Kathy's family extending a helping hand. That would certainly lend credence to Mrs Vanderlin's claim that she was grappling with financial difficulties."

Ruth shook her head, her intuition screaming there was more to the story. "All Kathy's rent payments are meticulously logged within the ledgers. According to them, she paid promptly on the fifth of every month, without fail." Ruth sat back, trying to piece together the puzzle. "Celia unequivocally stated that Kathy had missed several payments, and she threatened her with eviction." She rubbed her chin. "Which would tally with someone helping May out financially."

"Well, then we need to uncover the identity of the individual who made the payment," Alex said.

"That's our next lead," Ruth agreed, her resolve hardening.

"Right. But how exactly do we find them?" Alex asked. "Without access to her bank statements, we can't definitively prove if what Kathy's written here is accurate or not."

"Why would she falsify her ledgers?" Ruth wondered aloud. It seemed illogical. She took a picture of the page with her phone, capturing the anomalous entry, and of several more pages from the preceding and following months, clearly showing the consistent, on-time rent payments.

Evidence. Something tangible to work with. This could be the key, the breakthrough we need.

Now it was simply a matter of figuring out how exactly it connected to Kathy's murder, if at all.

They continued to pore over the ledgers, hoping to find more clues related to the mysterious deposit, or anything else that seemed out of place. But their painstaking efforts yielded nothing further.

The single large deposit remained a tantalising enigma.

Frustration gnawed at Ruth. Without those elusive bank statements, they had no solid evidence. The ledgers were certainly helpful, suggestive even, but they needed more concrete proof of foul play.

By the look on Alex's face, he had reached the same conclusion.

"We're not giving up," Ruth said, determined. "We will find answers."

They packed away the ledgers, carefully placing them

back on the desk in their original order, and closed the door to Kathy's office, leaving it exactly as they had found it.

Ruth and Alex stepped back out into the storm, which had intensified during their time inside. As they hurried back toward the Silver Thimble, the wind howled, the rain hammered down with renewed vengeance, and the darkness seemed even more oppressive than before.

Relief washed through Ruth as they stepped back into the café, removed their coats, and huddled around the warmth of the kitchen table. They recounted their findings to Greg and Reverend Michael.

"You uncovered a secret payment?" Greg asked.

Ruth nodded, trying to connect the disparate and sparse dots. "Twenty thousand pounds. That's a lot of money and would have meant she could easily keep up with her rent payments for at least a year, if not longer. It doesn't strike me as though her best friend, May, would have that amount lying about, not with her bookshop, but we can ask her."

A puzzled frown creased Reverend Michael's brow. "Mrs Vanderlin lied about the rent? Why?"

"We have no way to definitively prove anything at this juncture." Ruth leaned back in her chair, her mind wandering.

The silence stretched between them, broken only by the mournful howl of the wind.

Suddenly, a thought struck Ruth, a spark of inspiration, and she sat bolt upright, her pulse quickening. "Leana. The young woman in the candle shop." Ruth looked between the others. "She overheard a heated argument between Celia and Kathy."

"Leana mentioned something about Celia wanting Kathy out of her shop," Greg said. "But so what?"

"Our conversation was interrupted by Hattie's arrival,"

Ruth said with a sense of urgency. "We need to speak to Leana again, immediately. Find out what else she might have overheard."

10

Ruth, Greg, and Alex braved the tempestuous weather, battling their way through the narrow, winding village streets. The wind whipped at their coats, and the rain stung their faces.

"We shouldn't be out in this," Greg grumbled, his teeth chattering. "It's absolutely insane."

Ruth pressed on, despite the icy water now seeping into her socks. "Typical, my wellies are in the motorhome."

"Would you like me to cycle back to the garage and fetch them for you, Grandma?" Greg asked.

"Would you?" Ruth's eyebrows rose in mock surprise.

"Not in a million years," he retorted with a smirk.

"It could be worse," Ruth said.

"Oh yeah? How so?"

"At least there's no thunder and lightning." As if on cue, a deep, ominous rumble sounded in the distance, and Ruth winced.

Greg rolled his eyes.

Ruth refocussed on their imminent conversation with Leana. Several pressing questions gnawed at her: *Why would someone give Kathy such a substantial sum of money? Was it a loan, a bribe, or something else? And, if Kathy had sufficient funds to cover her rent, why did Celia Vanderlin lie?*

If there was only a way to trace the source of the mysterious funds and uncover the motive behind the payment, it might provide a crucial link to Kathy's murder.

Right now, the argument between Celia and Kathy, the one Leana had overheard, was Ruth's primary focus. *Why was Celia so vehemently adamant about Kathy vacating her shop? Was it simply a case of a ruthless, difficult landlady enforcing the terms of a lease, or was there something far darker, more malevolent at play?*

Ruth's gut instinct told her it was the latter.

The three of them reached Mystical Flames. Unlike the other shops, which were mostly dark and shuttered, lights and candles glowed within, casting a warm, inviting radiance across the rain-slicked cobblestones.

Greg's eyebrows rose. "They're open?" He looked around at the deserted street, his expression incredulous. "Why?"

"I've never known Hattie to ever close," Alex said. "Other than Julian, she's the first to open in the morning and the last to close at night." He looked down the street. "It's a crying shame Hattie's shop backs on to Julian's. If they'd been on the same street, in proximity to one another, she might have seen him last night or earlier this morning. May have been able to provide him with a concrete alibi."

With the rain now threatening to fully breach the inadequate protection of her coat, Ruth pushed open Mystical Flames' door. The tinkling bell announced their arrival—a welcome sound—and a wave of warm air enveloped them.

Ruth wrinkled her nose. The cloying, overpowering scent of incense and essential oils permeated the atmosphere, thick and almost suffocating, now magnified by the lack of shoppers coming and going, bringing with them much-needed gusts of fresh air.

Greg coughed, and his face contorted. "People actually find this sort of thing soothing? I can feel my eyeballs peeling like onions."

Leana, the young woman with long dark hair and the Edgar Allan Poe T-shirt, looked up from behind the counter, her eyes widening in surprise. "You're back."

"Where's your Aunt Hattie?" Ruth's gaze swept the rear of the shop.

"Had to run an errand," Leana replied, her voice hesitant.

"In this horrendous weather?" Alex said with apparent incredulity.

Leana's eyes darted to Greg, and her cheeks flushed a delicate pink. "She didn't say where she was going."

"We'd like to ask you a few more questions," Ruth said. "If that's okay with you?"

Leana closed the thick leather-bound book she had been reading, its cover adorned with strange, arcane symbols. Her expression turned suspicious. "I've already told the police everything I know."

"We'd be so grateful if you told us too," Ruth pressed, her tone encouraging. She had a brief flashback of all the times nervous-looking witnesses had sat opposite her in an interview room, recounting their observations.

Leana's gaze flickered between Ruth, Alex, and then Greg, as if she was trying to gauge their true intentions.

"We believe there might be something the police inadvertently overlooked earlier," Alex said. "Something seemingly insignificant that could potentially help us understand what really happened to Kathy."

"W-What really happened?" Leana bit her lower lip, and

her eyes darted to the rear of the shop. "What do you mean?"

Ruth took a different, more empathetic approach. "We know this is an incredibly upsetting time for everyone. But we want to make absolutely certain that nothing is overlooked, that the police have all the information, however trivial it may seem. We owe it to Kathy to uncover the truth, and to bring her killer to justice."

Leana stared at her, her eyes wide and uncertain. "Julian didn't do it?" she whispered, her voice filled with disbelief.

Ruth shook her head.

Leana's hand flew to her mouth, and then her expression softened. She nodded slowly, as if Ruth's words had confirmed something she had instinctively known all along. "What do you want to know?" she asked, her voice stronger now.

"Anything you can tell us," Alex said, "no matter how small, could make a difference."

"What about that argument you overheard between Celia Vanderlin and Kathy," Ruth prompted.

Leana stiffened at the creak of a door opening at the back of the shop.

Hattie swept into the room, a flamboyant whirlwind of colourful flowing scarves and jangling, clashing jewellery. Her expression faltered when she saw Ruth, Alex, and Greg standing before her. "What are you doing here?"

"We wanted to ask her a few questions about Kathy and Mrs Vanderlin," Ruth said, opting for the truth.

Hattie's eyes flashed with anger. "Absolutely not." She gave Leana a look of admonishment. "What have you told them?"

"Nothing," Leana murmured, her gaze fixed on the floor.

"We will not have anyone spreading unfounded, malicious gossip about Mrs Vanderlin." Hattie ushered Ruth, Alex, and Greg to the door. "Now, if you don't mind, we're closed."

Greg looked about the shop. "You're one of the only places still open."

"We're closed," Hattie repeated in a clipped tone. She flung open the door, exposing them to the full fury of the gale, and several candles around the shop sputtered, their flames extinguishing.

Ruth cast a final lingering glance at Leana, who pointedly averted her gaze. Defeated, Ruth stepped out into the storm. The door clanged shut behind them, leaving her with a profound frustration and a growing conviction that the truth was just out of their grasp.

The three of them headed down a rain-lashed street, turned a corner, and battled their way toward a roofed, open-sided picnic area next to the lake.

Stepping under it to shield herself from the downpour and gather her thoughts, Ruth stared out at the island barely visible through the swirling mist.

"We're no closer to finding Kathy's killer." Frustration gnawed at her insides. "We've reached a dead end."

"Maybe not." Alex nodded to a nearby alleyway.

A hooded figure hurried toward them, coat pulled tight against the wind. The figure joined Ruth, Greg, and Alex under the roof, lowered their hood, and glanced over their shoulder. Their face was pale in the dim light, eyes wide with a mixture of apprehension and urgency.

"Leana." Ruth stepped toward the young woman, hope flickering within her. "Are you okay?"

"I have to be quick," Leana panted, her breath misting in the cold air. "I told Aunty Hattie I was popping out to grab her a bite to eat."

Greg cocked an eyebrow. "In this weather?"

Leana's cheeks flushed. "She can't resist a steak sandwich," she said, the words tumbling out in a rush. Her gaze darted nervously in the direction of the candle shop, as if she feared Hattie would catch her at any moment.

"You told us before you overheard Kathy and Celia arguing," Ruth said, gently guiding Leana back to the subject she assumed the girl had come to discuss. "Can you elaborate?"

"I couldn't hear everything, only snippets." Leana gasped, her eyes widening in alarm. "Wait. You don't think the Black Widow murdered Kathy too?" She looked to Alex, her expression filled with a mixture of fear and morbid fascination.

He held up his hands, palms out. "Nothing of the sort. We're only trying to understand the events that led to her death. Every piece of information helps."

"What can you remember about their argument?" Ruth pressed, her gaze fixed on Leana's face.

She took a deep breath, and her fingers fidgeted with the silver ankh necklace at her neck. "Mrs Vanderlin seemed very upset. She kept saying Kathy was playing a dangerous game. That she'd regret it."

"Regret what?" Ruth asked.

"I don't know." Leana's voice was barely audible above the wind and rain hammering on the roof. The distant rumble of thunder echoed across the lake.

"Did Kathy say anything in response?" Alex said.

Leana's brow furrowed in concentration. "Something about . . . harassment? Kathy would expose Mrs Vanderlin's bullying, if she didn't leave her alone." Leana paused, her gaze fixed on a spot in the distance, as if she was replaying the scene in her mind. "But Mrs Vanderlin wouldn't back down. She was saying something about Kathy needing to go."

"Celia was trying to evict her?" Ruth asked. "Because she missed rent payments?"

A flicker of understanding crossed Leana's face. "Oh, she wasn't trying to evict Kathy, only force her to move shop."

Ruth's eyebrows lifted. "Within the village?"

Leana pointed to a vacant shop near the street corner, the windows dark and empty. "There. That's where they argued. I think Mrs Vanderlin was showing Kathy the shop, trying to persuade her to move there."

Ruth stared at Leana, confused.

"Do you know why?" Greg asked.

Leana shook her head. "But it must have been important. Mrs Vanderlin seemed quite insistent."

Celia wanted Kathy to move? Ruth thought. *What was her motive?* She looked to Alex, but his expression mirrored her own confusion.

"Mrs Vanderlin told Kathy it was in the village's best interests," Leana continued, her voice gaining confidence. "She wanted Kathy to move to the other side of the village. Said her shop didn't fit with the 'aesthetic' of the street." She made air quotes with her fingers. "But Kathy's shop looks fine where it is." She let out a breath. "Kathy refused to move any further, saying there was less foot traffic near that vacant place."

Greg peered down the street, scanning the row of shops. "It is farther back from the main square. Less likely to attract passing trade."

"Anything else?" Ruth asked Leana. "Any mention of money? Rent?" There had to be a reason behind Mrs Vanderlin's actions.

Leana glanced over her shoulder again. "Kathy said Mrs

Vanderlin was being a tyrant. She threatened to take Mrs Vanderlin to court for breach of the lease agreement if she tried anything funny." She looked between Ruth and Alex, her expression a mixture of fear and excitement. "I heard Oliver's name mentioned once too, so I can guess why Mrs Vanderlin wanted Kathy to move."

Ruth inclined her head. "You can?"

Greg and Alex stared at Leana with curious expressions.

Leana hesitated, then lifted her chin, a newfound determination in her eyes. "Oliver's business is going well, and he's keen to expand. So, I think that's why Mrs Vanderlin wanted Kathy out. To make room for Oliver."

Ruth glanced at Alex, who wore a stunned expression.

"Oliver Vanderlin. Celia Vanderlin's son." He shook his head as if trying to process this new information. "Now it makes sense. His shop is—"

"—next door to Kathy's," Greg finished for him. "We saw it when we first arrived." He looked to Leana. "It's an old furniture shop, right?"

Her cheeks flushed again, and she suddenly found her shoes incredibly interesting. "The Three Bears."

Ruth rested a hand on the young woman's shoulder, grateful for her courage. "Thank you, Leana. You've been a big help. Now go before Hattie catches you here."

A small smile finally touched Leana's lips. She pulled her hood back up, and with a final harried glance around, darted back out into the storm.

As Leana disappeared down the alleyway, Greg said to Ruth, "I bet I know who you want to talk to next."

She faced Alex, her mind already made up. The answer, Ruth was convinced, to Kathy's murder lay in the village's tangled relationships. Especially with Celia and Oliver Vanderlin. This small hint of a possible motive wasn't much, but it was a step in the right direction. "What can you tell me about Oliver Vanderlin?"

Alex blew out a puff of air, his expression troubled. "Well, I've had no direct dealings with him. Don't know much about Oliver, only mutterings and rumours."

"Seems to be the theme of this place," Greg said.

Ruth nodded and kept her attention on Alex. "Like what?"

"He supposedly undercut one of his competitors, forcing the only other furniture shop out of the village last year, but I suspect his mother had a hand in it—didn't renew the lease." Alex shrugged. "A while back, Oliver wanted some extra storeroom space, so he and his mother tried to bully May into handing over half of hers, and Mr Harris too, he owns the sweet shop, but Mr Harris threatened Celia with legal action, and they backed off. Eventually."

Ruth sighed, exasperated. "And you didn't think to bring this up earlier?" She fixed him with a stern expression. "From now on, please don't hold back any information, no matter how irrelevant you think it is. We need all the pieces of the puzzle."

Alex looked away, his gaze drifting toward the turbulent lake, then he refocussed on Ruth. "Oliver was devastated by his father's death, but he quickly stepped into his shoes, taking over the furniture shop. Seems he inherited his mother's ambition."

Greg leaned in to Ruth, his voice a hushed whisper. "This is getting dangerous, Grandma, and I don't mean the storm."

Ruth squeezed his arm, a thrill of excitement coursing through her, despite the gravity of the situation. "Let's see what Oliver Vanderlin has to say for himself."

Greg pinched the bridge of his nose, clearly not sharing her enthusiasm.

11

As Ruth, Greg, and Alex headed back out into the storm, the wind and rain seemed to have intensified, and the darkness had closed in further, but a glimmer of hope now burned within Ruth. They had a fresh lead, a new direction to explore, and with her unwavering resolve, she was determined to see it through.

The three of them, heads bowed, made their way to Oliver's shop. Ruth's mind raced, analysing every detail, every nuance of their conversation with Leana.

Oliver Vanderlin, an ambitious businessman, the son of the notorious Black Widow. *Could he be the one behind Kathy's murder?* The argument between Celia and Kathy, Celia's threats, Kathy's defiance... It seemed Oliver was the driving force behind Celia trying to evict Kathy.

A thought struck Ruth. She stopped abruptly under the shelter of a storefront, her hand gripping Greg's arm.

"What's the matter?" He glanced about, his eyes searching the street.

Ruth motioned for Greg and Alex to gather round, and

once huddled close, she said, "That twenty thousand pounds loaned to Kathy..."

Alex stared at her, then realisation dawned on his face. "You think it was a bribe?"

Greg's eyes widened. "From Celia? To get her to move?"

"Why would she do that?" Alex said, his voice filled with confusion. "She wanted Kathy's shop for her son, so why keep her afloat? And why would Kathy accept the money from her of all people?"

Ruth glanced about, ensuring they were still alone, despite the howling wind and the near-zero visibility. "Perhaps Celia wanted Kathy in her debt. Maybe she offered her the money with strings attached." She lowered her voice. "We can't rule anything out at this stage."

They pressed on, rounded a corner, and headed down another street.

The Three Bears' Home Furnishings looked out of place next to Kathy's elegant boutique. Its storefront was dark and imposing, the windows filled with oversized, worn furniture, like the dumping ground of several forgotten eras.

The shop's sign, depicting bears sitting on mismatched chairs, creaked ominously in the wind, the intended cheerful image strangely sinister.

Alex pushed open the door, and they stepped inside, the interior of the shop a welcome relief from the biting wind. It was dimly lit, with only a few strategically placed lamps casting long, eerie shadows across the cluttered space. The air hung thick with the scent of dust and old wood.

Shapes loomed in the darkness—the oversized furniture taking on a sinister presence. A grandfather clock sat in the corner, each tick echoing through the silent shop. The jumble of mismatched pieces crowded the space, creating a sense of claustrophobia that set Ruth's nerves on edge.

"He wants to expand this?" Greg muttered under his breath, scanning the clutter. "Why?"

Ruth shared his bewilderment. The shop seemed more suited to a gothic horror novel than a thriving business. It was hard to imagine anyone wanting to buy furniture from such a depressing, uninviting place.

A figure emerged from the back room, his footsteps echoing ominously in the cavernous space.

Oliver Vanderlin wore a confident smile and a tailored suit that accentuated his broad shoulders. "What can I do for you?" he asked, his voice smooth and friendly.

This took Ruth by surprise. She'd expected a man made in his mother's image.

"We'd like to ask you a few questions, Mr Vanderlin," Alex said. "If that's all right with you."

"I'm sorry, but now is not a good time. Could you please come back later? Thank you." Oliver turned to walk away, but Ruth stepped forward.

"We want to ask about Kathy Fellows."

Oliver stiffened. He slowly turned around, and his demeanour changed in an instant. His eyes lost their confidence, and his jaw relaxed. "Who are you?"

"Ruth Morgan." She extended a hand.

Oliver shook it with a hesitant grip. "Are you a police officer? Why are you asking about Kathy?"

"I'm a food consultant," Ruth replied, keeping her voice calm and steady, despite the way her pulse had quickened. "You weren't at the party last night for very long. Left early."

Oliver released her hand and stepped back, his eyes darting between Ruth, Alex, and Greg, his expression a mixture of confusion and suspicion. "What's a food consultant got to do with Kathy's murder?"

"I used to be a police officer," Ruth clarified, deciding to be upfront about her past. "Now I prefer to tackle culinary challenges rather than criminal ones." She smiled at Greg.

He rolled his eyes.

Oliver looked at Alex again. "I'm confused. Is this a joke?"

"No, sir. Mrs Morgan is assisting with some enquiries. Please answer any questions she may have."

Oliver lifted his chin. "I've already told the police everything I know. I'm sorry, but I have nothing more to say on the matter."

Oliver's not used to confrontation, Ruth thought.

Plus, there was something simmering beneath his pleasant exterior, a dangerous undercurrent.

Clearly picking up on it too, Greg moved closer to Ruth's side, his presence a silent, reassuring support.

Oliver eyed the young man with obvious confusion, then looked back at Ruth, a small amount of resignation in his eyes. "All right, you can ask your questions. But please make it quick. I have a business to run."

"Yeah, you seem really rushed off your feet," Greg murmured, glancing around the dusty, cluttered shop.

Ruth elbowed him gently in the ribs and flashed him a warning look.

However, Oliver didn't appear to have heard Greg's jibe, or care; his attention remained focussed solely on Ruth and Alex. He gestured to a rickety card table in a cramped corner.

Ruth and Alex sat down, the uncomfortable chairs creaking under their weight, while Oliver pulled up a seat opposite.

Greg remained standing, his arms crossed, his gaze fixed on the shop owner.

Oliver studied them for a moment, concern evident on

his face. "What do you want to ask about Kathy?" His voice was laced with caution. "I hope you're not implying I had anything to do with her death."

"Murder," Ruth corrected, leaving no room for ambiguity. "We're trying to understand what happened, what led to Kathy's murder, and we believe you could help us." She studied his reaction carefully, searching for any telltale signs of guilt or deception, any flicker of emotion that might betray his true feelings.

A bead of sweat formed on Oliver's brow, despite his attempts to appear calm and collected. "I— I should call my mother. I don't have to answer your questions, do I?"

Ruth held up a hand. "We're only having an informal chat, trying to understand what happened. Of course, DI Barnes has it well under control, but it couldn't hurt to ask a few more questions, could it? Everyone seems to have loved Kathy. Her death has shocked the entire village." Ruth leaned forward, her voice dropping to a conspiratorial whisper. "No one has anything to hide, do they?"

"I know what you're getting at." Oliver's lips trembled. "It's no secret Kathy and I once dated." He folded his arms. "I assume that's what this is about. You're digging up the past. Looking for dirt?"

He dated Kathy? Ruth's mind raced as it processed this new information. *Why did Alex not mention this before?* It seemed like a crucial detail, something that should have been brought to her attention immediately.

However, Alex too seemed surprised by this revelation, his eyebrows knitting in puzzlement.

Greg looked from Oliver to Ruth, and back again.

Ruth cleared her throat, refocussing her attention on Oliver. "In that case, you knew Kathy better than most. Tell us about your relationship. What was she like?"

"There's not much to tell," Oliver said, his voice flat and unemotional, which was odd, given the tragic circumstances. "We dated for a couple of years. It ended amicably. We remained on friendly terms." He gestured outside, toward the rows of shops lining the street. "We were neighbours, after all." Oliver sat back. "Ask anyone. They'll tell you the same."

Ruth opted to throw caution to the wind, to push him, to see how he would react. "But you had a disagreement with Kathy recently. About her shop space and your expansion plans."

"My mother deals with all that," Oliver said, dismissive, as if trying to distance himself from the issue. "But she said Kathy was being stubborn, unreasonable. She wouldn't budge, no matter what Mother offered. She always had to have things her own way."

Ruth leaned forward again, her gaze unwavering. "Some would say you had a motive to want her gone. To allow you to expand this shop."

Oliver's eyes flashed with anger for the briefest moment, his composure cracking, and then he relaxed. "That's ridiculous. Absolutely absurd. Who said that?" He folded his arms. "I would never hurt Kathy. I might have wanted her shop, but I would never resort to anything so horrifying, so barbaric." He frowned at Alex.

Ruth raised her hands for the second time and made sure to inject a conciliatory tone into her voice. "I didn't mean to offend, Mr Vanderlin. We're simply exploring all possibilities, trying to understand the sequence of events."

"I am not a possibility." His hands clenched into fists. "Julian murdered Kathy. He's a sick, twisted, bitter man, and I hope he gets what's coming to him. He was obsessed with her. Everyone knows that. Julian is the only one who would have possibly wanted that sweet woman dead."

"We have some cause for doubt about Julian's guilt," Alex said before Ruth could respond. "We're not ruling anyone out at this stage."

Ruth's gaze remained steady, her eyes locked on Oliver's. "Would you please explain this, Mr Vanderlin?" She produced her phone, displaying the picture of the deposit in Kathy's ledger, the mysterious twenty-thousand-pound payment. "We're curious to know who made this payment. Have you any idea where it came from? It's a rather large sum to be unaccounted for."

Oliver studied the image, his eyes widening as a flicker of surprise crossed his face. He then hesitated, seemingly weighing his options. Finally, he leaned back in his chair, his expression composed again, the picture of calm, collected innocence. "I have no idea."

"None at all?" Ruth pressed.

"I gather she was in financial trouble," Oliver said, his tone smooth again. "Missed rent. I didn't want to see Kathy lose her business, so my mother offered her a reduced rate on another shop. Kathy still refused to move, and that was the end of it." Oliver's gaze dropped to the table, and for the first time, his expression showed an ounce of humility, a flicker of something that almost resembled regret. "It was just a temporary setback, I'm sure. I wish Kathy had taken the offer." He looked out the window, to the deserted street outside, his voice softening. "And I do want to expand, that much is true, but I still didn't like to see Kathy go under."

Ruth stared at him, struggling to reconcile his words with his actions. Even though Oliver's story seemed as though he was hiding some deeper motive, there was still a hint of sincerity in his voice, a flicker of genuine emotion she couldn't quite dismiss.

However, Ruth still couldn't get over the fact that someone had murdered Oliver's ex-girlfriend, and he showed no outward signs of grief or distress.

The lack of apparent emotion was unsettling, but Ruth's time on the force had shown Ruth that people react to tragedy in different ways. Some grieve openly, while others internalise, presenting a stoic facade to the world.

Could he be telling the truth? she wondered. *Or is this an act, a carefully constructed lie to conceal his guilt, to deflect suspicion?*

"If you knew Kathy was in financial trouble," Alex said in a sceptical tone, "why didn't you help? Why did you still try to force her out? Was there more to your relationship?"

Oliver stood abruptly, his face flushed with barely contained anger. "I had nothing to do with Kathy's murder, and I resent your insinuations. Please, leave. *Now*."

12

Back in the warmth of the Silver Thimble's kitchen, Reverend Michael busied himself making more tea, coffee, and hot chocolate, while Ruth, Greg, and Alex huddled around the table, their faces flushed from the cold.

The aroma of rich, dark coffee and sweet, buttery pastries, usually a comfort, did little to dispel the unease twisting in Ruth's gut.

Oliver's demeanour, and his mother's bullying, painted a rather sinister new picture. This was about power, expansion, and ruthless ambition.

Was Kathy an obstacle in Oliver and Celia's path?

A sudden, sharp clarity pierced Ruth's mental fog. "Of course," she murmured.

Reverend Michael, ever attentive, peered at her with concern.

"We spoke to Oliver Vanderlin," Ruth said, accepting a steaming mug of tea from the reverend. She offered him an appreciative smile, attempting to project optimism that belied the turmoil within her. "He's quite the character, isn't he?"

Reverend Michael nodded slowly, his brow furrowed. "Driven, ambitious, and perhaps a little too eager to follow in his mother's footsteps." He joined them at the table, a weary sigh escaping his lips. "Word is, she plans on handing over the entire village to him in a few years."

"Did you know about his history with Kathy?" Ruth asked, casting a pointed sidelong glance at Alex.

Reverend Michael's gaze drifted toward the darkened café. "They dated for a couple of years." He looked back at them. "It ended badly."

Greg leaned forward. "Oliver said they remained friends. Split on good terms."

A fresh wave of suspicion washed over Ruth, hardening into a knot of certainty in her stomach.

"In that case, Oliver is not being truthful," Reverend Michael said. "There were accusations of infidelity, stolen money, and a bitter rivalry that has festered between them ever since."

"Stolen money?" Greg's eyes widened. "What happened?"

Reverend Michael hesitated, as if reluctant to dredge up the past. "It's a long and complicated story, but suffice to say, Oliver accused Kathy of stealing money from him after she caught him with another woman. Their relationship ended abruptly, and they never saw eye to eye again, except to exchange the odd heated word or two."

Can this be the root of Celia's animosity toward Kathy? Ruth wondered. "We told Oliver we found an entry in Kathy's accounts. A deposit of twenty thousand. He seemed genuinely surprised. Do you think he might have loaned the money to her, given their history?"

Reverend Michael snorted and folded his arms. "Oliver

would be the last person to lend anyone that kind of money. Especially not Kathy."

"As I suspected." Ruth leaned back. "My bet is Celia used the money to try and buy her out, to force Kathy to move her shop."

"Or leave the outlet village entirely," Greg murmured.

Alex appeared taken aback. "But it was in her ledger. She accepted the money."

"Not necessarily," Ruth said. "If Celia sent a direct bank transfer to her account, she'd have no choice but to receive it. Kathy would've kept a log of the payment to make sure her accounts remained straight."

"So if Grandma's theory is correct"—Greg rubbed his chin—"Kathy sent the money back to Celia?"

"It's a possibility," Alex conceded.

Reverend Michael looked between the three of them, his expression troubled. "Celia tried to buy Kathy out so Oliver could expand his shop." He blew out a puff of air.

"We should inform DI Barnes of what we've found," Alex declared, rising from the table. "There's enough probable cause for them to gain access to Kathy's bank statements. It'll take time, but they can ascertain where the money came from and where, if anywhere, it went."

As Alex left the kitchen, his slender silhouette disappearing into the main café, Ruth watched him go. Something wasn't quite right with him. She took a sip of her sweet tea as she mulled over their next move.

Oliver's desire to expand his business, his history with Kathy, the accusations of betrayal and theft—it all painted a picture of a man driven by quiet ambition, perhaps a thirst for revenge.

Ruth set down her mug. "I agree with Alex informing the police," she said, her voice firm with conviction. "That's the right thing to do, but we need more than suspicions and hearsay. We need concrete evidence of something that links Oliver or Celia to Kathy's death."

Reverend Michael nodded slowly, his expression thoughtful. "But what if they find out you're onto them? Celia's unpredictable."

Ruth inclined her head. "Is she capable of murder?"

"I'm not sure she'd go that far," Reverend Michael said. "Celia keeps her cards close to her chest. Oliver too. It's a trait he inherited from his mother, I'm afraid."

"Why pretend to be Kathy's friend, though?" Greg asked. "If he hated her so much, why not just admit it? Maybe Kathy found out something about him." He looked at Ruth. "Perhaps she stumbled upon something she shouldn't have, something that put her in danger."

What could Kathy have discovered? Ruth grappled with the possibilities. *Was it related to the supposedly stolen money from their past relationship, or something else entirely?*

"Whatever the case," Reverend Michael said, interrupting Ruth's train of thought, "we should all be wary of both Celia and Oliver."

"We'll be fine," Ruth assured him, though a sliver of doubt lingered in her mind. "We'll gather as much information as we can, discreetly, and then present our findings to the police." She stood. "I need to check on Merlin."

In truth, Ruth also needed a moment to clear her head, to process the disturbing revelations of the day, and to formulate a plan. The pieces of the puzzle were slowly coming together, but the picture they shaped was far from clear.

She walked to the stairs, intending to head up to her room, but stopped short at a hushed voice coming from the café.

Curiosity overriding caution, as it so often did with her, Ruth edged into the room a few steps.

Alex faced the window at the far end of the room, his back to her, phone pressed against his ear. He spoke in a low, urgent tone, his words barely audible above the rhythmic drumming of the rain.

Ruth strained to listen.

"Counterfeits," he said, his voice tight. "The operation... it's all falling apart." A pause, then: "The murder really complicates things. I don't know how long I can stop her from finding out."

Counterfeits? Operation? What on earth is Alex involved in? And am I the "her" he's referring to?

As Alex turned from the window, his face etched with a mixture of concern and frustration, Ruth darted back into the kitchen, her mind reeling.

Is he involved in something illegal? Is that why Alex was so keen to leave the investigation to the police? Is he trying to protect himself, or is there something more to it?

An impulsive idea struck Ruth, a risky gamble, but one she felt compelled to take. She marched across the kitchen and snatched her coat, scarf, and hat from the hook.

"Everything all right?" Reverend Michael asked, his kind eyes searching her face.

"What? Oh, yes. Fine," Ruth replied, forcing a smile in return. "I need to grab some fresh air."

"Now?" Reverend Michael's eyebrows rose in surprise.

"I won't be long." Ruth pulled on her coat, her fingers fumbling with the buttons in her haste.

"I'll come with you," Greg said.

Ruth hesitated. She wanted to insist he stay with Reverend Michael while she ventured out into the storm, but another part, the part that acknowledged her own limitations, recognised the value of having him by her side.

Besides, Greg was surprisingly resourceful, and his youthful energy might be what she needed to unravel the tangled threads of this increasingly complex mystery.

"Okay," she conceded, giving him a grateful nod. "But stay close."

Greg leapt to his feet and donned his coat.

"We'll be back as soon as we can," Ruth told Reverend Michael. And with that, she and Greg stepped back out into the storm's tempestuous embrace.

The wind howled around them, clawing at their clothes and whipping their hair as they headed up the street. Visibility was near zero, the rain a blinding curtain, but Ruth pressed on.

"What's happened?" Greg shouted above the roar. "Where are we going?"

Ruth darted into the shelter of a shop front for some temporary respite and beckoned for Greg to join her. "Alex portrays himself as a straitlaced, by-the-book type of guy, right?"

"Sure." Greg frowned. "So what?"

Ruth quickly explained what she had overheard, and repeating the fragmented phrases aloud only confirmed her earlier suspicions about Alex.

Greg stared at her, his initial confusion replaced by a dawning comprehension. "Should we confront him?"

"Not yet," Ruth replied, her gaze fixed on an intersection of streets. To the left, the road led down to the lake, a dark, churning expanse barely visible through the swirling rain. To the right, it snaked back into the heart of the village. "We have someone else to speak to first. Someone who could shed extra light on that twenty-thousand-pound deposit."

Without waiting for a response, Ruth jogged toward the intersection, careful to watch her footing on the slick cobblestones, with Greg hot on her heels.

Ruth had to take matters into her own hands, at least for now. DI Barnes seemed too quick to pin the blame on Julian, too eager to close the case without exploring all avenues.

As they reached the Storybook Store, Ruth squinted through the rain-streaked window, to discern if anyone was inside. The shop appeared dark and deserted, the door locked.

Disappointment washed over her, threatening to douse the flame of determination. Ruth was about to suggest they turn back, when a sliver of light inside caught her eye, flickering beneath the crack of the back door.

Greg knocked—"Hello?"—and cupped his hands around his face, peering through the glass. "Maybe they left the light on."

Ruth stepped back, looked right, and then jogged up the street, her boots squelching.

"Grandma?" Greg hurried to keep pace.

"This way." She reached a narrow alleyway and darted into it. At the end, Ruth emerged into an area behind the shops, a maze of overflowing bins, discarded boxes, and delivery entrances.

She stopped abruptly, and Greg nearly collided with her.

A delivery van was parked haphazardly in the yard, its back doors flung open, revealing stacks of boxes crammed inside.

Two burly men, one with a neck tattoo that snaked beneath his collar, carried more boxes from the shop and loaded them into the van.

"Is that the back of the Storybook Store?" Greg whispered.

Ruth nodded, her gaze fixed on the two men.

This didn't feel right.

Greg shielded his eyes from the rain. "Why is May sending a delivery in the middle of a storm?"

Ruth put a finger to her lips and watched.

As the men disappeared inside the shop again, she hesitated, torn between caution and a burning need to know more, but the desire for answers ultimately won out.

She crept closer, her attention fixed on the boxes stacked in the back of the van.

Greg trotted after her. "Grandma, are you freakin' serious?"

The tattooed man emerged from the shop. He spotted Ruth and Greg, now both frozen midstride, and his gaze hardened. "Who are you?"

Ruth tried to appear calm, to project an air of nonchalance, but it was Greg who piped up first.

"We were j-just passing by. W-Wrong turn." He gestured vaguely around them. "Nasty weather, isn't it?"

Ruth breathed out of the corner of her mouth, "Very smooth."

The dark alley left few possibilities of escape, and the man looming before them appeared anything but friendly.

His icy stare hardened further, his neck tattoo, a swirling pattern of skulls and flames, seeming to writhe in the dim light. "I'll ask again," he growled, his voice low and dangerous. "What's your business here?" He took a step closer, biceps bulging beneath his rain-soaked T-shirt, body language radiating aggression. "This is private property."

Ruth briefly considered karate chopping the man in the

throat and making a swift exit, but quickly discarded the idea.

At the moment the situation appeared ready to reach a breaking point, a calm voice cut through the tension.

"Mrs Morgan? What are you doing here?" May, the bookshop owner, strode outside, carrying a large box with relative ease, despite the fact it must be filled with books. She was clearly much stronger than her petite frame suggested. "I thought you would've gone home by now." May's gaze flickered between Ruth, Greg, and the tattooed man, then she slid the box into the back of the van. "Is there something wrong?"

The second burly man appeared behind her, carrying another box. He placed it into the van. Then, without a word, he closed the van doors with a loud, decisive double bang.

Ruth swallowed, looked between the men, the van, and May, trying to make sense of the situation. She let out a slow, shaky breath. "Thank goodness. I thought these gentlemen were robbing you." She winced at her own words, at how ridiculous they sounded. "Not that I thought you were criminals, of course," she added hastily, trying to salvage the situation.

"Very smooth," Greg murmured.

To her surprise, her awkward apology elicited half-hearted chuckles from the two men, their menacing aura dissipating in an instant.

"I donate overstock to charity." May smiled, her expression regaining its usual warmth. "Otherwise, I'd need ten shops' worth of space to store it all. And today was the only day they could collect. Despite the storm." She nodded to the workers, her expression grateful. "Thank you, gentlemen. Drive safely."

As the two men climbed into the van and drove off, disappearing into the rain, their taillights fading into the gloom, a pang of guilt twinged in Ruth's stomach. She had jumped to conclusions, letting her suspicions cloud her judgement. By the look on Greg's face, he felt the same way.

To be fair, the men didn't exactly look like typical charity workers, but Ruth reminded herself, not for the first time, that appearances could be deceptive.

May gestured toward the shop. "Come in out of the weather. You both look soaked through."

13

As they stepped over the threshold of the bookshop, Ruth sighed, grateful for the reprieve from the storm. She and Greg followed May through the warmth and the comforting aroma of old books, into an office that was even more chaotic than the shop itself.

The room was only ten feet square and cluttered with more books piled high on shelves, overflowing onto the floor, creating a labyrinth of paper and ink.

A single desk, covered in a jumble of papers, sat in the middle of the room, a lamp casting a warm glow on its surface.

Greg peered at a quirky collection of vintage toys and curios lining several of the uppermost shelves, which added to the room's eccentric charm.

Ruth couldn't help but feel a little overwhelmed by the sheer volume of . . . well, everything. It was hard to tell if it was organised chaos, or plain old-fashioned, regular mayhem.

A collection of antique dolls seated on a shelf above the desk drew her gaze. Their porcelain faces, frozen in expressions of wide-eyed innocence, seemed to stare back at Ruth, their painted smiles unsettling.

May indicated two comfortable armchairs in front of an electric fire, its bars glowing an inviting orange. "Please." She pulled up an office chair on casters for herself.

Ruth unzipped her coat and settled into one of the armchairs, the fire a welcome relief from the chill that had seeped into her bones.

Greg sat in the other, his gaze darting around the room, taking in the eclectic collection of objects.

May looked between them, her expression curious. "What can I do for you?"

"I hope you don't mind, but I wanted to ask you a few more questions." Ruth took a deep breath, steeling herself for the potentially awkward conversation. "I'm trying to understand Kathy's financial situation," she said, keeping her voice carefully neutral. "Particularly a deposit into her account not so long ago."

A flicker of surprise crossed May's face. "You've seen Kathy's accounts?"

Ruth swallowed. "A large amount. Twenty thousand."

"Twenty thousand pounds?" May blew out a puff of air, her expression thoughtful. "Wow. I know nothing about that."

"You have no idea who might have given her such a large sum?" Ruth pressed.

May pursed her lips, and then her eyes widened. "Now I come to think of it, Kathy did say something a couple of weeks ago about a 'lucky break' she'd had. She wouldn't elaborate, but she seemed quite pleased about it."

Calling it a 'lucky break' was an odd turn of phrase, Ruth mused, considering the money might have come from the Vanderlins. The inconsistency raised a fresh wave of doubt in her mind.

May hesitated, a troubled look, her gaze fixed on a point beyond Ruth's shoulder. "There's something else. Something I haven't told anyone, not even the police."

Ruth's heart skipped a beat. "The police?"

May looked between her and Greg, then sat back in her chair, her body language—raised shoulders, fingers twisting together—radiating tension. "Well . . ." She bit her lip, and her eyes filled with uncertainty. "You know what? It doesn't matter. I've said too much already."

"I assure you that whatever you confide will remain strictly confidential," Ruth said. "We're only trying to understand what happened to Kathy."

May looked toward the door, then back at Ruth. She screwed up her face, clearly wrestling with an internal debate. Finally, her shoulders slumped slightly. "Could the money have something to do with Oliver?"

"I'm not sure," Ruth lied, giving Greg half a glance. "What makes you ask that?"

May's eyes searched Ruth's, as though trying to gauge her sincerity. "Oliver—he's been acting strangely lately. Asking a lot of questions about Kathy, about her business, her finances." May's gaze darted around the room. "I saw Oliver and Kathy arguing the night before she died."

"At the party?" Greg asked, his voice filled with a mixture of curiosity and concern.

"After," May said. "I was on my way home when I spotted them outside her shop."

Ruth inclined her head. "What were they arguing about?"

"I couldn't hear everything," May admitted, her brow furrowed in concentration as she recalled. "Kathy was furious. She kept saying Oliver was 'playing a dangerous game' and he would 'regret it.'"

More threats, Ruth thought. *It's becoming a trend with these people.* "Regret what?" she asked.

"I don't know. Sorry." May shook her head. "But it sounded serious."

"Anything else?" Ruth said, frustration creeping in again.

May's expression turned apologetic.

A sharp voice cut through the silence. "What's going on here?"

Ruth's breath caught in her throat.

Celia Vanderlin stood in the doorway, her tall figure framed against the dim light of the shop beyond. Her face was a mask of disapproval; her eyes, cold and penetrating, bored into Ruth, then shifted to Greg, and finally settled on May. "Well?"

May rose from her chair, her usual cheerful demeanour replaced by a nervous flutter. "Mrs Vanderlin. What brings you out in this weather?"

Celia glared at Ruth. "I've been looking for you." Her perfectly coiffed hair had remained miraculously unruffled by the tempest outside. "I heard you've been harassing my son."

May dropped back into her seat, her hands clasped in her lap.

Ruth met Celia's gaze, a surge of defiance rising within her. She refused to be intimidated by this woman, whose every movement radiated an air of icy control and entitlement. "I'm not harassing anyone," Ruth said, her voice firm. "I merely asked your son a few questions about Kathy, as I'm simply trying to understand what happened to her. I thought Oliver could shed some light on the situation, perhaps offer a different perspective."

Celia's lips thinned into a tight, bloodless line. "How dare you. Oliver had nothing to do with her murder. I resent your insinuations."

May shuffled in her seat, clearly uncomfortable with the confrontation. "Mrs Vanderlin, please," she interjected. "There's no need for hostilities. Mrs Morgan has been nothing but polite and respectful. She is only trying to help."

Celia let out a short humourless laugh. "Help? By meddling in matters that don't concern her?"

Greg got to his feet. "Grandma is helping."

Celia ignored him, her gaze fixed on Ruth. She pointed a finger, her long manicured nail gleaming like a polished talon. "I'm warning you, Mrs Morgan. Stay out of our business. I won't tolerate anyone interfering in my affairs, or those of my family. This is a matter for the police, not some overglorified cook."

Ruth's gaze hardened. This woman's arrogance was infuriating. "Like I said before, what if they've arrested the wrong person?" she said, her voice unwavering. "What if the real killer is still out there, walking among us?"

"In this weather? No one's walking about, only you and your sticky beak." Celia's eyes narrowed to slits. "And as I have also said before, leave it to the professionals. You're playing a dangerous game, Mrs Morgan." Her voice dropped to a low snarl. "I'd advise you to tread carefully." Celia casually adjusted the fabric draped around her neck, the fabric catching the dim light of the office.

And that's when Ruth noticed it. The scarf: a luxurious gold silk. It was the same shade, the same delicate weave as she'd spotted earlier, snagged on a rivet inside the air duct. Her pulse quickened.

Could Celia be the one tampering with the CCTV recordings?

But why? To protect her son? And if it was her, why not use the spare keys Alex mentioned? Why go through all the trouble of sneaking through the air duct?

Ruth tried to maintain a poker face. "What a lovely scarf," she said to Celia as she got to her feet. "May I see it?"

She needed a closer look, to check for any telltale signs —a tear, a snag, anything that might correspond to the fabric left behind in the tunnel. After all, Celia's sudden appearance, her thinly veiled threats, the gold scarf—it all pointed to a deeper involvement.

Clearly cottoning on, Greg's eyes widened.

However, Celia's gaze lingered on Ruth. "I'll not have you causing any more trouble in my village. One more word out of line, Mrs Morgan, and I'll inform the police of your meddling, and have you escorted off the premises. Is that quite clear? If it wasn't for Reverend Michael, you'd be long gone." She shot a warning look at Greg too, then she spun on her heel and swept from the office, leaving a charged silence in her wake.

May, visibly shaken, sank back into her chair.

Celia's behaviour had only solidified Ruth's suspicions about the mother-and-son duo's involvement. Celia was hiding something too, and Ruth was determined to find out what. The CCTV tampering, the threats, the expensive scarf —it all pointed to involvement in this tangled mess.

Ruth zipped up her coat. "Thank you for your time, May. We're sorry to have disturbed you."

As she and Greg stepped back out into the storm, the wind and rain seemed to invigorate Ruth on this occasion, pushing her resolve onward. She had a new suspect to focus on.

Celia Vanderlin, the seemingly untouchable owner of

the village, was now firmly in Ruth's sights. And by the determined set of Greg's jaw, he felt the same way.

"Thank goodness you're all right," Reverend Michael said, his voice thick with relief as Ruth and Greg stepped back into the warmth of the Silver Thimble's kitchen. His kind face, etched with worry lines, softened as he took in their presence. "I was beginning to worry."

Ruth forced a smile, attempting to project a sense of calm she didn't quite feel. "We're fine. Just a little wet."

Greg removed his dripping coat and dropped into a seat at the table.

Reverend Michael hovered, his gaze flicking between them. "Did you manage to speak to May?"

"We did. And she's not the only person we ran into." Ruth peeled off her wet coat and hat, and hung them on a hook by the door. As she sat down at the table, the warmth of the café, now a familiar welcome contrast to the chill outside, seeped into her chilled bones. She recounted their run-in with Celia, highlighting the owner's thinly veiled threats and the suspicious gold scarf. "She might call the police on us," Ruth said, forcing a grim smile.

"Apparently, Grandma is causing trouble," Greg added with a wry smirk.

Reverend Michael's shoulders slumped, his earlier relief replaced with a heavy sigh. "You need to be careful, Ruth. She has eyes and ears everywhere."

"It was Celia in the air duct," Greg said. "She must be really desperate to protect her son."

The image of Celia's cold, calculating eyes, and the feel of her threatening presence, lingered in Ruth's mind.

The question now was whether Celia was willing to do more than merely tamper with CCTV footage to protect Oliver.

What if she was directly involved in Kathy's death too?
And how does Alex factor into all this?

Ruth's gaze drifted toward the inner door, sweeping over the now-deserted café beyond. "Where's Alex?"

Reverend Michael frowned. "I don't know. I haven't seen him since he left right after you did to check on things."

Ruth's heart sank. Alex's absence was unsettling, to say the least. She had hoped to confront him about the eavesdropped conversation. "Earlier, I overheard him on the phone."

"When he called the police?" Reverend Michael asked.

Ruth pursed her lips, choosing her words carefully. "I'm not sure it was the police Alex was talking to." When dumbfounded expressions greeted this proclamation, Ruth continued, "He mentioned something about 'counterfeits' and an 'operation falling apart.'"

Greg cleared his throat. "He's involved in counterfeiting? Alex? Seriously?" He gasped. "Do you think Kathy found out about it? Is that why she was murdered?"

But what is he counterfeiting? And who is he working with? The questions swirled in Ruth's mind.

Reverend Michael, however, seemed unconvinced. He waved a dismissive hand, his expression sceptical. "Alex is above reproach. He wouldn't get involved in such a thing. You must have misheard."

"Only one way to find out." Ruth motioned for Greg to follow her as she grabbed her coat, scarf, and hat.

They hurried back out into the storm, ignoring Reverend Michael's protests, the wind and rain lashing at them, and they made their way to the security office.

The door was locked.

"We have to get in." Ruth recalled the small open window she had spotted earlier. She circled the building, her boots squelching in the muddy ground, and found it tucked away in a wall, low to the ground, behind a bin. The window was tiny, barely big enough for a child to squeeze through, but it was their only option. "Greg, I need you to climb through here."

He hesitated. "But what if I get caught? It's breaking and entering. I could go to prison." He shuddered. "I wouldn't do well in prison."

That was true.

"You'd be fine in prison," Ruth lied, and then murmured to herself, "for about five minutes."

"What?"

"Nothing. Look, we have to try," Ruth said. "Alex could be hurt. We need to find him."

With a dubious expression, Greg flicked his gaze between Ruth and the window.

"He knows us," Ruth said in a reassuring tone, gently nudging her grandson toward the window. "It'll be all right. Just be quick."

Greg grumbled under his breath, something about his wayward grandmother and her crazy schemes, but he eventually sat on the ground and squeezed through the narrow window, feet first, disappearing into the darkness within.

Ruth raced back to the front of the building, and a moment later the door creaked open, and Greg beckoned her inside.

They entered the security office, the air thick with the hum of electronics. As before, the monitors displayed images from the various security cameras throughout the village, showing the deserted shops.

Alex's chair was pushed back, as if he had left in a hurry. And then Ruth saw it—the external hard drive, the one that contained the backup recordings of the CCTV footage, was gone.

Stunned, she and Greg stared at the empty space where the hard drive once resided.

"Where is he?" Greg said.

Ruth examined the desk closely, running her gloved fingers over the surface, hoping to find a clue, a note, anything that might indicate where he had gone. She searched the room, her eyes darting from the monitors to the filing cabinets, looking for anything out of place.

There was nothing.

Only the missing hard drive and Alex with it.

Ruth looked to the door and back again. *If Alex has taken the hard drive, where's he gone?* Then she pictured the layout of the outlet village—the staff car park was at the back of Julian's shop, which was on the other side of the complex.

The road from there followed the outer edge all the way round to the entrance, meaning there might still be time to catch him.

"Come on, Greg." Ruth ran up the steps and burst back into the storm, the wind instantly snatching at her breath. She took an immediate left, her boots slipping on the wet cobblestones, requiring a few panicked arm flaps to stay upright.

"Where are we going?" Greg shouted as they splashed through puddles and battled against the rain, his voice barely audible above the howling wind.

14

As she raced through the slick streets, Ruth pulled her phone from her pocket, her fingers fumbling with the wet screen. She dialled Reverend Michael, praying he'd answer quickly.

"Ruth?" His voice came through faint and distorted through the howling wind.

"What car does Alex drive?" she shouted.

"Excuse me?"

"*Car. Car.*"

"Cool seagull impression, Grandma," Greg said.

She shot him a withering look.

"He drives a Beetle, I think," Reverend Michael said, his voice still distant. "A Volkswagen."

Ruth took a hard right, squeezing between Sleeping Beauty's Mattress Market and a stack of empty crates, almost losing her footing on the slick stones for what felt like the millionth time. "Old- or new-style Beetle?" she shouted into the phone.

"Old. A dark blue one," Reverend Michael replied. "Ruth, are you—"

"Thank you." She hung up, sprinted across the village square, ignoring the curious glances from a few shopkeepers peering out from the safety and warmth of their shops, and headed down the incline of the main street, the wind now whipping at her back for a change, as if urging her on.

"Slow down," Greg gasped.

"No time." Ruth ran through the main entrance, across the drawbridge, her feet thumping against the wet wooden slats.

She darted in front of the gate just as a dark blue Beetle appeared, its headlights cutting through the rain-soaked gloom.

The car slammed on its brakes, sliding to a halt inches from Ruth. Startled, she held up her hands and staggered back, her heart pounding against her ribs.

Alex wound down his driver's-side window and stuck his head out, his face a mixture of shock and annoyance. "What's going on? I could have run you over."

Panting, she gestured for him to turn off the engine. "Get out of the car, Alex."

With a confused look, he switched off the car but didn't get out. "What's happening?"

Ruth threw open the passenger door, pushed the seat forward, and motioned for Greg to climb in. As soon as he was in the back seat, Ruth returned the passenger seat to its original position and clambered in beside Alex.

Now out of the rain, she took several deep breaths, trying to compose herself, and faced him. "So, how are you?"

"Fine. Thanks for asking." He glanced back at Greg, his expression unreadable.

Ruth inclined her head. "What are you up to?"

"What do you mean?"

Greg plucked the hard drive from the back seat and waved it in Alex's face.

"Ah. That." Alex ran a hand through his damp hair, his eyes fixed on the road ahead. "I was taking it to the police station. The copies Sergeant Nielsen has are corrupted. So I'm heading there now."

Ruth studied his face to gauge his sincerity.

Alex noticed her scrutiny and hesitated, perhaps weighing his options, deciding whether to tell the truth or feed them some complex charade. Finally, he let out a long sigh. "Fine." Alex opened the glove compartment and pulled out a small leather wallet. He flipped it open, revealing a police ID and badge. "Detective Constable Alexander Kensington."

Ruth took the ID and examined it closely. The photograph matched Alex's face, and the details seemed legitimate. "He's telling the truth." She handed it back to him.

"You're a cop?" Greg asked, his voice still laced with suspicion. "Why pretend to be a security guard?"

Alex returned the ID to the glove compartment. "I've been trying to gather evidence of a suspected counterfeiting operation within the village." He took a deep breath. "We believe it's been going on for many years." Alex leaned back in his seat, his face etched with weariness. "We've had our suspicions about this place for a long while, but we haven't been able to make any arrests."

"What are they counterfeiting?" Ruth asked.

"Designer clothes," Alex said, his gaze fixed on the rain-streaked windscreen. "High-end labels. The quality is exceptional. I've been attempting to identify the ringleader, but so far, no luck. We believe someone is using the village as cover for their operation. It's the perfect front."

Ruth's mind whirled. It was indeed an ideal location—a seemingly innocent, fairy-tale-themed outlet mall, nestled in the heart of the picturesque countryside, attracting tourists and local bargain-hunters alike. No one would suspect a thing.

This revelation threw everything into a new light. Suddenly, the arguments between Julian and Kathy, Celia's threats, and the mysterious deposit in Kathy's accounts all seemed to have greater meaning.

Did someone murder Kathy because she stumbled upon the counterfeiting operation, uncovered something she shouldn't have, something that put her in danger? Is Julian still involved? Or is it someone else entirely?

"I was brought in to identify the key players and uncover the extent of the operation," Alex continued. "I've been playing the long game, gaining the trust of the villagers, to blend in, to observe." He swallowed. "It's been a frustrating time."

Ruth nodded, a dawning understanding replacing her earlier suspicion. A security guard made perfect sense—able to go anywhere within the village without drawing suspicion, to observe without themselves being observed. And undercover work was a lonely and sometimes dangerous business.

"What about Kathy's murder?" Ruth asked. "Do you think it's connected to the counterfeiting operation?"

Alex sighed, the sound heavy with uncertainty. "I don't know," he admitted. "It's too early to say for sure. But it's a possibility." He met Ruth's gaze. "Now you can see why I didn't want to tell you. DI Barnes has already warned me not to investigate the murder and to stay in my lane. I'm to only focus on the counterfeiting, and report anything I may think is related. We're dealing with people who will resort to killing to defend what they have. You and Greg could be in danger. I've tried to warn you."

Ruth waved off the suggestion, and Greg tutted loudly at her dismissive gesture.

It all seemed too interconnected to be a coincidence.

Is Julian a victim of circumstance, or is he deeply involved in this mess?

"We need to work together," Ruth said, her voice firm with conviction. "Sounds like you could do with our help, and we need yours. We can pool our resources, share our information, and hopefully uncover the truth."

Alex looked at her, his eyes filled with trepidation. "I appreciate the offer, but I can't involve you. I shouldn't have even told you this much. DI Barnes will have my head."

"We're already involved," Ruth pointed out, her gaze unwavering. "And we'll stay out of the way of your colleagues," she added.

Alex's gaze flickered between Ruth and Greg in the mirror. He seemed to be weighing his options, considering the risks and the potential rewards.

"I can ask questions while you observe," Ruth continued. "As we were doing before. That way, you won't risk exposing your identity, and when it's over you can tell DI Barnes you didn't actively investigate the murder yourself, only kept an eye on us and how it relates to the counterfeiting. Same goes for Celia and Oliver—they'll think you're merely keeping an eye on me, making sure I don't cause any more 'trouble.'" She stared at him. "Well?"

"You won't leave me alone until I give in to your demands, will you?" Alex asked.

"Grandma never gives up," Greg said. "You're better off just going along with it and hoping we don't all get killed or in deep trouble."

Alex let out a long, slow breath. "All right, but you must promise me you'll be careful. If I say to back off, you have to do as I ask without question. No arguments. I'm the lead on this investigation. First sign of trouble, you're out of here, got it?"

"Oh, you needn't worry," Greg said, his voice dripping with sarcasm. "Grandma is fantastic at taking directions and advice. Always does everything everyone asks. You've never met anyone who respects authority more, and takes safety—"

"Yes. Thank you, Gregory." Ruth shot him a withering look, cutting him off before he could further undermine her credibility. She turned back to Alex, a determined smile on her face. "We'll be discreet. We'll be cautious. And we'll get to the bottom of this." She thrust out a hand, a silent offer of partnership.

Alex hesitated again, staring at Ruth's outstretched hand. Finally, he shook it. "I'll probably regret this."

"Where do we go next?" Greg asked. "Everything so far has resulted in dead ends."

Ruth's gaze shifted to the rain-streaked windscreen, her mind already racing ahead. "Julian. We need to find out what he knows, and how much involvement he's had."

"But Julian is in custody," Alex pointed out. "We can't waltz in and demand to speak to him. I'm not on the murder case."

"You can interview him as part of your counterfeiting investigation, though," Ruth suggested, formulating a plan.

Alex's brow furrowed, his expression thoughtful. "I suppose I could. But what good will that do? You can't come with me. My superiors certainly wouldn't allow a civilian to participate in a police interview."

"I have an idea on that front," Ruth said, a mischievous glint in her eye. "How about a phone conference?"

Alex's expression turned to disbelief followed by amusement. "A phone conference?" he repeated, as if he couldn't quite believe what he was hearing. "Ruth, that's ridiculous."

"Is it legal?" Greg asked.

"Ruth." Alex ran a hand through his damp hair. "This is a serious police investigation. I could lose my job if my superiors find out I was involving you. We can't take that risk."

"We can. Just don't get caught." Ruth held out her phone. "Tell Julian what we're trying to do for him, that we believe he's been framed. Ask his permission for me to talk to him. If he agrees, Greg and I will be waiting at the Silver Thimble for the video call. You can discreetly prop your phone up during the interview, so we can see and hear everything."

Alex hesitated, his gaze flickering toward the rain-lashed window again. He seemed to be considering the logistics, the potential risks, and the sheer audacity of her plan. "Fine," he said, the word heavy with resignation. "We'll try your phone conference. But if it doesn't work, or if it puts either investigation at risk in any way, we're back to square one. Understood?"

Ruth smiled, a surge of triumph coursing through her. "It'll work," she assured him. "I have a good feeling about this."

Alex nodded, hope creeping into the resignation on his face. He looked tired, the weight of his undercover operation and the murder clearly taking its toll.

Ruth climbed out of the car, helped Greg out too, and then they watched as the Beetle pulled away from the kerb, heading toward the main road, its taillights disappearing into the grey curtain of rain.

"How exactly did you do that?" Greg asked.

Ruth's mind already raced with questions she wanted to ask Julian. "Do what?"

"Convince a police officer to let you meddle with an active investigation?" Greg pulled his coat collar tighter against the wind.

"Oh." Ruth started walking back up the road. "Because Alex is desperate to make amends."

Greg trotted after her. "Make amends for what?"

"No idea," Ruth said, her voice light. "But whatever he did to be dumped here with this assignment, it must have been pretty bad."

Ruth and Greg hurried back to the Silver Thimble, the wind and rain battering them as they navigated the deserted streets. However, the chill no longer seemed to penetrate Ruth's resolve. A surge of adrenaline coursed through her, bringing a renewed sense of purpose. They had a lead, a chance to speak to Julian.

They reached the café and stepped inside, grateful for the warmth. The familiar aroma of freshly brewed coffee and baked pastries hung in the air.

"Reverend Michael?" Ruth called out.

He appeared from the café, his normally cheerful face etched with concern. "You're back." Relief was evident in his tone. "I was starting to think you'd been swept away by the storm. What's happened?"

"We're fine." Ruth peeled off her wet coat and hat, and hung them on a hook by the door. "We had a little detour. Now we need to set up Greg's laptop for a video call."

Reverend Michael's brow furrowed. "Who are you calling?"

"Julian," Greg said, already heading toward the stairs.

"How are you able to speak to him?" Reverend Michael asked. "He's in police custody."

Ruth stepped to him and whispered, "Alex is an undercover police officer." She wanted to gauge the reverend's reaction, see if he knew all along.

However, Reverend Michael's jaw dropped. "I can't believe it. Alex? Really?" When he seemed to notice Ruth's serious expression, he said, "He is? Why?"

"Something about a counterfeiting operation," Ruth said. "A long-term investigation."

Reverend Michael stared at her with a look of incredulity. "In the village?" He snorted. "Ridiculous notion."

"So was the idea of murder a few days ago, no?" Ruth shrugged. "Keep it to yourself. I shouldn't have told you, but with everything that's happened . . . Anyway, we'll let you know how we get on." As she climbed the stairs, Ruth hoped Julian would agree to the call, and that he could shed some light on the mystery surrounding Kathy's death.

But what if he won't answer our questions? What if he's too scared to talk?

Upstairs, Greg set up the laptop on the coffee table. The two of them waited anxiously for the call, the only sound the rhythmic tick-tock of a carriage clock on the mantelpiece.

Merlin curled up on Ruth's lap, a warm, comforting weight. As she absently massaged his ears, her mind drifted to a time when her late husband, John, had surprised her with a weekend trip to Paris. He'd known how much she loved art, so he'd booked them a private tour of the Louvre.

I miss his thoughtful gestures, his warm smile, the way he always knew how to cheer me up.

However, in typical John fashion, he'd arranged to meet an art historian who, like Julian, had been blamed for a recent crime—an art theft.

Despite only having met the guy once before, John had believed his innocence and insisted he and Ruth help him out. That had been the start of a weeklong adventure across France, hunting for clues, speaking to nefarious individuals in back-alley bars, and finally uncovering the truth—a much deeper plot involving a police chief, a politician, and a famous cat burglar.

John always knew how to get us into the most ridiculous situations, Ruth mused, finding solace in Merlin's steady purr.

However, she could never have imagined, during her first trip to Osborne all that time ago, that four decades later she'd be up to her eyebrows in a murder investigation.

John would've loved it.

Back in the present, Ruth frowned at the laptop screen. Thirty minutes had passed, and no call from Alex. *What's taking him so long? Did Julian refuse? Or has something happened to Alex? Has DI Barnes caught him out?*

A knot of unease tightened in her stomach. She glanced at Greg, who was tapping away on his phone, probably texting Mia.

Reverend Michael appeared at the door, his expression downcast. "While you were out, Mrs Vanderlin showed up." He cleared his throat.

Ruth widened her eyes. "What? Why? What did she say?" As if she couldn't guess.

"Accused me of stirring up trouble." He ran a hand through his thinning hair. "Said I should watch my back. Charming, right?"

"Did she mention Kathy?" Ruth asked.

"No, not specifically." Reverend Michael shifted his weight from one foot to the other. "But the implication was clear. I guess she wants me to stop encouraging you." He paused. "Mrs Vanderlin also said something rather odd. Something about 'protecting the village's reputation.'"

"Yeah, I'm not surprised," Ruth said. "Surely, solving a murder and bringing the real killer to justice would do just that."

Reverend Michael shrugged. "Anyway, thought you should know."

"Ignore her," Ruth said. "Don't take it personally."

In her experience, guilty people often did stupid things in a moment of panic and desperation.

As Reverend Michael left, Ruth's attention moved back to Greg's laptop screen. She was about to give up hope when it pinged. A small window appeared, showing Alex's face.

15

Under the harsh lights of the interview room, Alex appeared tired, his skin grey, his eyes bloodshot. "We need to be quick," he said, his voice low and urgent. "I've explained to Julian that you're assisting me with the investigation. He's agreed to speak to you."

Ruth's heart skipped a beat. *This was it—their chance to get some answers.*

A second later, Julian's face appeared, his eyes wide with fear and desperation. "Please, Mrs Morgan." His voice cracked with emotion. "I— I didn't kill Kathy. I would never do such an unspeakable thing. I've been set up. You have to believe me."

Ruth's gaze fixed on Julian's face. "We believe you," she said, trying to put some reassurance in her tone. "We'll do everything we can to uncover the real murderer."

Julian's shoulders slumped. "Thank you."

"Please explain what happened." Ruth steepled her fingers as she listened.

Julian took a deep breath, and his words tumbled out in

a torrent of fear and frustration. He recounted the events of the previous evening, his late-night work in his shop, his argument with Kathy, and the discovery of her body the following morning. "I found her like that." He shook his head, and his eyes glistened with unshed tears. "At first, I thought it was a sick joke. Kathy was dressed in the same way as the mannequin the night before. Wearing my dress. I couldn't believe it. Who'd do such a thing?" His voice cracked. "I mean, we argued, yes. But I would never, *ever*, in a million years, hurt Kathy."

"And then when you realised she was dead, what happened next?" Ruth asked. "You called the police?"

"No. I panicked." Julian looked down, his shame evident. "I'm sorry to say, I ran. I—" He wiped his eyes with the back of his hand. "Lost my mind." His voice choked again. "I'm—I'm a coward. I knew right there and then that someone was setting me up."

Ruth listened intently, her gaze fixed on Julian's face, searching for any flicker of deception. But she saw only fear, desperation, and a genuine plea for help. "What made you think someone was setting you up for Kathy's murder?"

Julian's eyes rose to meet hers. He hesitated, then whispered, "Kathy told me she knew something so bad it could bring the whole village down."

"Why would she say something like that to you of all people?" Alex's voice chimed in. "You hated each other."

Julian looked off camera. "I didn't hate Kathy, and it came out in the heat of one of our arguments." He cleared his throat. "Her actual words were, 'I know something so bad it'll bring this whole village down to its knees, including you and that stuck-up moron.'" He winced, then looked back at Ruth.

"Moron?" she asked. "Did she mean—"

"Mrs Vanderlin."

Ruth took a steadying breath as she pieced it together. "Did Kathy ever mention anything about counterfeiting?"

"What? In the village?" Julian's eyebrows shot up. "No." He looked off camera again, his expression questioning. "Is that true? Someone's doing that?"

Ruth winced and held up a hand, drawing Julian's attention back to her. "It's only one of my many silly theories," she lied, hoping to steer the conversation away from Alex's investigation. "Ignore me." She needed to refocus him. "What I mean to say is, what do you think Kathy knew that would be so damaging?"

"Enough to bring the village to its knees?" Julian shrugged. "She wouldn't tell me. Too busy shouting."

Ruth sighed as a fresh wave of frustration washed over her. "Can you remember anything else that might be useful?"

Julian shook his head, then his eyes widened. "Oh wait." He glanced around as if checking for eavesdroppers, then leaned in close to the camera, his voice barely a whisper. "Kathy had a diary."

Ruth leaned forward too. "Really?" They hadn't found anything like that at her shop. Where could she have hidden it? "What does it look like?"

"Leather-bound." Julian gestured with his hands, indicating a size of about six inches by four. "I—" He hesitated, a sheepish expression crossing his face. "Well, let's say I caught Kathy writing in it a few months back. When I went into her shop to have it out with her about her obvious animosity toward me. I wanted to make peace." He grimaced, the memory clearly unpleasant. "Anyway, when I opened her office door, she was at her desk, scribbling away.

I assume it was her personal diary because of the way she covered it up." His expression turned thoughtful. "So, if I were to guess, I'd bet Kathy wrote any secrets she had in there. Whatever dirt." He sat back.

"Where is it now?" Alex asked.

Julian's expression turned apologetic. "Sorry. No idea."

"Thank you," Ruth said. "You've been a great help. And don't worry, we're doing everything we can for you." After ending the call, Ruth sat in silence, mulling over what he'd said.

The mystery surrounding Kathy's death was far more complex than she'd imagined, and the revelation of her having a diary ignited a new sense of urgency. It may hold potential clues to unlock the truth behind her murder, or at least offer new hints. *If only we could get our hands on it.*

"We need to find that diary."

Greg, who had been engrossed in texting Mia again, looked up. "You really think Kathy wrote down anything linked to what happened to her?"

"Maybe." Ruth sat back, absently stroking Merlin, her fingers tracing his soft fur. "We'll wait for Alex." She pictured Kathy's shop and the office. "I didn't see a diary. I think she must have taken it to her house. Wherever that is."

"On the island." Greg pocketed his phone.

Ruth blinked at him, surprised. "Excuse me?"

"Kathy lives on the island. Several people do. In those cottages. I heard them talking at the party."

"Interesting." Ruth texted Alex, asking him to meet them by the lake, and then she stood. "Guess where we're going, Gregory?" Ruth beamed at him.

He groaned, a long, drawn-out sound of teenage suffering. "To the island? In this weather? How?"

"I spotted some pedalos shaped like giant swans." Ruth

straightened her face. "And we know how much you enjoy pedalling."

Greg let out another loud groan. "You'd better be joking."

Downstairs, they brought Reverend Michael up to speed. Then, they stepped back out into the storm, the wind and rain a relentless force now threatening to push them over should they not pay enough attention.

Ruth and Greg hurried down the deserted streets, heads bowed against the onslaught, their boots splashing through puddles that now reflected the lights of the streetlamps.

By the lake, they huddled under the roof of the picnic area, the wind howling around them.

Twenty minutes later, when they were about to retreat back to the Silver Thimble, Alex showed up. He stared out at the cottages, his expression troubled. "I'm not sure about this, Ruth. We can't search through someone's home without just cause."

Ruth shook her head. "You can't." She gestured between herself and Greg. "But we can." *Besides,* she thought, *what's the worst that could happen? A fine? A slap on the wrist?* It would be worth it if they found Kathy's diary. Ruth half shrugged, trying to appear nonchalant. "We'll take the risk of being prosecuted for trespassing."

Greg's eyebrows rose. "We will?"

"Do you have a key to Kathy's cottage?" Ruth asked Alex.

"Don't need one. As far as I know, they're not locked." He hesitated for a few seconds, his internal debate evident on his face, then let out a long breath. "Come on."

They followed him alongside the lake until they reached a pontoon with a small fishing boat tied alongside. Mercifully, it had a cabin to shield them from the worst of the weather.

Alex started the engine, Greg untied the boat, and moments later they were underway.

Despite the weather, the surface remained relatively calm in comparison, with the lake shielded on one side by the outlet village buildings, by a dense forest on the other.

A few minutes later, Alex deftly navigated them to a pontoon on the island. The three of them followed a narrow path that led to a row of cottages with thatched roofs and front gardens enclosed in picket fences.

"Which one's Kathy's?" Greg asked.

Alex opened the gate to a cottage with a red door and gestured them through.

Ruth held up a hand, stopping him. "Please wait here. Don't want you getting into trouble. We won't be long." She hurried up the path with Greg hard on her heels, opened the front door, and stepped into the cottage.

The sitting room had a low ceiling with wooden beams, two armchairs flanking a stone fireplace, a bureau, a sideboard, and a bookshelf overflowing with romance novels.

Ordinarily, it would have been cozy and inviting, but Ruth shuddered. The silence within the cottage was unsettling. The place felt cold and empty, devoid of life. A wave of sadness washed over her as she realised Kathy would never again curl up in one of those armchairs with a novel, or light the fire on a cold evening. Those simple pleasures, stolen from her.

The polished oak sideboard caught Ruth's attention. Framed photographs crowded its surface—snapshots of a life now cut short. Ruth approached, her throat tightening. There was Kathy as a young woman, arms around an elderly couple who must have been her parents. Another showed a teenage boy—a nephew perhaps—proudly holding up a fishing rod.

But what made Ruth's eyes mist over was a series of photos featuring Kathy and May together. Their friendship documented over decades: the two of them laughing on a beach somewhere sunny, windswept on the cliffs of Cornwall, arm-in-arm outside a London theatre, and sharing a chocolate birthday cake. In the last one, they sat at a card table, under a strange light shaped like a bunch of flowers. Both grinned at the camera.

All those years of shared memories, and now May was left to carry them alone.

"Such a waste," Ruth whispered, tracing her finger lightly over Kathy's smiling face. She took a deep breath. "We need to find that diary, Greg."

They began a systematic search, scanning every inch of the room. Ruth started with the bureau, carefully going through each drawer, rifling through files and folders, looking for anything that resembled a diary. Each item she touched felt sacred somehow. These were the everyday things Kathy had touched, organised, cared about.

Greg examined nearby shelves, then deftly sorted through a stack of envelopes by the door. "Bills, mainly."

The two of them searched high and low, methodical, in both the sitting room and kitchen. They checked under the chairs, behind the furniture, even inside the wastepaper basket.

Ruth and Greg examined every book, every magazine, every piece of paper, hoping to find a clue, a hidden compartment, anything that might indicate where Kathy had stashed her secrets.

But their efforts yielded nothing, and the diary remained elusive.

Frustration gnawed at Ruth. "Where could it be?" Her gaze shifted to the stairs. "It has to be here somewhere. Let's try upstairs." After all, if the diary did contain any important information, Kathy wouldn't have left it lying around. She must have hidden it somewhere safe, somewhere secure.

They headed up and found three doors. The first led to a bathroom, the second an empty spare room, and the third door opened to a master suite with a double bed, wardrobe, and bedside table.

Ruth checked the drawer in the bedside table, then turned her attention to the wardrobe. The top half held dresses, skirts, cardigans, trousers, and jackets, whereas the bottom was divided into shelves with a collection of neatly folded blouses, each one carefully arranged by colour and style. Ruth ran her hand over the soft fabrics, a pang of sadness hitting her. These were Kathy's personal belongings... clothes she'd chosen with care, worn to occasions both special and mundane. Ruth pictured her selecting an outfit for that final day, never knowing it would be her last.

"It's not right," she murmured to Greg. "All the life she had yet to live." Ruth closed the wardrobe and faced the room.

After searching everywhere, including under the bed, Ruth's gaze swept the room again. They had to be missing something. A hidden compartment, a secret drawer, a loose *floorboard*... anything.

Her eyes fell on a framed photograph on the wall in the upstairs landing, a picture of Kathy standing proudly in front of her shop, a radiant smile on her face.

Ruth left the bedroom and stepped to the wall where the photograph hung. She studied the image, a sudden intuition hitting her. "Kathy loved her shop. It was her pride and joy."

She ran her fingers around the frame, feeling for any irregularities, any hidden catches or mechanisms.

Not finding anything obvious, Ruth tapped the wall on either side, listening for a hollow sound.

Nothing.

She huffed and stepped back. "Maybe Julian is mistaken."

"We could try searching her shop," Greg said.

Ruth stepped into the spare bedroom, her gaze sweeping over the empty space. The room was bare, with not even a rug to cover the exposed floorboards.

She moved to the back window and peered out at a small garden, where a lone apple tree stood, its branches swaying violently in the wind. She wondered if Kathy had expected to harvest its fruit for years to come.

Greg joined her. "Maybe you missed it back at her office."

Ruth's gaze shifted to the horizon and Rapunzel's tower high above the village. She pictured Celia in her office, staring back at them. *Maybe she saw something that night and is keeping it to herself.*

As they headed back downstairs, Ruth's gaze fell on a small wooden coatrack by the front door. It held a few jackets, a scarf, and a hat.

"Wait a minute." Her eyes widened. "That hat."

It was a wide-brimmed, floppy straw hat, the same one Kathy had been wearing in the photograph upstairs. But there was something different about it now—it bulged in the middle and hung low, misshapen.

Ruth reached out and carefully lifted the hat from the rack. Her heart skipped a beat. Inside rested a small leather-bound diary. It was the size of a paperback novel, its cover worn and faded, its pages filled with Kathy's neat handwriting.

With Greg peering over her shoulder, Ruth riffled

through them until she found Kathy's last entries. As she read, her eyes widened. The last entry was dated the day before she died. *This is it,* she thought. *This could be the breakthrough we've been waiting for.*

Greg's eyes widened as he read. "Oh."

16

At the Silver Thimble, Ruth, Greg, and Alex huddled around the kitchen table with Reverend Michael. The leather-bound diary lay open before them.

The entries chronicled her life in the village since the start of the year: her family and friends, May in particular, her hopes, and her fears. They spoke of Kathy's love for her shop, her passion for the fashion industry, and her unwavering determination to succeed. A picture emerged of a woman who was not only tenacious, but also harboured growing suspicions about Celia and Oliver Vanderlin.

Several entries detailed the arguments with Julian, revealing a complex relationship filled with both animosity and a strange, grudging respect.

Mostly, they involved petty squabbles. Kathy had grown paranoid, convinced that Julian was trying to sabotage her business, even claiming he waited outside Kathy's Klassics to poach her customers. All this according to Kathy, and without any supporting evidence attached.

Ruth turned to the last page. "And then there's this." The

final entry, dated a day before Kathy's death, detailed a disturbing encounter with Celia. "'She threatened me,'" Ruth read aloud. "'Said if I didn't back off, she would make sure I regretted it. I informed her I'm in possession of evidence she doesn't want me to reveal if she knows what's good for her.'"

"Maybe it's evidence that Celia Vanderlin murdered her husband," Greg said.

Reverend Michael shook his head.

Ruth continued reading. "'I told her if she keeps threatening me, I'd have no choice but to hand over all the evidence I have to the police. I regret that now. I don't feel safe." Ruth looked up, her gaze settling on each of the men's faces in turn. "Seems she knew about the counterfeiting."

Reverend Michael's brow furrowed, concern etched into the lines around his eyes. Alex remained stoic, but a muscle ticked in his jaw, betraying his inner turmoil.

Greg appeared dubious. "But why didn't she go to the police anyway? Especially if she believed her life was in danger?"

"She did," Alex interjected. "She told me." He winced. "In a manner of speaking."

"Told you what?" Ruth asked, astounded by this sudden revelation. Something else he hadn't shared.

Alex glanced at Reverend Michael, looked away, and shook his head. "Doesn't matter."

"Oh, don't worry," Ruth said with a dismissive wave. "Reverend Michael knows you're an undercover officer."

Alex's face dropped. "*What?* You told him?"

Ruth shrugged. "He would've figured it out, what with all the running about we're doing. Now you're free to talk."

Alex pinched the bridge of his nose.

"Don't worry," Greg murmured to him. "You get used to Grandma after a while, and kind of go along with her shenanigans."

Ruth grinned. "Alex? You were saying something about Kathy?" She was eager to get the discussion back on track.

He sighed. "Kathy obviously didn't know I'm a police officer, so she was coming to me as someone she could trust. I got an anonymous note pushed under my door. At the time, I thought it was a prank."

"What did it say?" Greg asked.

Alex pulled his wallet from his pocket and extracted a folded piece of paper with a handwritten note. "This is a photocopy. The original is with evidence." He opened it and read aloud. "'I have proof you should see. Please meet me outside the Three Little Pigs BBQ at 7:15 tonight.'"

Ruth compared the writing to the diary, and they matched.

Kathy had been reaching out, seeking help, and no one had realised it in time. She'd planned to hand over the evidence to Alex.

"That was right before the party," Reverend Michael said, his voice filled with a mixture of sadness and disbelief. "If only you'd met with her."

"I tried to." Alex tossed the photocopy onto the table. "No one showed up. I waited ten minutes, then I went to the party."

"You didn't know who'd sent the note, so you couldn't confront Kathy about it," Ruth said, piecing together the sequence of events.

Alex's gaze remained fixed on the note. "If only I'd known it was from her. I wish she'd given me a hint."

"She likely didn't want to have you asking questions at the party," Greg said. "Perhaps that's why Kathy kept the note anonymous." He looked at Ruth. "So, we're still thinking one of the Vanderlins murdered her?"

Ruth tapped the diary page. "Which brings us to this." She cleared her throat and read the last sentence. "'I'm worried she knows about the evidence I have and will come looking, so I'm hiding it where she least expects.'"

Reverend Michael leaned in and whispered, "Where would Kathy have hidden something so crucial, something she knew the Vanderlins would be desperate to find?"

Ruth spun the diary around so they could all see.

Below Kathy's final entry was a series of abstract lines and dots, with an X in the middle. And beneath that drawing, she'd taped a key to the page.

Greg screwed up his face. "What's all that? Some sort of code? Where does that key fit?"

"It's a map," Ruth said, a thrill of excitement coursing through her. "A map of the village." Ruth studied Alex's reaction.

"You know what, I think you're right." He squinted, tracing the lines with his finger. "If I'm reading this correctly, and X marks the spot where Kathy's hidden the evidence, that's—"

"Oliver's shop," Ruth finished. "It's quite clever, really. Right under his nose. It's a far better hiding spot than her shop or house, where Oliver would surely look."

Greg blew out a puff of air. "Seems pretty risky to me. Why didn't she just hide it in May's bookshop? Among the thousands of books? Or just give it to May to hide on her behalf?"

"Kathy wouldn't have wanted to involve her best friend, and would not want to risk the book being sold with the evidence inside," Ruth said. "Or perhaps, whatever it is, it's not easy to hide in a book."

Alex stared down at the map. "I agree with you, Ruth. I don't see how this could mean anything else." He tapped the page. "There's no other orientation that lines up with the streets and shops." He indicated a small circle. "This is the wishing well in the village square."

A shiver ran down Ruth's spine at the thought of Kathy marking that spot, not knowing it would be the exact place people would later find her body.

Poor Kathy. She must have been terrified, knowing Oliver and his mother were after her, knowing she held evidence that could expose him and his mother's dark counterfeiting secret.

Alex unclipped a bunch of keys from his belt, flicked through them, and selected one. "This is to Oliver's shop." He held it against the key taped to the page. "They match. Kathy must have hidden the evidence when he was closed. Meant she could go back when he wasn't around and collect it again, should she need to."

"How did Kathy get a spare key?" Greg asked.

"They dated," Reverend Michael said. "Maybe Oliver loaned her a key then, and forgot to have her return it."

Ruth stood abruptly, her mind made up.

"Don't say it," Greg warned.

"We need to search Oliver's shop," Ruth said.

Greg threw his hands up. "And there it is."

"I don't see how," Alex said, his voice laced with caution. "DI Barnes is unlikely to approve a search warrant. Not with so little evidence to go on."

Greg snorted. "Have you even met my grandmother?"

Ruth beamed at him. "I'm sure we can think of some way around needing a warrant."

Greg gestured emphatically at her. "See?" he said to the others, and shook his head. "We're about to get into a lot of trouble."

Alex folded his arms and sat back with a contemplative expression.

"We can't wait until Oliver closes shop tonight. That would mean waiting too long." Ruth paced the kitchen, hands clasped behind her back. "So what we need is a distraction," she murmured, more to herself than the others. "Some way to get him out while we conduct a thorough search."

Alex frowned. "An illegal search."

"Not quite," Ruth said. "If Greg and I are already in the shop when Oliver's called away, let's say, we're browsing for furniture..." She winked.

"What about a fire?" Reverend Michael suggested. "A false alarm, perhaps. At Oliver's house?"

Alex gave him a disapproving look.

"It's too obvious," Ruth said. "He'll know he's been tricked and come rushing back before we've had the chance to search thoroughly." She continued pacing, her lips pursed, running through various scenarios, each one crazier than the last.

"What about a flood at one of his storage units?" Reverend Michael suggested. "Or at least the threat of one."

Ruth looked over at him, intrigued. "Oliver has storage units? Where are they?"

"On the outskirts of the village," Alex said. "Filled to the brim with more antique furniture. Ready for his expansion, I suppose."

Ruth stopped pacing, a plan forming in her mind. "That's it." She dropped back into her chair at the table and leaned forward. "Alex, what can you tell us about your undercover operation? Any recent leads?"

He hesitated, glancing furtively at Reverend Michael. "Actually, yes. We intercepted a communication a while back suggesting a delivery of counterfeit goods is imminent. However, what with the storm, we assume it's been delayed."

"Perfect," Ruth said, her excitement growing. "Mrs Vanderlin knows you're an officer, right?"

Alex groaned. "How could you possibly know that?"

"When we were in her tower, Celia said to you, 'When I agreed to you being here, you assured me there would be no trouble.'" Ruth cocked an eyebrow. "At the time, I thought it was an odd turn of phrase but dismissed it. She didn't say, 'When I agreed to your employment' or 'When I hired you.' I realise now, Celia was talking about agreeing to a police presence in the village."

"You could've confided in me," Reverend Michael muttered to Alex.

"No, I'm sorry, but I couldn't." He offered the reverend a weak smile. "That's not how it works." Alex turned his attention back to Ruth. "Mrs Vanderlin was fully aware."

"Which could explain why you haven't managed to uncover the counterfeiting," Greg said. "If the Vanderlins are in on it together?"

"If Celia's aware of your real reason for being here, Alex," Ruth continued, "then it's a safe bet her son does too. She would've told him. So, we'll make sure Oliver knows you suspect one of his storage units is being used as a drop-off point. We'll pretend you're staking it out right now."

"How exactly do you plan on doing that?" Alex asked, his voice laced with scepticism. "He's already suspicious of our snooping. He won't fall for it."

He was right. A direct approach could backfire. They needed a more subtle, indirect way.

"Oliver might believe it if the information about your surveillance doesn't come from us," Ruth said. "We'll plant a rumour. A rumour that will reach Oliver's ears without us having to directly involve ourselves. Something outlandish."

Greg's brow furrowed. "Leana? She seems to have a knack for gossip."

"Close," Ruth said. "But Oliver might not believe her."

"Who then?" Greg asked.

"Hattie," Ruth said. "Ironically, she seems to not like gossip coming from anybody else's mouth." She smiled. "Bet she'd go running to Oliver at the drop of a hat though."

"Absolutely not," Alex said. "We're not involving anyone else in this." He glanced at Reverend Michael. "Too many people already know I'm an officer. I've risked far too much already. DI Barnes is going have my guts for—"

Ruth held up a hand, cutting him off. "We won't tell Hattie what we're really doing," she said in a placating tone. "We only need someone other than the four of us to tell Oliver you're scoping out his units. He won't trust one of us going to him, nor Leana. It must be Hattie." Ruth took a breath, thinking it through. "In fact, to make sure it doesn't get back to us at all, we will go one further." She looked at Greg. "We'll ask Leana to tell her Aunty. She can be the one to pass on the news that Alex is watching one of Oliver's units, waiting for an illicit delivery."

Reverend Michael chuckled. "Oliver will hit the roof if he thinks he's being implicated in any counterfeiting."

"That's the plan." Ruth half smiled.

"He'll be worse if he really is involved," Greg added.

Ruth refocussed on Alex, hoping he'd go along with the plan. "The rumour will reach Oliver's ears without him suspecting we had any hand in it, or that it's merely idle gossip. We'll need to make sure it's convincing, though." Ordinarily, she'd feel a twinge of guilt at the lie, but considering Oliver's suspected involvement, Ruth would make an exception. "Leana already thinks Celia murdered her husband, so it won't be a stretch for her to believe Oliver is up to something nefarious. Besides, we're not lying to Leana about that part, are we? Only keeping her from directly getting involved with what we're investigating." She let out a breath. "I'm sorry, but it's this or nothing. We're in a hurry. Not enough time to think of a better plan."

Alex nodded slowly, even though his expression was reluctant. "It's risky, but worth a shot, I suppose."

"Go to one of Oliver's units," Ruth said before Greg had a chance to tell Alex all her plans were risky, whether thought out or not. "Act as if you're waiting for people to show up."

"I must be crazy for doing this." Alex stood and zipped up his coat. "You do know it's my investigation, right? I'm the lead officer on this. You're supposed to be assisting. That's what I agreed to. Grudgingly, I might add." He shook his head. "I'm dreading having to write a report."

Ruth gave him a wry smile.

Alex sighed. "Make sure Oliver knows I'm at unit eighteen. There's a bicycle shed across the way. I can watch from in there."

"Eighteen," Ruth repeated. "Got it." As Alex left, a twinge of foreboding gnawed at Ruth's insides, but she quickly shook it off. *This is it,* she thought. *We're on the verge of uncovering the truth. No time for doubts. Find Kathy's evidence of the Vanderlins' counterfeiting involvement and get out of there.*

"Thank you for all you're doing to help," Reverend Michael said to Ruth, breaking her from her thoughts. "I don't know what we'd do without you." He placed a hand on Greg's shoulder. "You too, young man. Thank you."

"Don't thank us yet." Ruth pulled on her coat and handed Greg's to him as he rose from the table. "We still have to find that evidence."

Reverend Michael lifted his chin, his eyes shining. "I have faith in you." His gaze darted to the door. "Is there anything I can do to help?"

"I don't think so," Ruth said. "Just be ready with warm beverages when we return."

"That, I can do."

17

Ruth and Greg left the Silver Thimble and headed toward Mystical Flames. The rain had eased slightly, reduced to a persistent drizzle, as they made their way to the shop. The wind, however, still whipped through the narrow streets, ensuring the village remained deserted, the going tough.

"I hope this works." Greg pulled his collar up against the cold.

"It will," Ruth assured him, though a flicker of doubt danced in the back of her mind. After all, Leana seemed like a lovely young woman, and Ruth didn't want to manipulate her, so they'd have to tread carefully in what they revealed. "I'm sure this will go well. After all, we have a secret weapon."

They reached the corner of the street and stopped.

"What secret weapon?" Greg's brow furrowed.

Ruth pointed to the candle shop. "You."

"Huh?"

"I think it's pretty clear Leana likes your rugged Gregness."

"Cool. So?"

"You can go in there without raising suspicions," Ruth said.

"You want me to use my charm to get Leana to help us?" Greg asked, incredulous.

"I'm not telling you to be her boyfriend."

"Good. I already have a girlfriend. Don't need another."

Ruth gave him a pointed look.

Greg glared at her, murmured a few naughty words, and then marched to the candle shop. The bell tinkled above the door as he disappeared inside.

As Ruth waited, she thought of a time when she had to use her own wiles to extract information from a reluctant witness. It had been years ago, during her first big case as a police officer.

She'd been assigned to track down a missing husband, and the only lead Ruth had was a grumpy old bartender who refused to talk. She had spent half a day in a dimly lit pub, nursing a lemonade, slowly winning him over with charm and dry wit, only to find she'd been in the wrong pub, schmoozing the wrong man.

Her fellow officers had never let Ruth forget that one.

It had been a valuable lesson in not only the subtle art of persuasion but also checking you had the right address in the first place.

The bell above the candle shop door tinkled again, drawing Ruth back to the present moment, and Greg beckoned her over.

Ruth hurried across the street and slipped inside.

Leana stood behind the counter, her expression wary. "You want my help with what exactly?" Her eyes darted to Greg and then nervously toward the back room. "I don't understand."

Ruth glowered at Greg. "What did you tell her?" When she received an awkward shrug in reply, she refocussed on Leana. Ruth opted to get straight to the point, but not reveal too much, and certainly not tell her why they wanted Oliver away from his shop while they searched it. "We'd like you to get the word out that one of Oliver's units is under surveillance."

Leana gestured for Ruth to lower her voice and indicated Hattie was in the back office. "Yeah, he said that part. What for?"

"Counterfeiting," Ruth continued in a whisper. She then painted a picture of Julian, wrongly accused, languishing in jail, and the real killer still at large—a conspiracy through and through. Ruth finished up by appealing to Leana's sense of justice, her fascination with true crime, reminding her that this was a real-life mystery unfolding before their very eyes.

Greg chimed in, adding a touch of dramatic flair to the narrative. "We're talking about bringing down a criminal mastermind."

Slightly over the top, but it seemed to work because Leana's eyes widened, and a flicker of excitement replaced her initial apprehension.

"Julian's behind a counterfeiting operation?" she said, looking puzzled. "Here?"

"Not Julian," Greg said. "Could be Oliver."

Leana's jaw dropped.

Ruth grimaced, but pressed on. "All you have to do is tell your Aunt Hattie that Alex is watching one of Oliver's units, waiting for a delivery of counterfeit goods. Unit eighteen."

Leana looked even more puzzled. "Why Alex?"

"He's a police officer," Greg said before Ruth could come up with a plausible excuse.

Ruth tensed.

Leana's eyeballs almost popped from their sockets. "He is?" Then her expression turned serious. "Can't say I'm surprised. Alex has always had that look about him. Seen him following people about, acting all suspicious. Are you sure he's not the one doing the counterfeiting?"

"Will you help us?" Ruth asked, trying to steer the conversation back on track.

"I don't know. Aunty Hattie might not believe me." Leana stared into the distance, biting her lip. "Mind you, she has always been suspicious of the strange goings-on around the village." She looked back at Ruth. "Only the other day, Aunty Hattie told me Alex was up to something. I guess this is what she meant. It turned out to be true." Leana shook her head. "I have no idea how she knew. She always seems to know. It's uncanny. Aunty Hattie knows everything."

"Then she must suspect there's counterfeiting going on," Greg said. "It won't be news to her."

"Maybe," Ruth agreed. *Although, if that were the case, why hasn't Hattie reported it to the police?* "We can talk to her properly about it later, after we've done this little mission."

"Mission?" Leana asked, her eyebrows raised. "Are you spies now?"

"We only want to expose the truth." Ruth hoped she wasn't laying it on too thick.

Leana shrugged. "Aunty Hattie has never said anything to me about that." She paused, then met Greg's gaze, a hint of a smile on her lips. "All right. I'll help."

Relief washed over Ruth. "Thank you, Leana." She squeezed the young woman's hand. "You won't regret this."

As Leana headed toward the back of the shop, Ruth turned to Greg and whispered, "What exactly did you say to her?"

"That we wanted her to tell Hattie about Alex watching Oliver's unit." Greg shrugged. "She seemed really confused, so that's when I came to get you."

Ruth rolled her eyes. "Well, it's done. Now, let's go and find that evidence."

A few minutes later, she and Greg stood outside The Three Bears' Home Furnishings shop, with its dark, imposing facade.

"And now for the tricky part," Greg murmured.

Ruth's mind had already raced ahead, picturing their search. Even she had to admit this was a risky plan, with plenty that could go wrong, but they had come too far to turn back.

Greg peered through the window. "He's in there. Alone, I think."

Ruth took a deep breath, steeling herself for the confrontation. "Right, let's do this."

The bell above the door jangled as they entered Oliver's furniture shop, a jarring contrast to the light tinkle of the candle shop's bell. The sound was swallowed by the cavernous space, filled with dark, looming shapes of furniture.

Oliver looked up from behind his desk, his eyes narrowing.

Ruth forced a smile, hoping it didn't look as fake as it felt. "We're so sorry to bother you again, Mr Vanderlin." Her voice dripped with faux sweetness. "We're here on a completely different matter. You see, my grandson"—she nudged Greg—"is off to university in September, and he's in desperate need of furniture for his student accommodation."

"Desperate," Greg murmured. "Can't imagine having to

sit on the floor." He swallowed and avoided Oliver's suspicious gaze.

"And you've chosen my shop?" Oliver said. "In the middle of a storm?"

Ruth gestured vaguely outside. "Well, yours is one of the few still open, and we were so impressed with the... extraordinarily unique selection you have on offer. We couldn't resist popping in. Besides, we're on a tight budget, and we heard you have some incredible deals."

Oliver seemed to consider this for a moment, his suspicion replaced by a flicker of greed. He gestured toward the cluttered showroom. "You're in luck. I do have a wide range of furniture to suit all tastes and budgets." He rose from his desk, a predatory gleam in his eye. "What sort of thing are you looking for?"

Ruth and Greg exchanged a glance, a silent communication passing between them. They had him hooked.

"A desk?" Greg suggested. "And an office chair, I suppose."

"A bedside table," Ruth added. "He'll need one of those."

Oliver led them deeper into the labyrinth of furniture, and pointed out various pieces, extolling their supposed virtues with a practised sales pitch.

He showed them a wobbly legged desk that looked as though someone had backed a van over it, a moth-eaten armchair, and a wardrobe with wonky doors. Greg feigned enthusiasm, asking questions, testing the furniture, and generally keeping Oliver occupied, while Ruth discreetly scanned the room. She searched for any sign of where Kathy might have hidden the evidence.

As Oliver droned on about the merits of a chipped coffee table, Hattie burst into the shop, her colourful scarves billowing behind her. "Oliver," she called. "May I have a word?"

"Excuse me," he grumbled to Ruth and Greg, and strode over to her. "What is it? Can't you see I'm busy?"

Hattie spoke to him in hurried whispers, her words inaudible to Ruth and Greg. Oliver's face contorted with anger, his carefully constructed facade crumbling.

Hattie offered him a grave nod. "It's true."

"That's ridiculous," Oliver said, his voice rising. "I have nothing to do with such things."

Ruth winked at Greg, a surge of triumph coursing through her. The plan was working.

However, instead of leaving in a hurry as they had hoped, Oliver turned to them, his eyes blazing. "Get out of my shop."

Ruth stood rooted to the spot, unsure how to react to his sudden outburst. Her mind raced, trying to process the abrupt shift in his demeanour. She shot Greg a sidelong glance, her eyebrows raised in a silent question. He shrugged, his expression mirroring her own bewilderment.

"I beg your pardon, Mr Vanderlin?" Ruth feigned indignation. "What's happened?"

"I said get out." Oliver's voice, sharp and cutting, punctuated each word with a rising anger. His face, normally pallid and drawn, now flushed a dangerous shade of crimson. He thrust a finger at the door. Oliver looked at Hattie. "You too."

Hattie appeared utterly bewildered. "M-Me?" she stammered. "I— I don't understand." Her eyes darted between Oliver, Ruth, and Greg, while her hands fluttered nervously with her scarves, a mismatch of clashing colours.

Oliver's face contorted. "*Go.*"

Hattie, her face ashen, didn't need telling twice. She

bustled from the shop without a backward glance, almost tripping over the threshold, her hasty retreat a stark contrast to her earlier confidence.

Oliver wheeled back to Ruth and Greg, his eyes narrowed to slits, his chest puffed out, head high. "*Move.*"

Ruth, her heart a frantic drumming against her ribs, grabbed Greg's arm and pulled him toward the door. "Come on," she said, her voice low and urgent. "Clearly, he's having a bad day."

"A bad day?" Oliver took a step toward them, his presence suddenly overwhelming in the small space. "I know you're working with that fool Alex." Clearly, his mother had told him. "You can't pin anything on me. I've got nothing to do with the supposed counterfeiting. Leave. Before I call the real police and press charges."

No sooner had they stepped foot outside, the cold, damp air a shock after the stifling atmosphere of the shop, than Oliver slammed the door, the sound like a gunshot in the quiet street. The force of it made them both jump.

Greg stared at Oliver through the glass. "That went well." He faced Ruth. "What's plan B?"

"I have no idea." A wave of frustration washed over Ruth. They had been so close, and now her only idea lay in ruins.

"Did Hattie know we were trying to get Oliver out of the shop?" Greg asked, voicing the question that had been nagging at Ruth. "You think Leana told her? Figured it out?"

Ruth pursed her lips as she watched Oliver retreat into the gloomy interior like a bat back into its cave. "I don't think she'd—"

Greg nudged her. "Grandma."

Leana jogged up to them, her face flushed, her breath coming in ragged gasps. Rain plastered her hair to her forehead. "I'm so sorry," she said, her voice filled with genuine mortification. "I don't know what happened."

"What did you say to her?" Ruth asked.

"I did exactly as you told me," Leana said, her words tumbling out in a rush. "But when I explained to Aunty Hattie, it's almost as if she already knew you were up to something." Her brow furrowed in confusion. "She went straight to Oliver."

"Perhaps Hattie overheard our conversation," Ruth suggested, trying to make sense of the situation.

Leana shook her head, her wet hair flinging droplets of water. "Aunty Hattie was in her office with the door closed." She glanced at Oliver's shop, a flicker of fear in her eyes. "I — I want to help. Let me make it up to you."

"You don't have anything to make up for," Ruth said, her voice soft. "Go back. It's fine. We'll figure something else out."

"Please?" Leana lifted her hood and looked between them, her dark eyes pleading. "I do not believe Julian killed Kathy. There's something not right about this whole thing. I know there is. I must help." Her voice was filled with conviction.

Ruth sighed, her resolve weakening in the face of Leana's earnest desire to help. "Okay," she conceded, giving in to the young woman's persistence. "Let's meet Alex at his security room." Perhaps, with a bit of distance and time to think, they could come up with a new plan.

The three of them hurried back through the rain-lashed streets. The once charming village now seemed menacing, the darkened windows like watchful eyes.

When they finally reached the security office tucked away beneath the giant beanstalk, and finding the door unlocked, Greg hurried off to get Alex. Inside, Ruth stared at the CCTV monitors. She tried to come up with other ways to get Oliver out of his shop, but now he suspected they were up to something, it would be a million times harder.

18

When Alex finally returned to the security office with Greg, concern etched his face. "What went wrong? Greg said Oliver's on to us. How?"

"Aunty Hattie seemed to know you were pinning the counterfeiting delivery on him," Leana added.

Alex's eyebrows shot up. "What? How?" He looked to Ruth, his eyes searching hers. "He knew you tried to get him out of his shop?"

"I'm not sure," Ruth said, truly baffled by the events. "Only that we're working with you on the counterfeiting operation."

Greg's expression darkened. "Why would Hattie grass on us? And how does she know what we were doing?"

"Two very good questions," Ruth said, her mind already racing ahead to formulate a new plan. "But one thing at a time—we still need to get a look inside Oliver's shop."

She had to think, to find a solution, and quickly.

What has Kathy hidden? Is it something that can lead us to her killer? Or is it something else entirely unrelated? Could Kathy have been involved in the counterfeiting? Unlikely. But then again, Ruth didn't know Kathy, only what the other shop owners and her best friend said. *Is it really far-fetched?* After all, she was purportedly in financial trouble.

Alex dropped into the office chair with a heavy sigh and glanced at the CCTV monitors, his gaze lingering on the image of Oliver's shop. "Now he's onto us, there's no way to get him out of there." He looked defeated, the weight of the situation pressing down on him.

A spark of an idea flickered in Ruth's mind. "He still doesn't know our original plan was to get him out of his shop. He just thinks we were trying to pin the counterfeiting on him."

"We could fake a medical emergency," Greg suggested.

"Oliver doesn't care about anyone but himself," Leana muttered.

"Yes, he does," Greg said. "His mother."

"I'd rather not involve Celia," Ruth said. "Besides, Oliver would figure out he'd been lied to in a heartbeat."

"Make up a story about a TV crew wanting to feature his shop on a show," Alex said. "Play to his narcissistic ego."

Ruth smiled, appreciating the suggestion, but dismissing it.

"What about an unusual furniture find?" Leana said. "I'll pretend a local antique dealer has uncovered an incredibly rare piece and Oliver needs to get there before it's sold."

"Might work if we knew his specific interests," Ruth said, "but have you seen his shop? He doesn't strike me as being particularly concerned with fine antiques." She paced back and forth, her hands clasped behind her back. "We need something that plays to his greed, or fear of being implicated in the counterfeiting scheme."

She recalled the way Oliver had reacted to the mention

of counterfeiting—a flash of fear in his eyes, quickly overridden by anger.

"Power outage?" Alex suggested. "Anything that affects the running of his shop on top of this storm might tip him over the edge. The fuse boxes are nearby. He'd probably come to investigate, and I could try to hold him up while you search."

Ruth considered the idea, and then said, "We need something stronger. He mistrusts you."

"The feeling's mutual," Alex muttered.

The room fell into silence, the only sound the rhythmic hum of the computer and the wind howling outside, rattling the window.

Our plan needs to realistically provide enough time for Greg and me to search thoroughly, Ruth thought. *This might involve secondary distractions or delays. Oliver is already wary, so the ruse must be convincing and exploit his existing anxieties or motivations, but what exactly?* She gnashed her teeth, frustration growing.

Think, Morgan. Think.

Ruth stopped pacing as an idea suddenly formed. She faced the others, a glimmer of hope building within her. "What if we don't make Oliver our direct target?"

"What do you mean?" Greg asked.

"Perhaps I could stage a loud argument with a disgruntled customer outside Oliver's shop," Leana said, clearly cottoning on to what Ruth had in mind. "Draw him out to investigate." She looked to Alex. "Security could get involved, escort the disruptive customer away."

"I like the idea of you two working together," Ruth said, "but with that plan, we'd need to involve another person, not known to Oliver."

"The whole village is still on shutdown because of the storm," Alex said, his voice doubtful.

He raised a valid point. They needed someone who wouldn't arouse suspicion, someone Oliver wouldn't recognise.

Leana's shoulders slumped, her brief moment of enthusiasm fading.

After a few minutes' more contemplation, Greg said, "What about a raid?"

Ruth blinked at him, momentarily confused, and then she understood. "A police raid? Of course. That's brilliant, Gregory."

He shrugged. "It's been known to happen."

Leana's eyes darted between them. "I don't get it."

"I think I do." Alex folded his arms.

It was an audacious plan, another risky gamble, but Ruth already loved the idea. *Now to iron out the details...*

She resumed pacing, putting together the elements of their new strategy. "Alex, using his police credentials, stages a 'raid' on a nearby shop, creating a commotion and drawing Oliver out of curiosity." She glanced at Alex, gauging his reaction. "You can then subtly detain Oliver, giving Greg and me time to search."

Alex shook his head, his expression dubious. "That's madness."

"To be fair," Greg said, "most of Grandma's ideas are pretty nuts. This one sounds fairly tame in comparison."

Ruth smirked. "It's your idea."

Greg held up his hands. "I just knew what craziness you were about to suggest."

Ruth refocussed on Alex. "You could pretend to have a warrant to search Kathy's shop." That would really get Oliver all hot and bothered. He knows you're an officer." She knew it was a long shot but could almost see the gears turning in Alex's mind. Ruth looked to Leana. "And you can let slip to the other shop owners that Alex has a tip-off about hard evidence of something or other lurking about. He's starting with Kathy's shop, and they're next."

Leana nodded. "What evidence, though?"

"Well, we can't tell anyone else about the counterfeiting." Ruth paused, a sudden thought striking her. "Leana, say the police are coming round to the idea of Julian being innocent, and Alex is helping them hunt for evidence that would reveal the real killer."

"And people will be terrified the murder may get pinned on them," Leana said.

"Including Oliver," Greg added, a satisfied grin spreading across his face.

The three of them looked to Alex.

However, given his deep scowl, he didn't seem overly convinced by their devious plan.

Ruth let out a slow breath. "What's your objection?"

He cocked an eyebrow. "Everything."

"What? All of it?" Greg asked with incredulity.

Alex sighed. "I can't go round pretending to have a warrant to search people's premises." He glanced at Leana, and said through tight lips, "I would lose my job."

"Because you're an undercover police officer," Leana said, her tone matter-of-fact.

Alex glared at Ruth. "You told her too?"

Ruth pointed to Greg.

"Thanks, Grandma," Greg murmured, taking a step away from Alex.

Alex rolled his eyes. "As I was saying, I'm supposed to be incognito. Most people here think I'm a security guard. Up until you two came along."

Ruth nodded, acknowledging his concerns. "Valid points."

"Thank—"

She held up a hand. "Don't do it with your police officer hat on at all. Do it as the Osborne Outlet's security guard." She knew she was pushing him, testing the limits of his cooperation, but they were running out of options, and time was not on their side.

Alex stared at her, his expression unreadable. He was clearly weighing the risks against the potential rewards.

Ruth continued, "Leana, make sure not to let slip Alex works for the police, but make out he's looking for evidence under his security guard role, helping them, and when he finds it, he'll let the authorities know, and they take it from there." It was a fine line they were walking, a delicate balance between truth and deception, but she believed it could work.

"I can do that," Leana said.

Ruth looked back to Alex. "How does that sound?"

"Like it could go very wrong." He stood, a reluctant acceptance in his posture. "Let's give it a shot."

Relief washed over Ruth. They had a plan, a risky one—some would say rather thrilling—but a plan nonetheless.

Twenty minutes later, Leana worked her magic, her words like carefully placed dominoes, setting off a chain reaction of gossip and speculation through the outlet village. She had the shop owners buzzing with the news Alex was onto something, her voice a carefully modulated blend of urgency and discretion.

They gathered under awnings, huddled together, gossiping, their voices a low hum of anxiety and curiosity. Alex, playing his part to perfection, opened Kathy's shop and began his fake search of the premises, his presence a clear indication that something significant was happening.

And then, as if on cue, Oliver appeared, drawn out by the commotion like a rat smelling discarded food. "What's going on?" He glared into Kathy's shop. "What is he playing at now?"

The woman in the yellow raincoat, the one who had discovered Kathy's body, hurried up to him and whispered in his ear, her words rapid and animated.

Oliver's jaw clenched.

Leana caught Ruth's eye and winked.

"Come on, Greg, now's our chance." Ruth grabbed his arm, her chest tight with a mixture of excitement and trepidation. With Oliver distracted, they slipped into the Three Bears' Home Furnishings, careful not to set the bell above the door clanging.

Ruth looked about, taking in the cluttered interior, the looming shapes of furniture, and pulled a pair of gloves from her pocket. "Let's get to work."

The two of them began a systematic search of the shop, their eyes scanning every nook and cranny, every shelf and drawer.

Greg started with the desk from earlier, carefully sifting through the piles of papers that had been left in the drawers, old invoices and receipts, his brow furrowed in concentration. "What are we looking for exactly?"

"No idea," Ruth admitted as her gaze swept across the room. "Guess we'll know when we see it."

She focussed on the right-hand side of the showroom, her eyes scanning the cluttered displays, searching for anything out of the ordinary, anything that might have been overlooked. She ran her fingers along the dusty cabinets, feeling for hidden compartments or loose panels.

The minutes ticked by, punctuated by the odd glance out the window to make sure Oliver was still distracted, the silence broken only by the rustling of papers and the occasional creak of the floorboards under their feet.

Ruth opened the front of a grandfather clock in the corner of the room, its pendulum long since stilled, but found it empty. She huffed out a breath, a wave of frustration washing over her. They needed to find something, and soon.

She moved to the back room, her eyes scanning the cluttered space within. Boxes overflowed with old furniture parts, dismembered limbs of chairs and tables, tubs of screws, and cushions stacked against the wall.

A workbench covered in tools sat in the middle of the room, a chaotic jumble of hammers, saws, and chisels, but it didn't look like anyone had used it in decades. A thick layer of dust coated the surface, undisturbed.

Frustration gnawed at Ruth. "Where could Kathy have hidden the evidence?" she murmured. "It has to be here. Somewhere obvious." She turned her attention to the boxes, carefully opening each one, sifting through their contents. But her efforts yielded nothing of interest, only more dust and discarded remnants of furniture.

Greg joined her, his expression mirroring her own disappointment. "Anything?"

Ruth murmured, "It has to be here."

"Maybe Kathy didn't hide anything in the shop after all," Greg suggested. "Perhaps she changed her mind."

Ruth considered this for a moment. It was possible, of course. But something about Kathy's final diary entry suggested urgency, a feeling she was in imminent danger. "I don't think so."

They had to be missing something obvious. Something right under their noses.

"Oliver might have already found it, then," Greg said.

Ruth looked around the room again, scanning every inch of space, every shadow, corner, and crevice. "It's not in here. Let's search the shop again. We must have missed it." She refused to give up.

No sooner had they slipped back into the showroom than the front door opened, and Oliver returned, his footsteps heavy on the worn floorboards.

Ruth's heart leapt into her throat, a surge of adrenaline coursing through her veins. Before she had time to think, she dived behind an oversized tatty leather sofa, its worn cushions providing a meagre hiding place.

Stunned, and clearly panicked, Greg squeezed into an old wardrobe and pulled the doors closed.

Oliver marched across the shop, his face twisted with anger, and a phone pressed to his ear. "Mother?"

19

Oliver's voice, laced with frustration, reached Ruth behind the sofa. She lay still, her heart pounding in her chest, and strained to decipher his words.

It seemed Oliver's ire was mostly focussed on Alex, the raid on Kathy's shop, and something about being framed. "What can he possibly hope to find?" Oliver said, his voice tight with barely suppressed anger. "He's trying to pin her murder on me, I know he is . . . No, Mother, I will not calm down. This is serious. I bet it has something to do with that Morgan woman." The sound of his agitated pacing receded as he moved farther into the back room.

This was their chance. With Oliver's attention diverted, they could slip away. Ruth glanced at the wardrobe, and its doors creaked open a fraction. Greg's wide eyes peered out. She signalled for the pair of them to make a hasty retreat.

Ruth then crawled on all fours, keeping low to the ground, heading toward the front door. The shop, once merely cluttered, was now a labyrinth of potential obstacles. Every piece of furniture taking effort to crawl under or around.

The shop stood eerily quiet now, the only sound the muffled rumble of Oliver's angry voice and the rhythmic thump-thump-thump of her own heart.

Greg dropped in behind Ruth, also crawling like a baby, and they wound their way through the shop. Together, they navigated the treacherous terrain—under tables, weaving between chairs and behind cabinets.

Finally, Ruth reached the front door, her hand outstretched, fingers inches away from the handle. But then the wonky-legged card table caught her eye—the one they'd sat at to speak to Oliver.

At the time, Ruth's focus had been on him, and she hadn't spotted the odd light fitting shaped like a bunch of flowers above their heads. But now Ruth had some distance, she recognised the location from one of Kathy's photographs with May.

She stared up at the light fitting, transfixed. The faint outline of a rectangular object was barely visible through the frosted, multicoloured glass.

Kathy's evidence?

It had to be.

But why there? Why not hidden somewhere more secure?

Unless Kathy hadn't had time to hide it properly. Perhaps she had been interrupted. Or maybe Kathy had chosen that spot because it was the least likely to be found by a customer. A hiding place in plain sight. A place she remembered with May.

"What are you doing?" Greg whispered, frantic. "Let's go." He waved her on.

Ruth glanced over her shoulder. Oliver was still pacing the back room, his voice a muffled, irritated drone. She pointed to the light fitting.

Greg looked bewildered, unsure what she wanted him to

do. His eyes darted from the light to his grandmother, then back again. He mouthed, "What?"

Ruth pointed again, more insistently this time, and mimed reaching up. His lanky frame could easily stretch up to the light and retrieve the envelope.

Greg seemed to finally understand her meaning. He shook his head in a firm refusal, and mouthed, "Too risky."

Ruth nodded, urging him to reconsider. *Oh, for heaven's sake,* she thought. *He knows we can't leave without it.*

Greg shook his head again, more vehemently this time. "He'll catch me," he breathed, his eyes wide with a mixture of fear and defiance.

Ruth began to crawl toward the table, determined to retrieve the envelope herself.

Greg reached her side and whispered, "Fine. I'll get it."

Ruth grinned. "Thank you."

"Whatever." Greg scurried over to the card table, stood and cautiously climbed onto it. The table rocked precariously under his weight, threatening to send him tumbling to the floor or into a stack of furniture.

Ruth winced and bit her knuckle, her eyes darting between Greg and Oliver. Each creak of the table legs was like a gunshot in the silence, and Ruth held her breath.

Greg stretched his hand up, his fingers brushing the light fitting. Just a little further. He strained, his fingertips now barely reaching over the top.

The table swayed again, and Greg wobbled, his face a mask of concentration, beads of sweat forming on his forehead. He pulled out an envelope just as the table lurched violently.

Greg let out a muffled yelp as he lost his balance, his arms flailing wildly, but by some miracle he dropped to the floor double-footed, bending his knees to absorb the impact.

Ruth's head snapped toward the back room as Oliver peered out. "What was that?"

Greg cowered under the card table, the envelope now between his teeth, his eyes wide with terror.

Blood pounded in Ruth's ears, her body frozen. *Oh no,* she thought. *We're done for.* All their sneaking around had been for nothing. They were about to be discovered, and there was nothing she could do about it.

"What, Mother?" Oliver said into the phone. "Nothing. Something falling over again. I'll look in a minute. I know, I know. That's why I need that other shop." He headed into the back room again.

Ruth let out a juddering breath, and her body sagged with relief. Greg, red faced and sweaty, crawled over to her, his chest heaving. "Well done," she whispered, plucking the envelope from his mouth.

He glared at her. "Can we go now?"

"Absolutely." Ruth turned back to the door, opened it, and they slipped outside.

Back in the security room, Ruth, Alex, Greg, and Leana gathered around a table. The brown envelope, now bearing Greg's teeth marks, lay in the middle.

All four of them stared down at it, their faces illuminated by the desk lamp.

"This is what you've been looking for?" Leana leaned forward, her hands clasped in front of her, her eyes fixed on the envelope. "Is it evidence that Celia murdered her husband, and that Oliver had something to do with it too?"

She looked positively hopeful. "They did in Kathy because she found out?"

Alex snatched up the envelope. He tore it open and slid out a single sheet of folded paper. As he read the contents, his eyes widened, his expression shifting to surprise.

"What is it?" Leana whispered.

"Definitely some evidence Kathy left behind." Alex held it out to Ruth. "But it's not what we expected."

Ruth took the paper from him and scanned the contents. A soft, "O-kay. Hmm," escaped her lips.

"So?" Greg asked with more than a hint of impatience. His eyes darted from Ruth to the paper. "What is it?"

"Kathy hadn't uncovered evidence of Celia murdering her husband. Sorry, Leana." Ruth laid the document on the table for the others to see. "But she found something with regards to the counterfeiting operation."

On it was a printed image of a box a twelve inches square tipped over on its side, with fabric clothing labels spilled across the ground. The picture was grainy, the colours muted, but the tags, ready for someone to sew them into garments, were clearly visible: Gucci, Prada, Chanel—all designer brands, all highly sought after.

"Does anyone know where this picture was taken?" Ruth asked.

"Judging by the plain, dark tarmac," Alex said, "looks to be the rear of the shops."

The corner of a faded yellow marking, a loading bay designation, added weight to his assessment. The area was nondescript, utilitarian, a place of deliveries and dispatches, away from the prying eyes of customers.

Above the image, written in Kathy's distinctive cursive, were the words: 'Delivery came at *4pm.*'

Ruth looked to Alex, her gaze searching his.

A rare smile touched his lips, along with a glimmer of triumph in his eyes. "Finally, I get a break. And this doesn't look to be out the back of Oliver's shop. It's on the other side."

"Wait. Does this mean he didn't kill Kathy?" Greg looked from Ruth to Alex, his brow furrowed in confusion. "What do we do now?"

"You do nothing." Alex snatched up the paper and slid it back into the envelope. He then motioned to the door with a jerk of his head. "If you don't mind, I need to call DI Barnes and update him with this new development." His voice came out sharp and abruptly dismissive.

Ruth opened her mouth to protest, but Alex held up a hand, stopping her for a change.

"Thank you," Alex said. "All of you. You've been a great help. I'll take it from here." He marched from the security office, his steps purposeful, his back straight.

Shocked by his shift in demeanour, Ruth hesitated, and then she got a grip and hurried after him. *This is wrong,* she thought. *We should still be working together.*

Outside, she called, "Alex. Wait."

He kept marching through the storm, his retreating figure a dark silhouette.

Ruth increased her pace, eager to catch up to him, but not so keen to slip on the wet cobblestones. "Alex, please."

At the corner of the street, he wheeled on her. "I appreciate your help up until now, but this is a police matter. It's always been a police matter, Mrs Morgan." His expression was serious, almost angry, his eyes blazing with emotion. "I'm asking you nicely—please back off." Alex stuffed the evidence into his pocket, shielding it from the rain. "I've waited a long time for a break in the case."

"We can continue to assist you," Ruth said. "Where exactly do you think that photograph was taken?"

He must've known exactly where, given his abruptness.

Alex opened his mouth to answer, clearly thought better, and closed it again. "I promise to update you once it's over." And, with that, he marched away, his figure disappearing into the gloom.

Ruth stared after him, resisting the urge to catch up to Alex again and make him see sense, but she knew it would do no good.

Something in that image had rattled him.

No, *rattled* was the wrong word. Alex appeared angry.

Why does that photograph make him so upset?

Ruth turned on her heel and hurried back to the security office with a sense of unease.

Back in the warmth and comfort of the Silver Thimble's upstairs apartment, Greg and Leana sat on the sofa, while Ruth stared out the window, hands clasped behind her back.

Reverend Michael, ever the attentive host, supplied mugs of steaming tea and set them on the coffee table before settling into an armchair. "Let me get this straight," he said, his voice a low murmur. "Alex has some evidence of counterfeiting, but he won't let you help him anymore?"

Ruth nodded, her gaze fixed on Rapunzel's tower. "He was adamant."

"Alex obviously knows where that picture was taken." Leana stroked Merlin, who was curled up on her lap.

The streetlights flickered on, casting a warm glow on the wet cobblestones.

"He wants the police to handle it from here on," Ruth said.

"So they should," Greg said. "Whatever it takes to get Julian out of jail, right?"

Ruth shrugged.

Truth was, it bothered her *not* to be involved in the investigation, and she itched to know what else Alex was uncovering at this very moment. *But why wouldn't he let us help?* she wondered. *What's he suddenly afraid of?*

"Dinner will be ready in an hour." Reverend Michael stood. He stretched, and then looked at Leana. "Are you staying?"

Ruth smirked. "She's not going anywhere." And nodded to Merlin, who was now fast asleep on the girl's lap, his purring a soft rumble.

"If it's all right?" Leana asked Reverend Michael. "I'll text Aunty Hattie."

"Of course it is." He tapped Greg's arm as he passed him. "Steak, chips, mushrooms, and peas. Sound good?"

Greg nodded and practically salivated at the prospect.

Ruth returned her attention to the window and darkening sky. *Where's Alex? What is he getting up to?* The village was quieter now, every shop closed, the streets deserted, the wind easing.

Has he called DI Barnes? Are they currently arresting a new murder suspect? How long before they release Julian?

She yawned and dropped into the armchair, slouching into the cushions, eager for Alex to return and explain. *But what if he doesn't?* a nagging voice whispered in her mind. *What if he's keeping something from us? Something important?*

However, Alex didn't return. Not in time for dinner, not after, and certainly not that evening.

As Ruth sat in bed that night, reading Mrs Beeton's latest

jaunt into culinary oddities, an uneasy feeling settled in the pit of her stomach.

Something felt off.

But what? she wondered. *What am I missing?*

The next morning, Ruth, Greg, and Reverend Michael sat at the kitchen table, finishing up their breakfast, when Leana hurried through the back door, her cheeks flushed, her eyes wide.

"He's gone," she panted, her breath coming in ragged gasps. Leana leaned against the doorframe, her hand on her chest. "I ran all the way here."

"Good morning, Leana." Ruth smiled and gestured to a pot of tea. "Hot beverage?"

Greg rolled his eyes. "Who's gone?" He carried on munching his bowl of cereal and toast.

"Alex, of course." Leana pushed herself off the doorframe and staggered into the kitchen.

Ruth blinked at her, her smile fading. "Alex is gone?"

"Gone where precisely?" Reverend Michael asked with a confused expression.

Leana shrugged. "No idea."

"Hold on." Ruth turned in her seat to face the girl properly, her full attention now on Leana. "You'd better explain from the beginning." She gestured to an empty chair.

Leana dropped into it and took a few deep breaths. "When I got up this morning, I thought I'd see Alex. Find out what happened."

"But he doesn't live here, does he?" Greg asked, his mouth full of toast.

Leana shook her head. "I mean, see him at his security

office. He's normally one of the first to arrive. Unlocks the gates. Does his rounds."

"And then drops in here for his coffee," Reverend Michael said, nodding in agreement. "Right after Julian, usually."

Ruth motioned for Leana to continue.

She swallowed. "His security office was open, but he wasn't there."

"On his usual round?" Reverend Michael asked.

"I don't think he's been back to the office since yesterday," Leana said. "It was unlocked and just as we'd left it."

Ruth's chest tightened. "Go on."

"I thought, what with everything that's happened recently, he might have forgotten to lock the security office," Leana continued. "Because he arrested someone and then went back to the station?"

Reverend Michael poured her a glass of orange juice.

"Thanks." Leana sipped. "But Alex's car is still here." She set the glass back down. "So I went to open Mystical Flames, and that's when I told Aunty Hattie he was missing. I didn't tell her about anything that happened yesterday," she quickly added. "Only that I noticed Alex wasn't in his office, and his car was still here, but that I don't think he left the village last night."

"And?" Ruth leaned forward, her elbows on the table, her hands clasped in front of her.

"Aunty Hattie made out like it was nothing, and said, 'Don't you worry your pretty little head about Alex, dear. I know exactly where he is. And I know what he's been up to.'" Leana's expression intensified, her eyes locked on Ruth's. "Aunty Hattie showed me a picture on her phone of Alex sneaking into the back of May's shop."

"May?" Greg's eyebrows lifted.

Both Ruth and Reverend Michael looked at Leana with quizzical expressions.

"Alex and May," Leana said. "Aunty Hattie says they have a thing. They're together."

This, Ruth had to admit, caught her by surprise. "They are?" She'd not gotten the slightest hint of anything like that going on between them.

Mirroring her own shock, Reverend Michael's eyebrows lifted even higher, his mouth forming a small 'o' of surprise.

"But that's not the really odd part." Leana looked between them. "How did Aunty Hattie get that picture? I didn't go back to Mystical Flames until after dinner. Aunty Hattie was working on the accounts, so I locked up the shop. Which was long after Alex must have arrived at May's." Leana took a breath. "Which means—"

"Hattie wouldn't have left Mystical Flames unattended to take the picture," Ruth said in realisation. "They're on opposite sides of the village. She was working late."

Leana gave a vehement nod.

Greg frowned. "I don't get it."

"Me neither." Reverend Michael sat back.

Suddenly, Hattie's mysterious third eye made complete sense to Ruth.

She's not psychic. Not in the slightest.

20

Ruth, Greg, and Leana hurried toward Mystical Flames, the rain finally abating, leaving behind a damp, glistening, and quiet village. The cool air carried a freshness that invigorated Ruth, and anticipation built within her.

They reached the candle shop. Ruth pushed open the door, the tinkling bell announcing their arrival. The scent of incense, though still strong, no longer seemed as cloying as before, pushed aside by Ruth's newfound determination. Or maybe she was just getting used to it. Either way, the smell didn't bother her as much now.

Hattie stood behind the counter, polishing a candlestick. She looked up as they entered, her eyes narrowing. "What do you want?" She shot Leana a look. "You're supposed to be unpacking stock."

"We need to talk," Ruth said, keeping her voice firm but still polite.

However, given her scowl, Hattie wasn't pleased to see her. She placed the candlestick on the counter. "I have nothing to say to you." She plucked up a second candlestick. "If you're not here to buy something, I suggest you—"

"It's about Alex," Ruth said.

As if Hattie doesn't already know.

Sure enough, her eyes now filled with a mixture of suspicion and defiance. "What about him?"

"Leana told us you have a picture of him visiting May yesterday," Ruth said, opting for a direct approach.

"Oh, did she?" Hattie sniffed and threw another angry glance in Leana's direction.

"Please, just show them," Leana said in an exasperated tone. "It's important."

Hattie's face reddened, her earlier composure cracking. "I don't know what you're talking about," she snapped. "You're making things up. You and your conspiracy theories."

"I'm not trying to cause trouble." Leana stepped forward, her expression hardening. "Mrs Morgan wants to understand what's going on. She's here to help."

Ruth smiled inwardly. The girl had a good heart.

"How did you take that picture of Alex?" Ruth asked. When she didn't get a response, she added, "He's missing, and we're worried about him. We need to know if Alex is safe."

Hattie hesitated, and her gaze flicked between Ruth, Greg, and Leana. She seemed to be torn between concern about Alex and no doubt her desire to protect her own secrets.

Ruth had a hunch about what she might be hiding, and why she was so reluctant to help, but only wanted to directly accuse Hattie as a last resort. The proof would be in that photo. Whatever the case, she wasn't backing down.

Clearly realising this, Hattie let out a sigh, and her shoulders slumped. She pulled her phone from her pocket, navigated to the image, and held it out for them to see.

As Ruth had expected, due to the visible pixelation, the black and white image, and the angle showing the edge of a computer monitor, Hattie had taken a picture of a CCTV screen.

Also, the CCTV image wasn't at head height, but from up high, looking down. And, the icing on the cake—it had a date and timestamp in the corner. *Yesterday evening, just after 7pm.*

"This wasn't captured from one of the new cameras," Ruth said to Hattie. "You have access to the old security system, don't you? You took a photo of the screen."

"What old system?" Leana asked with a look of puzzlement. When Hattie stepped back and pocketed her phone, Leana said, "Wait. That's how you know so much about people? You spy on them?"

Leana has a point. Ruth frowned. It was one thing to have access to the old security cameras, but quite another to use them to spy on the villagers.

What else has Hattie seen?

"Please," Ruth said to her. "You have to show us. It's vitally important." For a brief moment, she wondered if there were any of the old cameras with a direct view of the murder scene.

Hattie huffed. "I don't have to show you anything." She pointed to the door.

Ruth crossed her arms, defiant. She wasn't going anywhere until she got some answers.

"Someone could murder Alex," Greg said. "And you're holding back information that might mean we can stop them."

"He's with May," Hattie retorted. "Not a killer."

Greg held up his phone. "I'll call the police and let them know you won't help. They won't be happy about you withholding evidence."

Hattie glared at him. "You think if I had evidence about Kathy's murder I wouldn't tell anyone?"

Ruth held up a hand, wanting to bring the temperature back down before it got into a shouting match. "Please. We really need to see that old CCTV system. We must find Alex."

Hattie huffed. "Fine. Whatever. If it means you'll leave me alone, I'll show you." She stepped around the counter, grumbling under her breath as she went. "I don't know what you hope to prove. What they get up to in private is their business."

That is pretty rich, given the fact Hattie blatantly spies on people, Ruth thought, but she bit her lip.

Hattie led them to the back of the shop, through a door into a storeroom.

They marched single file past shelves lined with boxes of candles, crystals, and incense sticks, their aromas mingling.

Hattie stopped at the far end and shoved several shelves aside, revealing a jagged hole in the plasterboard wall, with a curtain hanging behind it. "I was fixing a bracket when I found this." Hattie pulled the curtain aside and stepped into a dark space ten feet on each side. "This is the old security room." She gestured to a door opposite. "It's boarded up from the other side."

A small desk sat in a corner of the room with an old computer monitor displaying twelve images from around the village, but mostly inside shops.

Greg pointed to a view of the village square. "You can see the other side."

Ruth glanced at Hattie. "Do you have recordings from the night someone murdered Kathy?"

Hattie shook her head and pointed to an empty metal rack with wires. "No way to record anything." She clicked buttons on a keyboard. "Some have audio." Sound played through a small speaker—voices. Hattie motioned to a shop interior with two women talking about the weather.

Now Ruth understood how Hattie had known of their plan and real reasons to get Oliver out of his shop.

"You literally spy on everyone," Leana said.

Hattie screwed up her face. "Stop saying that. I don't spy. How dare you."

Greg frowned. "What do you call it, then?"

"I . . . observe. Keep an eye on things. I'm doing the village a favour."

Observe? Ruth raised an eyebrow. *That's one way of putting it.*

She picked out the same view of the back of May's shop. "You were sat here last night when Alex went in there?"

Hattie crossed her arms. "Yes."

Ruth's gaze shifted to the empty racks. "And you don't know if he left because these are live views only, no recording."

Hattie nodded.

Ruth let out a slow breath.

Even so, Hattie's secret access to the old CCTV system gave her a unique perspective on the village and its inhabitants. She could have seen things, heard things no one else had.

"Did you notice anything suspicious the night of Kathy's murder?" Ruth asked. "Or at any time since?"

"I'm not in here all the time. Can't watch everything." Hattie hesitated and lowered her voice. "I'm sorry. I do wish I'd seen who murdered Kathy, though." She lifted her chin. "I can't believe it was Julian."

"Any idea who, then?" Greg asked.

"No. Everyone's nice."

"Almost everyone," Leana muttered as on one view Celia Vanderlin marched into Oliver's shop.

Ruth's gaze shifted to the CCTV image showing the back of Kathy's shop. "Right." Ruth forced a smile at Hattie. "Thank you. Big help." She marched from the room.

"You won't tell anyone about this, will you?" Hattie called after her. "Especially not Mrs Vanderlin."

But Ruth kept marching—through the shop and into the street. She had more important things to worry about than Hattie's secret.

Greg and Leana hurried to keep up.

"It could all be unrelated to what's happened," Greg said.

"You really think that?" Leana asked as they rounded the corner and headed up an incline. "Alex just decided to take a day off in the middle of his investigation? After what he said last night about leaving it up to him?"

Greg looked to Ruth.

Leana was right. With Alex missing, concern gnawed at her. Plus, Hattie's nonchalant attitude about his disappearance only fuelled her desire to uncover the truth.

I have to find him.

May, the quiet bookshop owner, seemed an unlikely romantic partner for the stoic security guard, but Ruth had learned over the years that appearances could be deceiving, despite every molecule in her body refusing to believe their connection.

May is hiding something. Ruth was sure of it. *But what?* She remembered the way May had looked at her when she asked about Alex, the slight hesitation, the way her eyes had darted away. *She was lying.*

With a renewed sense of purpose, Ruth continued her march toward the Storybook Store. The streets were still mostly deserted, the shoppers yet to return.

Good, Ruth thought. *That will make things easier.*

Outside the bookshop, she spun to face her young companions. "Wait here, please."

Greg furrowed his brow. "Not likely."

Ruth held up a hand. "If Alex and May have been seeing each other and keeping it from the rest of the village, that means they think it's a delicate matter, and don't want other people to know."

Greg shrugged. "So what?"

"She's more likely to talk if your grandma goes in alone," Leana said. "I get it. Three of us might put her off."

"Precisely." Ruth took a breath. "I won't be long." She pushed open the door and stepped into the bookshop. May wasn't behind the counter. Ruth called, "May?"

No answer.

Only an eerie silence.

Where is she?

With trepidation, Ruth moved deeper into the shop, past table displays and between bookshelves crammed full of novels.

"May?"

"Hello."

Ruth jumped and spun around.

May, clutching a stack of books, smiled. "Sorry to startle you, Mrs Morgan." She noticed Ruth's expression. "Is something wrong?"

Ruth gathered herself and glanced about. "Have you seen Alex?"

"Alex? No. Why?"

Something in May's clipped response sent alarm bells ringing. She was definitely lying.

"He's missing," Ruth said. "No one's seen him."

May inclined her head. "Missing? Are you sure?"

"Have you seen him?"

"Not for a couple of days," May said. "Is there something wrong?"

Ruth opened her mouth to answer, knowing May had lied to her, and to confront her with the fact Hattie had seen Alex enter the back of May's shop last night, when something made Ruth stop herself. It was too soon. She needed more information before she threw accusations at her.

Even so, an uncomfortable shudder ran down Ruth's spine, and she took a few small steps backward.

"Are you okay, Mrs Morgan?" May set the books on a nearby table. "You look pale." She asked this without the slightest hint of any real concern.

Ruth swallowed. "I'm fine." She forced a tremulous smile. "Can I use your bathroom?"

May inclined her head, eyes cold. "It's not really for custo—"

"I'm so sorry," Ruth interrupted. "An emergency." She pulled a face. "The Silver Thimble is so far away. Wouldn't ask otherwise. I'll be quick."

May let out a breath. "Of course. This way." She led Ruth to the back of the shop, through a door, and down a short hallway. At the end sat three doors. May stopped at the one on the left. "In there."

"Thank you." Ruth slipped inside, closed the door, and turned the simple lock. It clicked shut with a reassuring solidity. She then held her breath and pressed an ear to the door.

May's footsteps retreated, followed by the muffled sound of the other closing door. Ruth waited a few seconds more, unlocked the bathroom door, and slipped back out into the hallway.

The other door at the end had an emergency bar and obviously led to the loading bay. This was the one Alex had used. However, there stood another door opposite the bathroom.

Bingo.

Ruth crept over to it, finding the door slightly ajar, and she pushed it open.

The room beyond was twenty feet on each side and cluttered, filled with cardboard boxes stacked high against the walls. Books overflowed from them, creating a chaotic landscape of paper and ink. *But where are the clothes?* Ruth wondered. She'd seen the men carrying boxes from May's shop, and they'd seemed light, as if they were filled with clothes, not books. *Has May moved them all?*

Ruth searched the room for any sign of Alex. But he wasn't here.

Disappointment washed through her, and she was about to leave when a small white label caught Ruth's eye. It lay on the floor, partially obscured by a stack of books.

Ruth bent to pick it up. It was a clothes label—a designer tag. She looked about, but it seemed to be the only one. *Where are the rest of them?*

As Ruth straightened, a voice, cold and sharp, cut through the silence.

"What are you doing?"

Ruth's heart leapt into her throat. As she turned back to

the door, she surreptitiously slipped the label into her pocket.

May glowered at her.

"S-Sorry," Ruth said, trying to sound casual and failing. "I went straight ahead instead of taking a right."

May's eyes narrowed. "That's not what you're doing," she said, her voice laced with suspicion.

Ruth stared back at May, fully aware she blocked the only escape route. "I'm not?"

"No." May took a step closer, her gaze unwavering. "You're looking for Alex. You think I lied." She gestured around the storeroom. "Satisfied? Like I said, I haven't seen him."

"Sorry," Ruth murmured. "I saw the door was open. I do love a good book, though." She forced a smile, hoping May would buy her weak apology.

To her relief, May's expression softened, and she stepped aside, allowing Ruth to pass.

Ruth hurried back through the shop, her mind racing.

May definitely knew what had happened to Alex.

As she stepped back out into the street, Greg and Leana hurried over.

"Find anything?" Leana asked.

Ruth took a deep breath. "May's the counterfeiter."

Greg's eyes widened. "How do you know?"

Ruth gestured, and they walked back in the direction of the Silver Thimble. "Apart from the suspicious men carrying boxes from her shop yesterday . . ." Now the fact they'd seemed light made sense—they were packed with clothes, not books. "I found this." She pulled the label from her pocket and handed it to her grandson.

"Do you think she killed Kathy?" Leana asked in a whisper.

"One thing at a time," Ruth said. "We need to figure out what she's done with Alex."

"She probably murdered him," Greg said as he studied the clothes label.

Leana screwed up her face. "Don't say that." As they rounded the corner and the familiar café swung into view, she looked to Ruth. "Alex will be okay, right?"

Ruth balled her fists. "He'd better be."

21

Back at the Silver Thimble Café, Ruth placed the fabric designer clothes label on the kitchen table. "What do you think?"

Reverend Michael leaned in. "Is that one of Julian's?"

A knot of unease tightened in Ruth's stomach. She could picture the inside of May's shop, the neat rows of books, the storeroom. It all seemed so normal, so innocent. There didn't appear to be enough space for a big-time counterfeiting operation.

"You didn't find Alex, I take it?" Reverend Michael continued, his voice pulling her back to the present.

"No sign of him," Ruth confirmed, her gaze fixed on the label. "Only that. On the floor in May's bookshop."

"May's b—?" Reverend Michael's eyes widened, his usual calm demeanour replaced with a look of disbelief. "You really suspect she's involved in the counterfeiting? May?"

Greg scrolled through the internet on his phone. "Blimey," he muttered, flipping through pages of information on the designer brand. "This stuff's expensive." He looked up at Ruth. "Like, seriously pricey."

"That's why the counterfeiters have targeted it," Leana said.

"Yeah, but this is a high-end designer label. Extremely difficult to replicate." Greg tapped the part of the label with a shimmering A-shaped logo. "Requires specialised equipment and expertise. It seems it's part of their brand protection policy. This is serious stuff."

Reverend Michael picked up the label, his long fingers turning it over and over, angling it in the light. "A bit like the hologram on money?"

"I doubt May has access to that sort of thing," Ruth said. "The equipment needed." The image of May, with her beehive hair and prim cardigans, flashed in her mind. It was hard to reconcile that image with the sophisticated operation Greg was describing.

"It could be a real label," Leana suggested, her voice thoughtful. "But stolen. You know, from the original factory. Taken by the box load."

"Or made to order overseas," Greg added, his eyes still glued to his phone. "And then shipped here."

"Hold on." Reverend Michael placed the label back on the table and looked at Ruth. "Just because you found a single item that may or may not be linked to counterfeiting, it doesn't automatically mean May has anything to do with it, surely?"

"No. Of course not." Ruth blew out a puff of air. "But it's all very suspicious." She shrugged. "Alex goes missing. Last seen at May's shop. And then I find this."

"You think he caught her?" Reverend Michael asked. "And then May... what?"

"I don't imagine she killed him." The thought of Alex,

with his gruff exterior and surprisingly kind heart, lying dead somewhere didn't sit well with her. "Not yet, at least."

Leana's eyes widened. "Why not?"

"Because doing that would draw attention back to Kathy's murder," Ruth said. "Another dead body would make the police re-examine the evidence they have against Julian." She shook her head. "I think— I *hope* May has Alex tied up somewhere until she figures out what to do with him. That's my best guess."

She needed to believe that, for Alex's sake, and for her own. Ruth couldn't bear the thought of another life lost.

She stood and paced the kitchen.

Reverend Michael watched her, his expression a mixture of concern and bewilderment. "How on earth is May, a seemingly ordinary bookshop owner—and rather petite, I might add—involved in kidnapping a burly security guard twice her size, murder, and also something this sophisticated?" He jabbed a finger at the label. "And not to mention the fact she then somehow pinned Kathy's murder on Julian?"

"That's what we need to find out," Ruth said, her resolve hardening. "We'll start with the counterfeiting. If May really is doing that, she'll need somewhere to carry out her operation, undisturbed. She has labels. Those labels need to be sewn into garments."

"How about one of the storage lockups?" Leana suggested.

"Too obvious." Ruth continued pacing, sifting through the possibilities. She remembered the layout of the village, the various shops and their potential back rooms, the alleyways and hidden corners.

Greg looked up from his phone. "What about an empty shop?"

Ruth shook her head, dismissing the idea. "Too obvious." Then, the memory of the men loading and unloading boxes at the back of May's shop popped into her thoughts again. In hindsight, their actions took on a new significance.

It means there has to be some secret room in May's shop, but where?

There was only enough space back there for the storage room and the bathroom. Ruth had been through both, albeit briefly, and had seen nothing out of the ordinary.

She had to have missed something.

"We need to find him," Ruth murmured to herself. "There has to be a hidden—" The words caught in Ruth's throat as another memory, sharp and clear, surfaced. She spun to face the others, her eyes wide with sudden realisation. "He has blueprints. Alex. In his security room. Plans of the entire village." She looked at Greg, her voice urgent. "He showed some of them to us, remember?"

"Alex said he had blueprints dating back decades." Greg rose from the table. "They'll tell us if there's a hidden space behind May's shop."

Ruth, Greg, and Leana hurried through the village, and had just turned the corner leading to Alex's security office, when two figures blocked their path—Celia and Oliver Vanderlin.

Celia looked about ready to explode. "There you are," she snarled. "I hear you've been causing all sorts of problems, despite my warnings to the contrary." Her cold eyes slid to Leana, Greg, and back to Ruth. "I want you out of my village."

Both Greg and Leana opened their mouths to fire back, but Ruth jumped in first. "Happy to leave. Once we've dealt with a little issue." She went to step round them, but Oliver mirrored her.

"What issue?" Celia said through tight lips. "What exactly are you interfering with now?"

Ruth let out a slow breath. "We're about to uncover the counterfeiting."

Celia's eyes narrowed to slits. "Oh really? The very thing Alex and the police have spent years trying to do, and along comes a busybody and solves it in five minutes."

"Something like that." Ruth forced a smile. "Now, if you'll excuse us." She squeezed past Oliver, with Leana and Greg hard on her heels.

As they hurried away, Celia called after them. "I'll have Alex escort you from the village, immediately." She glanced about. "He's not in his office or answering his phone. Where is he?"

"We'll let you know the moment we find out," Ruth said, and headed through the door, hoping Celia and Oliver wouldn't follow.

Back in Alex's security office, the familiar hum of electronics greeted them. The air was thick with the scent of dust and stale coffee, a testament to Alex's long hours spent monitoring the village.

Ruth's gaze immediately shifted to the monitors, but the images were the same as before—deserted streets, empty shops—no Alex.

She walked to the other end of the desk, scanning the piles of papers and documents that covered its surface. Finding a few blueprints that looked promising, Ruth unfurled them and spread the first out across the surface. She used Alex's coffee mug and a stapler to pin down the corners, and then leaned in for a closer look.

Ruth traced the narrow lanes and outlines of the shops,

comparing the now familiar layout in her mind's eye. "This is different. The old layout, before the refurbishment." She tapped a spot behind the shop where Mystical Flames was now located. "Look. Old security room. The one your aunt found."

Julian's current shop was located on the other side. Little did he know his neighbour spied on the rest of the village from behind the wall in his storeroom. Ruth wondered if Julian had ever suspected, if he had ever felt the prickle of being watched.

"Here's May's shop." Leana pointed to it.

Greg, meanwhile, examined the equipment. "This system is basic," he muttered. "No wonder someone was able to tamper with it."

Ruth looked up at him. She'd almost forgotten about that. Her gaze flitted to the air vent, but then she refocussed on the blueprint, and May's shop in particular. "The layout was different back then. It's hard to figure out." The outlet village hadn't been here when she first visited Osborne some four decades ago, so Ruth had no mental note to compare the layout to. Not that she could've remembered that far back anyway. She went through the other blueprints until she found the modern plan. Ruth then set it next to the other, comparing the two.

"It's really confusing." Leana's brow furrowed in concentration. "They've moved walls about. Extended the bookshop out into these old storerooms."

Greg joined them at the desk.

"But what's this?" Ruth folded both blueprints into squares, until only the bookshop layout was visible on each, then set them back on the desk, side by side.

All three of them leaned in further, squinting, their

heads close together, eyes darting from one blueprint to the other.

"Here." Ruth traced her fingers over the old blueprint, and then the new. "There's a space missing. It looks like it's part of the shop next door, but there are no doors marked."

"A room without doors?" Greg said, his tone a mixture of surprise and intrigue. "Like the old security room?"

"Why wouldn't they repurpose the rooms, though?" Leana asked. "Why board them up? That seems like a waste of space."

"Could be all manner of reasons," Ruth said. "But it looks like they divided the shops up more equally during the renovation, which left a few areas left over. Maybe Celia plans to reuse them one day. Who knows." She jabbed a finger at the blank space on the new blueprint. "Point is, there's a hidden room, and I bet that's where May has been carrying out her counterfeiting operation."

Greg straightened. "And where she has Alex."

Leana stared at the blueprints. "How do we get into that room?"

"The door used to be here." Ruth pointed to the corner of the back wall in May's bookshop. "But there's shelves now."

"Perhaps one of them swings out of the way," Greg suggested.

Ruth pictured the large bookcases, their shelves laden with boxes. "I doubt it. Too big and heavy." She leaned in closer still to the blueprints, taking in every detail, searching for a clue. "Besides, you can see it from the front window. It would be too obvious if May kept using that way in." She ran her left finger over the old blueprint, while her right traced the same lines over the new. Ruth stopped, hovering over a small rectangle on the new blueprint. "Here."

Greg's brow furrowed. "The bathroom?"

Ruth groaned. She had been a few feet away from the secret room, and not known. Her focus at the time had been solely on sneaking into the storeroom. She had been so close to Alex and not realised.

"What's the plan?" Greg asked.

Ruth stared at the blueprints, and then a slow smile swept across her face.

"Oh no," Greg said, his voice full of dread and impending doom. "I know that look."

Leana glanced between them, her expression curious. "What look?"

"The one that says we're about to do something extremely reckless, dangerous, and stupid."

"Don't be ridiculous, Gregory." Ruth marched to the door. "It's not at all stupid."

As they hurried back toward the Storybook Store, Ruth remembered a particular case from her days on the force, a seemingly simple burglary that had spiralled into a complex web of deceit, involving a respectable antique dealer who ran a lucrative side-hustle fencing stolen goods. He had seemed so upright, so honest, a pillar of the community. Yet, beneath that facade of respectability, he had been living a double life.

Ruth's husband, John, had worked with her as a consultant on all things history and antique related, and with his sharp, analytical mind, John had been instrumental in cracking the case.

He'd noticed an antique clock displayed prominently on the suspect's dining room mantelpiece. It had seemed out of place, too grand for the otherwise modest home. And it had also turned out to be a stolen item the dealer had kept.

That one object had unravelled the whole operation.

Turned out, the clock's rightful owner was a prominent London businessman, and they'd reported it stolen, among many other items, a few years prior.

Ruth missed John's steady presence, his quiet support. Now, more than ever, she wished he were here. She could picture the look on his face, a mixture of amusement and concern, as she explained her plan. He would have called it "brilliantly bonkers." Which was rich, given the crazy shenanigans he'd so often got them into.

Ruth used the memory to fuel her resolve. She would find Alex and expose May.

They reached the bookshop.

Greg peered through the front window. "How will we get into the secret room?"

"All three of us can't," Ruth said. They needed a diversion, something to lure May away from the shop, giving them time to search for the hidden room. "Leana, how good are you at acting?"

Leana looked bewildered. "At what?"

Greg, clearly sensing what Ruth had in mind, let out a low groan.

Ruth chose to ignore his pessimism and remained focussed on Leana. "We need to create a scene, something to draw May's attention while I sneak out back." She looked to Greg. "You and Leana will have a loud argument near the front door, something about a birthday present for a friend. Escalate it to the point where May has to intervene."

Greg looked dubious. "An argument? Are you serious? I'm terrible at arguing."

"What are you on about?" Ruth said, exasperated. "You argue with me all the time."

"No I don't."

"Yes, you—"

Greg smirked, a playful glint in his eye.

"Just do it, please," Ruth said, her voice softening. "This is important. We have to find Alex."

Greg sighed, but nodded in agreement. He shot Leana a wry smile. "Ready to fight?"

Leana grinned.

With the plan in place, Ruth followed them into the shop, then circled round the far edge of the bookshelves, keeping out of May's direct line of sight, where she currently stood behind the counter, labelling a pot of pens.

Ruth positioned herself near the back of the shop, ready to make her move.

Greg and Leana took their positions by the front door, their faces already set with mock anger.

"We can't buy her this." Leana waved a fitness book in his face, her voice rising, each word laced with theatrical outrage. "She'll think we're trying to say something."

Greg, feigning indignation, said, "Like what? She's always telling us to exercise more."

Leana snarled, "Which is a good thing."

"Right," Greg retorted. "But her advice is always terrible." He screwed up his face. "Jogging backward? Is she serious?" Greg snatched the book from Leana's hands. "At least with this she'll give advice that won't see people winding up in hospital."

"We're not buying her that." Leana reached for the book, but Greg pulled away. "Give it here."

"Please." May hurried from behind the counter and over to them. "Let me help."

However, Leana leapt at Greg. They wrestled with the book, and knocked over a display stand, sending novels flying in all directions.

"Now look what you've done," Leana shouted.

Seizing her chance, Ruth darted through the back door, hurried along the corridor, and stepped into the bathroom.

With the blueprints fresh in her mind, Ruth faced the tiled wall opposite the sink. A mirror hung on it, so Ruth ran her fingers around the outer edge and lifted it from its hook.

Finding nothing out of the ordinary behind, Ruth set the mirror back and scanned the rest of the wall.

Near the door was a coat hook. It looked ordinary enough, but... Ruth tugged it one way, then the other, but that didn't reveal anything either.

She huffed and stepped back, her heart racing, fully aware she didn't have much time. "Where are you?" She muttered, searching the tiles, and looking for any sign of a hidden mechanism.

Then, she saw it—an almost imperceptible difference in the grout around one of the tiles above the sink. It was barely noticeable, but to Ruth's trained eye, it stood out like a beacon.

She pressed her fingers against the tile, pushing gently at first, then applying more force. With a soft click, a section of the wall swung inward, tiles and all, revealing a narrow dark opening.

Ruth activated the torch function on her phone and stepped into a room fifteen feet long by ten wide. Down the left-hand wall were empty shelves, with worktables running along the right with several sewing machines.

However, not only was the room free of counterfeit garments or labels, but there was also no sign of Alex.

Disappointment washed over Ruth. She had been so certain this was where May had been hiding Alex. But the room was empty.

Her gaze swept the space again, searching for any sign of another secret door, a hint of a second room, anything that might indicate another level of concealment. There had to be something more.

On the floor, near one of the sewing machines, lay a torn piece of fabric, a gold silk. It was identical to the scrap she had found in the security room air duct. And scattered across the floor near the back wall, shimmering in the weak light of her phone, was a fine dusting of red glitter—the same shade as the speck she had found on the pedestal in the village square.

Ruth's heart pounded, and she took pictures of both, careful not to disturb the evidence. May had tampered with the CCTV, and she was the one who'd murdered Kathy. The realisation hit her with the force of a physical blow. May, with her innocent facade, was a cold-blooded killer.

She took a few more pictures to be sure, and then pulled the card from DI Barnes from her pocket. Ruth attached the photos to an email explaining as much as she could in the briefest way possible and sent them to him. This evidence was key to proving Julian's innocence.

Once done, she was about to leave when a voice boomed, "What are you doing?"

Ruth froze, her blood turning to ice. The tattooed man from the delivery van stood in the doorway, his eyes narrowed, his arms crossed. He took a step closer, his imposing figure blocking her escape. The guy was even bigger up close, his muscles bulging beneath his tight T-shirt.

As Ruth stared back at him, her mind raced. She had been so focussed on finding evidence, she hadn't considered the possibility of someone else being here. She wanted to think fast, to come up with a plausible explanation, but he'd see through her excuses. Her mind was blank, her usual quick, some would say world-renowned wit failing her in this moment of crisis.

Indeed, the other delivery guy escorted a sheepish Greg and Leana from the bookshop. Their attempt at a diversion had clearly failed.

A voice cut through the silence. "Well, well, well." May stepped into the room, a chilling smile playing on her lips. "Look what the cat dragged in."

22

May and her goons bundled Ruth, Greg, and Leana into the back of a delivery van. The vehicle lurched forward, its engine sputtering as it navigated the familiar roads of the outlet village.

Where are they taking us? She glanced at Greg, his face pale but determined, then at Leana, whose eyes were wide with fear and defiance. *Stay calm. Think this through.*

A few minutes later, the van pulled up outside the gingerbread house at the far side of the outlet village.

Ruth's brow furrowed. She remembered the building from their arrival. Plastic swords, dragon figurines, and cheap, glittery costumes filled its windows, but it didn't look like a shop, not anymore.

They were unceremoniously hauled from the van and shoved through the back door of the building. Ruth stumbled, catching herself on a stack of boxes.

Greg grabbed her arm. "Are you okay?"

Ruth nodded, forcing a smile. She needed to reassure him, and herself.

They found themselves in a brightly lit space, far larger than the hidden room behind May's bookshop.

Indeed, this was no quaint village shop; it was a mini factory floor with sewing machines and the back wall filled with boxes overflowing with fake designer clothes, shoes, and handbags.

This is where they moved the operation. The sheer scale was impressive. It wasn't a few fake handbags; it was a full-blown counterfeiting enterprise. And May, the seemingly harmless shop owner, was at the heart of it.

And then she saw him. Alex, slouched in a chair at the far end of the room, his hands bound.

Relief washed over Ruth. *He's alive.* His eyes met hers, a flicker of apology in their depths. Alex appeared unharmed, but his shoulders slumped, his usual confidence gone.

Ruth's jaw tightened. *I have to get him out, get them all out.* This wasn't only about solving a murder anymore.

Before Ruth could take another step, the tattooed man relieved Greg, Leana, and her of their phones. His hands were rough, his grip tight. Ruth caught a glimpse of another faded tattoo on his wrist—a skull.

A knot of dread tightened in her stomach. Their lifelines to the outside world were gone. And that was when she noticed something else—May had put on a brown coat with a scarf made of the same gold fabric they'd found in the air duct leading to the security room. Not only that, but she'd tied the scarf with a single knot, the same as on Kathy's body.

As May and her men turned to leave, Ruth called after her. "You murdered Kathy." It was a desperate attempt to buy time, hoping DI Barnes had received her email and was on his way. "Why did you kill her? Did she uncover what you were doing?"

May turned slowly, her face a mask. Her eyes, usually warm, were now cold. "I didn't murder her," she said, voice flat. "That was Julian. Nothing to do with me."

"You pinned it on him," Ruth retorted, her anger rising. *How can she lie so easily?* "Why? Did he uncover your operation too? Like Kathy?"

"I have no idea what you are talking about," May said, her deadpan expression unwavering. It was as if she had no emotion at all. "I liked Kathy. She was my best friend. Thought Julian was a nice guy too. I hope he rots for what he did to her."

Ruth shook her head in disgust. *She's a monster.* "What about all this?" Ruth gestured around the room, at the machinery, the fake goods.

May sighed, a theatrical display of weariness. "When I realised someone might be onto us, I moved our gear here, hoping I could convince them to back off or join us. It seemed logical at the time." Her tone held a cold pragmatism, as if she were discussing a minor business inconvenience.

Sudden realisation hit Ruth. "You gave Kathy that twenty thousand pounds. It *was* you. Kathy found out about your counterfeiting and confronted you. The twenty thousand was a bribe to shut her up."

May's eyes hardened. "I already told you I have no idea what you're talking about."

"And what happens now?" Alex strained against his bindings.

May hesitated, a flicker of something unreadable crossing her face before she shrugged. It was a small gesture of someone who had made a decision that had sealed their fate. "Time for us to leave." She gave them a wink, so casual it sent a wave of annoyance through Ruth.

May and her henchmen left, slamming the door shut behind them.

Greg hurried over and rattled the handle. "Great. Now they'll get away."

"Not necessarily." Ruth untied Alex, her fingers fumbling with the thick, tightly bound ropes. Alex winced as she worked, but didn't complain. "They have our phones."

Leana stood near Greg, her arms wrapped around herself. "How does that help?"

"That stupid family tracking app your mother made us install," Ruth said to Greg. She scanned the room, searching for any possible escape. An air vent, another door, anything. But the room was sealed tight. A locked metal panel secured the display windows from the inside.

"Of course." A spark of hope ignited in Greg's eyes. "We can track the phones using my laptop."

"That's if they don't throw our phones out right away," Leana said.

"They won't." Alex rubbed his wrists. "May likes to cover her tracks. She wouldn't risk someone finding discarded phones in the village. She'll wait until they're some distance away." He looked to Ruth. "My guess is they'll return soon, with more men, and get rid of us."

"Time is of the essence." Ruth turned her attention to the door. "Anyone have a way to open this?"

"Stand clear." Alex, his face set with determination, wheeled a trolley with a heavy sewing machine bolted to it into the middle of the room.

Ruth, Greg, and Leana moved aside.

Alex crouched low, his muscles coiling. He gripped the handles of the trolley, his knuckles white, and then he charged. He ran full pelt at the door, the trolley a makeshift battering ram.

The trolley slammed into the door, cracking the frame.

The impact jarred Alex's arms, but he didn't falter. He backed up, and charged again. And again. Each impact sent vibrations through the floor. The door creaked under the relentless assault. The room filled with the sounds of splintering wood and Alex's grunts of effort.

With one final crash, the door gave way, bursting open.

Ruth didn't hesitate. "Well done, Alex," she shouted over her shoulder, already racing through the opening and heading in the direction of the Silver Thimble.

"I will see if I can cut them off at the entrance," Alex yelled back.

"I'll come with you." Leana rushed after him.

"Be careful," Ruth called.

Greg's longer legs quickly caught up with her. They hurried through the narrow, twisting streets of the outlet village. Each corner they turned, each narrow lane they dashed through, brought them closer to stopping May.

Ruth and Greg reached the Silver Thimble, where Ruth, breathless, panting, chest heaving, leaned against the wall.

Reverend Michael rushed to greet them, his face etched with worry. "Are you all right?" He looked between Ruth and Greg. "What happened?"

Ruth spoke in short, clipped sentences, explaining the situation while Greg ran upstairs to fetch his laptop—May's counterfeiting operation, their capture, Alex's quick thinking, their escape, the tracking app.

Reverend Michael gaped at her. "May? She's really involved in all this?"

Greg bounded down the stairs and set up his laptop on the kitchen table, his fingers flying across the keyboard. A map of the village appeared on the screen, a blinking red dot marking the location of their phones. "May and her goons are heading toward the main road," he said, his voice urgent. "Just as Alex thought." Greg's eyes then widened. "Wait. No, they're not." He jabbed a finger at the screen. "They've turned around."

Sure enough, the dot had changed direction. It was now moving away from the main road, heading back through the village.

"They're going the back way out." Reverend Michael leaned over Greg's shoulder, his eyes fixed on the screen. "Through the delivery gate. I'll call the police, but they will never get here in time. May will escape."

"Not if we can help it." Ruth pointed to the map. "They'll have to take the long way round." Her fingers traced the narrow lanes. "We can use this shortcut. It's not far."

"We're going after them?" Greg said, aghast.

"Need to buy time for DI Barnes and the police to get here." Ruth grabbed her coat. "Reverend, tell them to hurry. We'll meet the officers at the delivery entrance instead. We'll find some way to block May's escape." She threw open the back door. "Let Alex know too."

Ruth and Greg ran into the damp air. They had an opportunity to stop May and bring her to justice, and Ruth wasn't about to let that chance slip away.

Their feet pounded the cobblestone streets as they took a left, right, left again, rushing past shops, weaving in and out of bewildered shoppers returning to the village after the storm. A few hurried along, their heads down, their collars turned up against the wind.

"This way," Greg shouted, diving into an alleyway between the Crystal Goblet and Jack's Magic Beans.

Ruth's leg muscles burned as she tried to keep up, and her lungs threatened to explode.

Greg veered sharply to the left, heading toward the back of the village, and Ruth followed, her mind racing, trying to calculate the best route to the delivery gate. "Go left." Her breath came in ragged gasps.

Greg did as she asked, his longer legs easily keeping a steady pace. "Are you sure?"

"Yes, it's this way."

"No." Greg glanced over his shoulder. "I mean, you really want to confront them? We could get murdered."

"No choice," Ruth said as they dived past overflowing dustbins, the stench of rotting food momentarily filling their nostrils. "The new CCTV covers the back gate."

"Well, that's a relief," Greg muttered.

If they could stop the van, they could trap May and her accomplices until the police arrived.

Ruth and Greg reached the back of the village, the fairy-tale-themed shops replaced by a utilitarian landscape of loading bays and storage units. The delivery gate, a large metal structure, loomed ahead.

Greg skidded to a halt, his gaze fixed on it. The gate was closed, not locked.

Ruth bent double, a stitch in her side, lungs on fire. She glanced back. No sign of May's van.

"We made it," Greg said, relief evident in his voice. "Now what?"

Ruth's chest heaved as she scanned the area, searching for anything they could use. Her gaze fell on a stack of wooden pallets. "Help me with these." She rushed toward them.

Greg, though looking initially confused, quickly understood her plan. They worked together, dragging the heavy pallets to the gate, their muscles straining with the effort. Each pallet was awkward and unwieldy, splinters digging into their hands.

They positioned them in front of the gate, wedging them against it, creating a makeshift barricade. It wasn't much, but it would at least slow May down.

As Ruth and Greg finished, an engine sounded in the distance, growing louder with each passing second.

"They're coming," Greg said, his voice tense.

Ruth's heart pounded. "Get ready."

"For what?" Greg looked at her askance. "Are we fighting them?"

"We need to stall them until the police arrive, or they'll get away." Ruth's voice was firm, her gaze fixed on a pair of headlights cutting through the gloom.

The van was moving fast, eager to escape the village, but the driver clearly spotted the barricade, and the van slid to a halt, its engine sputtering.

The driver's-side door then flew open, and the tattooed man emerged, his face contorted with anger. "How did you get out?"

Ruth stood her ground, despite the fear coursing through her. "I want to talk to May."

A full ten seconds passed before the passenger door opened, and May stepped out, her expression unreadable. She was followed by the shorter, but equally menacing burly man.

Ruth kept her attention on May, waving Greg back, but he didn't move.

"This is pointless, Mrs Morgan," May said, her voice calm, but with an undercurrent of steel. "You can't stop us. We'll merely set up somewhere else."

The tattooed man started moving pallets aside, while

the other took a step toward Ruth and Greg, cracking his knuckles.

"You're right, we can't stop you leaving," Ruth said. "But at least do the right thing."

The burly guy took another step toward them.

May held up a hand. "Which is?"

"You've framed an innocent man for murder."

May's composure cracked—a flicker of anger crossed her face. "Julian killed Kathy," she said, her voice sharp.

"The scarf." Greg waved a finger at the scarf around her neck. "*You* tampered with the security footage."

May's eyes narrowed. "Again, I have no idea what you're talking about."

The tattooed man finished with the pallets and joined his friend.

As if on cue, Alex bounded round the corner. "You're under arrest."

The men squared up to him instead, fists raised. The tattooed man stepped toward Alex, a menacing grin on his face.

However, May's focus shifted to Leana, who had followed him. "What lies have you and your silly aunt been spreading? What conspiracy theories now?"

The wail of police sirens pierced the air.

"It's over," Ruth said.

May's eyes darted between Ruth, Greg, Leana, and Alex, and the approaching sirens. A flicker of desperation crossed her face, but it was quickly replaced by a cold, hard resolve.

She turned to her two henchmen, a silent command passing between them.

They understood.

The tattooed man lunged at Alex, wrapping his powerful arms around him, and Alex struggled to wrestle free. The other man charged at Greg, a roar erupting from his throat. Greg, though startled, stood his ground. He raised his arms, in a defensive stance. The man, however, was too strong. He grabbed Greg, and threw him aside, sending him sprawling to the ground.

Greg landed with a thud, his breath knocked out of him.

Fury surged through Ruth. "How dare you." She lunged toward the man, but May stepped in front of her, blocking her path.

"Don't even think about it," May said.

Leana helped Greg to his feet as the man shoved the pallets aside and opened the gates.

Ruth held May's gaze. "You won't get away with this."

May shook her head, as both men now wrestled with Alex.

Leana, clearly seeing an opportunity, rushed at May from behind, and leapt onto her back. She wrapped her arms around May's neck, attempting to pull her over.

May, caught off guard, stumbled, her arms flailing as she tried to dislodge Leana. "Get off me."

Ruth rushed forward and grabbed May too, adding her weight to Leana's. May's muscles strained as she tried to fight them off.

Meanwhile, Greg, having recovered from his fall, rushed to help Alex. He grabbed the tattooed man's arm in an attempt to pry him free, but the teenager's weak frame had little effect. He was no match for the larger man's strength.

Suddenly, May twisted her body, using her momentum to break free from Ruth's grip and shake Leana off, then turned and ran, sprinting toward the delivery gate.

Police cars, their blue lights flashing, screeched to a halt in front of her, blocking any chance of escape.

A split second later, several police officers helped Greg

and Alex with May's goons, cuffing them and leading them away, their protests falling on deaf ears.

Greg bent double, panting. "I'm never doing that again." He clutched his side.

Alex patted him on the back, breathing hard, his face flushed.

DI Barnes emerged from the lead police car, his face grim. He surveyed the scene, his gaze lingering on Ruth, then on May. "May Thomas," he said, his voice authoritative, "you're under arrest for suspected counterfeiting and murder."

May didn't resist as Alex approached. He handcuffed her, and led May toward one of the police cars.

As Alex placed her in the back, she turned to Ruth, her eyes filled with a mixture of anger and resentment. "You can't prove I killed anyone because I didn't do it."

Alex slammed the door on her. "Watch us." He nodded to Ruth. "We'll catch up tomorrow?"

She smiled. "See you then."

The police cars pulled away, disappearing into the distance, and the village fell silent.

"Are you two all right?" Ruth asked Greg and Leana, her voice hoarse. She felt drained, both physically and emotionally.

The girl nodded.

Greg let out a long breath. "Well, that was intense. Wait until I tell Mum what happened."

Ruth glared at him. "Don't you dare."

23

The next day, at the Silver Thimble, Greg struggled down the stairs with his and Ruth's cases, and finally dumped them on the kitchen floor with a heavy thud.

The café itself buzzed with the morning rush. Ruth, ever the helpful soul, even if she did say so herself, helped Reverend Michael serve.

Although, with his swift, practised efficiency, he didn't need much assistance—he had it all well under control.

It was actually rather impressive—he moved like a mini whirlwind, clearing tables and serving customers with a grace that suggested years of juggling plates and dealing with customers, rather than as a man of the cloth.

"Ready to go?" Ruth asked Greg, sliding the last plate into the dishwasher and flipping it shut.

He shrugged and leaned against the counter. "Can we get a taxi?"

Ruth wiped her hands on a tea towel, a mischievous glint in her eye. "Absolutely not."

"Come on. It's not as if we need the exercise." Greg yawned. "Please? I'm knackered. We've spent the last few days running around." He then let out a dramatic sigh for emphasis.

"Which means we're used to it by now," Ruth said, her tone brooking no argument. "Besides, we have to return the tandem bicycle to the garage. Think of it as a leisurely victory lap."

"A victory lap that involves pedalling a contraption designed to kill us," Greg muttered under his breath. "May and her henchmen left their van behind," he said, looking hopeful. "We could use that. I'm sure they wouldn't mind. After all, they're hardly in a position to complain, are they?"

Ruth opened her mouth to retort when Julian appeared in the doorway.

He held a large bouquet of flowers tied with a red ribbon. The scent of lilies and roses filled the small kitchen, momentarily masking the lingering aroma of bacon and coffee.

"I hope I'm not interrupting anything important?" Julian asked, his sheepish gaze shifting between Ruth and Greg.

"Of course not." Ruth waved him in with a polite smile. "Greg and I were discussing how much we'll enjoy cycling back to the garage. Isn't that right, Gregory?"

He shot a pointed look at the cases, then back to her, silently questioning why a taxi was out of the question.

Julian extended the flowers to Ruth. "For you," he said, his voice soft. "A small token of my immense gratitude."

Ruth beamed and took them, burying her nose in the blooms and inhaling deeply. "They're lovely. Thank you, Julian. But you really needn't have gone to the trouble."

"You saved my life," Julian said, his eyes shining with sincerity. "I can't thank you enough. I owe everything to you and your grandson."

Reverend Michael bustled into the kitchen, laden with a

precarious stack of plates, swiftly followed by Alex and Leana.

Ruth gestured to them, her smile widening. "You can thank these two as well. They were a massive help."

"Thank you," Julian said, turning to face the newcomers. He looked between everyone. "Stop by my shop any time. Pick out anything you like. Consider it a lifetime discount, a small way to repay your kindness."

"Only doing my job." Alex glanced at Ruth. "But thank you. Glad you're home."

Leana smiled. "Me too."

Reverend Michael rested a hand on Julian's shoulder. "Indeed. It's good to have you back, Julian," he said, his voice filled with relief. Then, with a nod to the others, he left the kitchen to serve more patrons.

Julian bowed and followed the reverend out.

Leana glanced at the cases, then at Greg. "You're leaving?"

"I'm afraid so." Ruth plucked the small white card from the flowers, her fingers tracing the elegant script. "Greg and I have a family wedding to—" She gasped.

Greg stepped to her, concern etched on his face. "What's wrong?"

With trembling fingers, Ruth held the card out to him.

Greg squinted as he read. "'Dear Mrs Morgan, Thank you for all you've done. I'm forever in your debt. Sincerely, Julian.'" He shrugged. "So what?"

Ruth set the card on the table, then opened her phone and navigated to the pictures of Kathy's diary. She placed the phone next to the card and stepped back.

Greg, Alex, and Leana leaned in, their eyes darting between the card and the phone image. Realisation slowly dawned on each of their faces.

Eyes wide, Leana waved a finger at the card and phone image. "Same handwriting," she whispered. "It's an exact match."

Ruth nodded, her mind spinning.

Could it be? Have I been wrong all along?

Reverend Michael reappeared. When he spotted everyone's shocked expressions, he said, "What's happened?" Ruth showed him the card and the diary images. Reverend Michael stared for a moment, a frown creasing his brow, and then he gasped. "Julian?"

Alex looked to Ruth. "Julian wrote Kathy's diary. But why? So that means…"

"I can't believe this," Reverend Michael murmured, his face pale.

"Julian did murder Kathy after all," Greg said. "And then planted evidence to make us think it was May."

Leana rubbed the back of her neck, her expression a mixture of confusion and disbelief. "Why, though? I mean, I know Julian and Kathy didn't get along, but why kill her?"

"And why frame May?" Reverend Michael said.

Those were good questions, the ones that echoed in Ruth's mind, demanding answers. *What was Julian's motive? What did he gain by killing Kathy and pinning it on her friend May?*

Ruth paced for a moment as she pieced together what they'd learned. Fragments of conversations: Kathy and Julian's arguments, Celia and Oliver; snippets of observations like the snagged scarf fabric, and even seemingly insignificant details like the flowers. It all began to coalesce, forming a clearer picture.

"Julian wants to take over May's counterfeiting business," Ruth said in realisation.

"How do you figure that?" Alex asked.

And then something else clicked—a missing piece of the puzzle that made everything fall into place. "Of course." Ruth's eyes widened. "Julian's been using Hattie's secret CCTV room to spy on May." She looked between them. "That's how he knows about her operation." Ruth focussed on Leana. "And that is why Julian moved into the shop behind your aunt's. The vacant one opposite Kathy. Julian needed access to that old security room, to those cameras." Ruth shook her head. "I bet he burned down his own shop on purpose, to make sure Celia agreed to moving him there. He's been planning this for months, maybe years."

Reverend Michael dropped into a chair. "I can't believe this. I trusted Julian. Was utterly convinced he was innocent."

Greg nodded slowly. "I think you're right, Grandma. Julian watched May, learned her routines, her contacts, everything."

A knot of unease twisted Ruth's stomach. "But at some point Kathy also found out what May was doing. They were best friends, after all. Confronted her about it. Kathy probably agreed to stay silent at first, but she then threatened to tell someone. Julian, wanting to take over May's operation, feared Kathy would expose it, so he had to silence her." Ruth looked between them. "Julian deliberately set it up so fingers would point in his direction first."

"The Tudor rose next to Kathy's body," Greg exclaimed.

Ruth nodded. "That made the police arrest him first."

"Why?" Leana frowned. "That's risky."

Ruth looked at Alex. "If Julian had access to the old security cameras, I think he must have figured out you were investigating. Julian then planted the fake evidence, making it appear as though May carried out the deed, knowing Alex would likely investigate." Ruth sighed. "We played directly into his hands."

"The twenty thousand pounds was not from May?" Leana asked.

"I bet there was no twenty thousand," Greg said. "If Kathy was behind on her rent, like Mrs Vanderlin insists, Julian saw a chance to plant what looked like a bribe in her ledger, making it look like she was involved with May somehow."

"But her bank account won't show the deposit," Reverend Michael said.

Greg shrugged. "Doesn't really matter. Even if Celia shows she never paid her rent, it was only designed to push us all in May's direction. Julian only wanted us to catch May in the act, and there's enough evidence to put her away."

"Murder will mean she stays out of Julian's way for a long time," Alex said. "I'm guessing Julian has her contacts. That's all he really needs. He'll start fresh with the counterfeiting once the dust settles."

"Probably plans to leave the area and set up somewhere else." Ruth scrolled through the images of the ledger on her phone. "Different ink." She showed Alex.

"What about Celia Vanderlin?" Greg asked. "Did she know May was doing the counterfeiting or not?"

Alex folded his arms. "Perhaps Celia confronted May, and that's when she moved her operation, and messed with Julian's plans. He couldn't have Celia exposing May before he was ready." He looked at Ruth, his expression hardening. "We will take Mrs Vanderlin in for questioning. Oliver too. We'll get it out of them."

"It seems like a lot of people have been holding on to secrets around here," Reverend Michael murmured.

"Julian gave a gold scarf to May," Ruth said to Alex. "Left

a snagged piece of it in the air duct. More planted evidence. My bet is the new CCTV hasn't been tampered with, which is why you couldn't find signs of it. As you pointed out, too technical. But that didn't stop Julian making it look like someone *could* have."

"How did she not notice it was snagged?" Greg asked. "May, I mean. Would be pretty obvious."

Ruth shook her head as a clearer picture formed. "Julian saw Kathy as a loose end, a liability. I think he tried to deliberately harass her, force Kathy out of the village—the arguments, scratched door, bins falling over, dead rat on her car . . . a campaign to get rid of her. He probably thought Celia would throw Kathy out for missed rent, but Kathy became too much of a problem, so he had to take care of her. He used Kathy's murder to frame May. Kill two birds with one stone."

The room fell silent, the weight of Ruth's words hanging heavy in the air. The implications painted a picture of Julian as a cold, calculating killer, willing to do anything to achieve his goals.

"But how do we prove it?" Leana whispered.

"We have the handwriting," Alex said. "And a possible motive, but we need concrete evidence, something that links Julian to the murder."

"We'll find the evidence," Ruth said, determination once again her driving force. "If Julian's been using the old CCTV system, there has to be a way he's accessing it. We'll start with that." She looked between them. "It means going back to Hattie's shop one more time. We know Julian's been using her secret CCTV room. We need to find out how."

Back at Mystical Flames, Hattie had outdone herself in preparation for the expected influx of returning customers. At least ten incense sticks and twenty scented candles burned, filling the shop with enough toxins to scrape flesh from bones.

Ruth fought back the urge to cough as she, Greg, Alex, and Leana approached the counter.

Hattie looked up and smiled, her eyes crinkling at the corners. "Well done, Mrs Morgan," she gushed. "It's so good to see Julian back where he—"

Ruth held up a hand, cutting her off midsentence. "Can we take another look at the security room, please?"

Hattie's face fell, her smile vanishing as quickly as it had appeared. "I— Why?"

"Please, Aunty Hattie," Leana said. "It's important. We think Julian's been spying on everyone, and he might have something to do with Kathy's murder."

"Julian? That's absurd," Hattie scoffed, shaking her head. "He wouldn't hurt a fly. He's a kind, gentle soul. You must be mistaken." When she seemed to notice everyone's serious expressions, her face paled. "Really? He'd do such a thing?"

"That's what we want to find out," Alex said.

Hattie's shoulders slumped, and she let out a shaky breath. She then led them to the back of the shop, through the storeroom, and to the jagged hole in the wall. Hattie pulled aside the curtain, revealing the hidden room beyond.

24

Ruth, Greg, Alex, and Leana followed Hattie into the hidden room, their eyes adjusting to the dim light. The old computer monitor flickered, displaying grainy images of the village. The cameras, strategically placed throughout the square, provided a panoramic view of the shops.

Ruth walked slowly around the room, running her fingers over the walls, checking the blocked-off door, for any signs of a hidden entrance. She examined the old brickwork, but found no obvious way Julian could've gotten in. Ruth faced Hattie. "Did you ever let Julian—"

"Of course not," Hattie said before she could finish the sentence, her voice defensive. "Only I know about this room. No one else has been in here."

"Are you sure?" Alex asked, searching Hattie's face. "Maybe he found out somehow? Spotted you coming in here?"

Hattie lifted her chin, her expression defiant. "Positive. I'm always careful. No one knows about this room, except for the four of you, now."

Alex folded his arms and leaned against the wall, a sceptical look on his face. "Your theory must be wrong, Ruth."

Ruth's gaze shifted to the equipment. "There has to be a way he's accessing these feeds."

Greg examined the empty rack, his fingers tracing the wires and cables, his brow furrowed in concentration. "This system is ancient," he muttered, shaking his head. "It's a miracle it still works. It's all analogue, no digital interface, no way to access it via a network either."

"He must have added something." Ruth's eyes fell on a thick cable running from the back of the computer, disappearing through a small hole in the wall, one they hadn't noticed before. It was barely visible, tucked away in a dark corner, but it was there. "What's this?" She pointed to the cable.

Hattie leaned closer to examine the cable. "I don't know," she said. "I've never noticed it before."

"Which means it could've been there a long time," Ruth said. "I bet it leads to Julian's new shop."

Greg faced the blank wall. "He must have rigged up some way to connect to the system, a way to tap into the feeds. That's how he's been doing it."

Ruth waved a finger at the wall. "We need to look on the other side."

"Julian's shop?" Leana asked. "But he's there. He'll see us. He'll know we're onto him."

Ruth leaned into the monitor and focussed on the camera view of the loading bays, scanning the grainy image. "His back door is open," she said, urgent. "He must be up to something, maybe getting rid of evidence."

Sure enough, Julian emerged, threw a box into a skip, and returned to the shop, but left the door ajar.

"We need to hurry." She spun to Alex and Leana. "Can

you two please keep Julian busy while Greg and I sneak into the back of his shop?"

Greg blinked. "We're doing what now?"

"We need to see where that leads." Ruth waved a finger at the cable.

"Right." Greg swallowed. "But he's a murderer. If he catches us, he might—"

Ruth waved off the suggestion, her mind made up. "Alex will be there. He and Leana will keep Julian distracted. We'll be in and out before he even knows it." She glanced at the monitor again and the open door. "We'll look for evidence and let you know as soon as we find something."

Alex balled his fists. "Come on, Leana."

They headed to the front of Julian's shop, while Ruth and Greg raced to the loading bay. Ruth peered around the back door as Alex and Leana entered the shop and approached Julian, engaging him in conversation, drawing his attention away.

"Now," Ruth whispered.

She and Greg slipped through the back door and darted into a storeroom on the right, a cramped space packed full of boxes, bolts of fabric, mannequins, and sewing equipment.

Greg squatted at the end of the rack and pulled aside a box, his eyes searching for the cable. "Yes," he said, his voice triumphant. "It's here." Pushing more boxes aside, and pulling some away from the wall, he followed the cable back toward the door.

Ruth lifted a tub full of fabric scraps out of the way.

A modern laptop sat toward the back of the shelf, its screen dark, but a small green light on the side indicated it was in sleep mode. The CCTV cable went into a black box, and then another cable connected it to the laptop.

"Keep a lookout," Greg whispered. He carefully opened the laptop, and images of the security cameras popped up on the screen, a live feed from Hattie's hidden room.

Ruth stepped to the door and turned an ear to it, listening for any sign of Julian. "See if it's recording."

"I think we can do better than that." Greg navigated to the video files.

Ruth glanced back, and a gasp escaped her lips. On the shelf, next to the laptop, was a tub of spilled glitter. Its particles matched the same size and shade as the flake she'd found at the wishing well. It was a tiny piece of evidence connecting Julian to the murder scene, and he could argue it had come from the week before, but it was another nail in his coffin.

"Here," Greg said, his voice filled with excitement. "Julian's kept loads of files. He's been recording everything, for weeks, maybe even months."

Ruth let out a sigh of relief. He'd made a huge error in judgement. "Julian's been so sure he won't get caught, he hasn't completely covered his tracks."

"Or he was keeping them as backup, use them to blackmail May if his plan didn't work out." Greg clicked on a file, and the screen filled with a grainy image of May's bookshop. The date and timestamp indicated it was from several weeks ago. "You were right—Julian has been watching her for a long time." Greg pointed to a list of files.

He then fast-forwarded through some of the footage, stopping at various points, showing May receiving deliveries, meeting with the tattooed man, and going about her daily routine. All the recordings had audio.

Greg brought up an image that showed her storeroom.

Ruth leaned in closer, her eyes glued to the screen. They watched as May entered, followed by the two burly men.

They carried boxes, the same ones Ruth had seen in the back of the delivery van.

"He's got it all on tape," Ruth murmured. "The counterfeiting operation, everything. This is how he planned to take it over. Julian knows everything. He's been studying May, learning her weaknesses, waiting for the right moment to strike."

"But Kathy nearly ruined it for him." Greg continued to scroll through the files, finding more recordings, each one revealing another piece of the puzzle. "And he killed her for it."

There were conversations between Julian and Kathy, their arguments escalating in intensity. And then, a recording from the night of the party, showing Celia arguing with Kathy about the missing rent payments.

Ruth blew out a puff of air. "He's got dirt on everyone." She had to admit she was impressed, albeit grudgingly. "But where's the recording of the murder itself? There has to be something, some evidence that proves Julian did it."

Greg continued his search, his brow furrowed in concentration. He navigated through folders, opened and closed files, scanning the screen for any sign of the crucial recording. And then, he found a video file of interest. He swallowed. "This might be something." Greg clicked on it, and the screen filled with a black-and-white image of the village square, the wishing well in the middle, the shops lining the perimeter.

The timestamp read 23:58 PM, the night of the murder.

A figure emerged from the shadows, dragging something heavy behind them. It was Julian, his face contorted with effort. He struggled to move a bulky object wrapped in a dark cloth, a large, shapeless bundle.

Greg tensed. "Kathy."

Ruth rested a hand on his shoulder.

Once Julian had reached the pedestal, he unwrapped the object, revealing Kathy's lifeless body, her pale skin ghostly in the dim light.

Despite knowing what was coming, Ruth's breath caught in her throat. "He did it," she whispered with a mixture of horror and relief. "He really did it. We have him. We have the proof."

The overconfident fool had kept every recording. Maybe he planned to delete it soon, but they'd got there before him.

Julian positioned Kathy's body, already dressed in the flowing purple gown, with a green silk scarf around her neck, deliberately tied with one knot. He tied her up there, arranged her limbs, adjusted the fabric, making sure she was displayed in a specific way, like any other mannequin.

Once finished, Julian stepped back, surveying his work. A sinister smile crept across his face.

"Sick." Greg screwed up his face. "He's enjoying it."

"He wanted to make it look like May framed him at this point, and not the other way around. Made sure everyone saw Kathy in his dress. Had them convinced he'd been framed."

The recording continued, showing Julian disappearing into the shadows, leaving Kathy's body on display in the village square, a gruesome attraction.

Ruth sighed. "That's enough. We have everything we need."

Greg closed the lid on the laptop, his eyes filled with a mixture of anger and sadness.

Ruth indicated for him to take the laptop, and once he'd disconnected it and tucked it safely under his arm, she took a deep breath and stepped out of the storeroom.

Alex and Leana were still talking to Julian, their voices calm and steady, keeping him engaged. As Ruth approached from the back of the shop, Julian's smile slipped from his face, replaced by a look of suspicion and unease. He glanced at the laptop under Greg's arm, his eyes widening.

"We know you framed May for Kathy's murder," Ruth said, making an effort to keep her voice calm and businesslike, despite the anger searing through her. "We know you're trying to take over her counterfeiting operation. You've been planning this for months, haven't you? Studying her, learning her routines, waiting for the right moment to strike." She sighed, shaking her head. "And we know you're the one who murdered Kathy. She was a loose end, wasn't she. A liability you couldn't afford."

For a few seconds, Julian looked as if he was going to maintain his act, but instead he lifted his chin. "She gave me no choice. Kathy would ruin everything and expose May before I was ready. And as for May? She's a fool," he snarled, his voice filled with contempt. "She has no idea how to run a business. She's sloppy, careless." He glanced at Alex. "I'm surprised you didn't catch her sooner." He looked back at Ruth, lip curled. "I'll make it bigger and better than she ever could."

"You won't do anything." Alex pulled a set of handcuffs from his back pocket. "You're under arrest for the murder of Kathy Fellows."

Julian lurched past him, knocking Alex aside and making a run for the door. However, Leana, quick as a flash, stuck her foot out, tripping him up and sending him sprawling to the floor.

Alex was on him in a heartbeat, his knee pressing into Julian's back, and pulled his arms behind, cuffing him as he read him his rights. Julian struggled, cursing and spitting, but Alex's grip was firm, unyielding.

Ruth leaned against the counter. "Well done, Leana," she said, filled with admiration. "That was quick thinking."

Greg nodded his approval.

Leana glanced at him, her cheeks flushed, and she muttered, "Thanks."

Alex hoisted Julian to his feet, his grip tight on his arm. Julian glared at them, his face contorted with hatred.

Greg held up the laptop. "All the evidence you need is on here."

Alex stared at the laptop, then back at Julian. A mix of emotions played across his face—anger, betrayal, and a hint of sadness. "We helped you," he said. "We trusted you." He took the laptop from Greg, nodded at Ruth, and led Julian from the shop.

Ruth let out a long, slow breath, the tension draining from her body. It was finally over. They had caught the real killer. They had solved the mystery. But, as Alex and Julian disappeared from view, a wave of unease washed over her, a feeling that something still wasn't quite right.

"What's wrong?" Greg asked.

"Nothing. I'm sure it's fine. Tired, I guess." Ruth shook herself. "It's been a long couple of days."

And that was an understatement.

25

Reverend Michael loaded Greg up with bags of pastries, pies, cakes and buns, while Ruth sat at a table in the corner of the café, finishing her tea.

Alex stepped back into the Silver Thimble, made a beeline for Ruth's table and sat opposite. "I'm glad I caught you before you left. I've told DI Barnes everything you've done to help."

"How did he take it?" Ruth asked, unable to keep the curiosity from her voice. "My meddling?"

"He's not happy, but we have a suspect in custody . . . *again*." Alex shook his head. "Right after Kathy's murder, DI Barnes gave me explicit instructions not to investigate. He wanted to do that himself. No one else. Least of all me. His orders were quite clear."

Ruth chuckled. "A big feather in his cap, and likely the only chance he gets in a small place such as Osborne."

"That's why I backed off and allowed you to investigate," Alex said.

Ruth cocked an eyebrow. "*Allowed* me?"

He half smiled. "The laptop is in evidence, and the

investigating team are at Julian's shop now." Alex took a breath. "We've taken Mrs Vanderlin in for questioning, but I've already spoken to her on the way to the station. Your hunch was right—Celia did suspect May was behind the counterfeiting and confronted her about it. May denied it, of course, but Mrs Vanderlin didn't come to us with her suspicions. Instead, she kept it quiet, fearing bad publicity. And then when Kathy was murdered, she grew fearful for her own safety, and that of her son's, so she kept her mouth shut. Well, that's her story anyway." Alex shook his head. "Mrs Vanderlin is in a lot of trouble. If she'd come to us sooner..."

"And Oliver?" Ruth asked.

"Mrs Vanderlin claims he knows nothing about it, and judging by his reaction, that seems to be the case, as far as we can ascertain. But we'll be keeping an eye on him."

"What about May's gold scarf?" Ruth said. "Was it snagged?"

"It was," Alex said. "Apparently, she noticed it after Julian had gifted it to her. He said he'd replace it. He gifted several gold scarves, one of the others to Mrs Vanderlin for her birthday."

"Then he likely tossed the roll of gold fabric away." Ruth inclined her head. "Will you tell me before I go?" She leaned forward. "Something has bothered me about you from the day we met. I know you're a good man, but you're hiding something. I feel it in my bones." She studied his face. "For a fleeting moment earlier, I thought you might be in on it with Julian." She sat back again, still watching him carefully. "Of course, I realise that's ridiculous."

A flicker of a frown crossed Alex's features. "I would never—" His gaze dropped to the table. "That's actually why I'm glad I've caught you. I had to tell you before you left."

"Tell me what?"

"I remember you," he murmured.

Ruth stared at him, unsure how to reply.

What on earth is he talking about?

"And your husband. John." Alex's eyes rose to meet hers again. "He was a nice guy. I liked him."

Ruth's stomach did a backflip, and she unstuck her tongue. "How did you know John?"

"When you stayed here," Alex said. "In the village. At the B&B." He paused, his eyes searching hers as if gauging her reaction. He then added, "My parents owned it."

"But that was—"

"Forty-four years ago," Alex said.

Ruth let out a low whistle. "Which would've made you..."

"Eight years old."

Ruth widened her eyes. "You were the little boy with the red trousers and the matching suspenders?" *Oh my word. The little scamp with the mischievous grin. I remember him.*

Alex's cheeks flushed. "Mum made me wear those. You don't know how glad I was once I'd grown out of them."

Ruth chuckled and shook her head. She recalled the brash little boy always up to mischief, playing with his toy cars on the stairs. Several guests had almost come a cropper, and he'd received quite the scolding from his mother. A vivid memory surfaced: little Alex, sitting in the dining room, his lower lip trembling as his mother reprimanded him for leaving his toys scattered about. He'd looked so dejected, clutching a small car in his hand. "Why didn't you say something sooner?"

Alex's face turned serious again. "I didn't mean to steal it. I found it on the back steps. I played with it and was going to give it back, but you'd already left." He shrugged one shoulder, a hint of the mischievous old Alex peeking through. "I was embarrassed. Thought you'd think I'd stolen it." He pulled an object wrapped in a handkerchief from his pocket and slid it across the table to Ruth, his hand lingering on it for a moment as if reluctant to let go.

"Wait." She stared down at it, and her breath caught. "I think I know what this is." She couldn't believe it.

"I'm really sorry," Alex said. "I feel terrible. Always have." He looked genuinely remorseful, his eyes pleading for understanding. "I hoped you'd come back the next year."

Ruth swallowed, her eyes filling with tears. "You kept hold of it all this time?" A wave of emotion washed over her —disbelief, nostalgia, a touch of sadness for the young boy who had carried this secret for so long.

"I tried to find you. Looked on the internet over the years. Tried to remember your face." Alex sat back. "Do you know how many Ruth Morgans there are in this country? I must have emailed at least twenty of them. None were you. And you and your husband never left an address. Paid in cash."

Ruth forced a tremulous smile. "And John is a common name too."

Alex sighed. "When I met you at the party, I was stunned." He shook his head. "I thought it couldn't be you. And then when you mentioned you'd visited Osborne before, I knew it had to be. But I struggled to find the best time to tell you, what with everything that's happened." He leaned forward, his tone earnest. "I was so deeply embarrassed, and I promise I didn't take it on purpose."

Ruth touched the back of his hand. "I believe you. And I'm so happy to have it back after all these years."

They sat in silence for a moment, the only sound the

chatter of patrons and the rustle of bags as Greg came and went, loading their tandem's trailer.

Finally, Alex stood, his stoic expression returning. "It was nice to meet you again, Ruth Morgan. I guess it's fate." He nodded, then said goodbye to Greg and left, disappearing through the café door.

Greg dropped into his vacant chair, breathing heavy. "All loaded." His eyes fell on the object wrapped in a napkin. "What's that?"

With trembling fingers, Ruth carefully unfolded it to reveal a silver compass, a couple of inches across.

"That's cool." Greg leaned in. "Did Alex give it to you? Why?"

Ruth turned the compass over to reveal the engraving on the back. It read:

To John,
    With this, you'll never get lost again.
    All my love,
    Ruth

Greg's eyes almost popped from their sockets. "What? You're kidding. This was Grandad's?" He looked back at the door. "Why did Alex have it?"

"John was forever losing his way," Ruth said wistfully. "He couldn't navigate a supermarket without ending up in the frozen aisle, when all he wanted was a packet of biscuits." She smiled. "I gave him this compass for our first anniversary. I thought it would be a practical gift, but also a symbol of our journey together." She shrugged. "Corny, I know." A wave of sadness then washed over Ruth, the weight of John's absence squeezing her heart. She traced the inscription with her fingertip, the familiar words a bittersweet reminder of their love, and life's fragility.

Ruth reflected on the events of the past few days, the dark secrets they'd uncovered beneath the seemingly idyllic surface of the Osborne Outlet Village.

She acknowledged the dangers she faced, the risks she took by sniffing out mysteries, but it only reaffirmed her commitment to uncovering the truth, and helping people as much as she could.

Ruth pocketed the compass and got to her feet. "Come on, Greg." She picked up Merlin in his kitty backpack and slipped her arms through the straps. "Before it starts raining again."

However, as they left the Silver Thimble, stepping back outside, the sun finally broke through the clouds, casting a warm, golden light over the quaint, fairy-tale-themed buildings. The outlet village was peaceful once more.

Ruth took a deep breath, filling her lungs with the fresh air. She then motioned to the waiting tandem bicycle, and its trailer laden with their cases and bags. "Ready?"

Greg grumbled under his breath.

"Good, good." Ruth looked over her shoulder. "Ready, Merlin?"

There came a raspy meow in reply.

As they cycled away, with Greg at the front, steering this time, Ruth would never look at a mannequin, scarf, or a clothes label the same way again.

Thank you for reading!

If you've not yet read the Ruth Morgan series prequel:
MURDER ON THE OCEAN ODYSSEY

OUT NOW

To be notified of FUTURE RELEASES in the Ruth Morgan series, click on the author name "Peter Jay Black" at Amazon, and then "Follow" in the top left of the author profile page.

Or visit peterjayblack.com

We would be incredibly grateful if you could leave a star rating or review. Your invaluable support is vital to the Ruth Morgan Mystery Series' success and can make all the difference.

BIBLIOGRAPHY

PREQUEL
MURDER ON THE OCEAN ODYSSEY

As a freelance food consultant, Ruth Morgan travels Britain, advising restaurants, cafes, and hotels on their menus and recipes. So when she's hired to work on board the Ocean Odyssey, she looks forward to gaining her sea legs.

However, when someone throws the captain overboard on the first night, Ruth and five other mysterious passengers discover they've sailed into a death trap, and it's clear the killer won't stop.

On a ship now adrift in the middle of the ocean, with no way to call for help, the dire situation forces Ruth to dust off her amateur sleuthing skills. She wants to help her fellow guests survive through the next three days, but can she unmask the killer before she becomes their next victim?

BOOK ONE
MURDER AT VANMOOR VILLAGE

Trapped in a quaint British village by an unforeseen detour, Ruth Morgan's idyllic escape takes a sinister turn when an artist goes missing and a landlady tumbles to her death.

Warned by the police not to leave Vanmoor, Ruth's sleuthing instincts take over as the mysteries pile up. The discovery of the artist's car in an abandoned tunnel paints a grim picture, but a shocking twist emerges – the body in the driver's seat is a stranger.

Tension in the village thickens like clotted cream, death lurks behind every painted smile, and with the stakes rising quicker than the bistro's pastries, can Ruth unravel the mystery before it's too late, or has she bitten off more than she can chew?

BOOK TWO
MURDER ON IVYWICK ISLAND

Ready for some family catch-up time before her next food consulting job, Ruth Morgan arrives at Ivywick Island. But no sooner does she step foot off the boat, than her sister asks for help locating a missing will. Without it, Margaret and her husband are about to lose their home and everything they've worked for. Ruth agrees, not only out of loyalty, but for the chance to atone for past mistakes where she put her love of solving mysteries before family.

However, there's far more at play than a simple document, and things take a nasty turn when Ruth finds their beloved butler murdered.

With a riddle obscuring the will's hiding place, and every choice Ruth makes bringing her family closer to danger, can she solve the puzzles before the killer strikes again?

BOOK THREE
MURDER ON THE FINSBURY FLYER

When an old acquaintance invites Ruth Morgan and her grandson to take a working trip on board the Finsbury Flyer —a modern steam train with Victorian charms—Ruth is excited to look over the chef's menu and give advice where needed.

However, before she's had the chance to step foot inside the kitchen, a murder derails the relaxing getaway and turns it into a tragedy. It's clear there's a sinister plan in full swing.

With Ruth's reputation threatening to veer off the tracks, she must use her amateur sleuthing skills to solve several puzzling conundrums: How did the killer reach the victim unseen? Who is the most likely suspect? And why has a seemingly innocent person copped to the crime?

BOOK FOUR
MURDER AT HADFIELD HALL

When someone invites Ruth Morgan and her grandson to a fun and spooky encounter at a theme park, they're eager to get their teeth sunk into a once in a lifetime experience.

However, determined to flush out his sister's killer, their paranoid host invents a series of elaborate games for the guests to play, and the enjoyment quickly turns deadly.

With each new challenge threatening to overwhelm them, and every twist and turn a matter of life or death, can Ruth and Greg make it through the weekend, or are their mystery solving days numbered?

BOOK FIVE
MURDER AT THE OSBORNE OUTLET

When Ruth Morgan arrives at the Osborne Outlet, expecting to consult on cakes, not crime, she finds more than discounted shoes: someone has murdered a shop owner and posed them like a mannequin.

The police have their suspect - the victim's bitter rival. But Ruth, relying on her sharp ex-cop instincts, and her reluctant grandson, believes they're wrong.

Beneath the Tudor facades and designer discounts lie deadly secrets, simmering feuds, and a hidden counterfeiting ring. Can Ruth expose the real killer before they close shop for good?

∽

Printed in Dunstable, United Kingdom